A
LAIRD *for*
CHRISTMAS

A LAIRD *for* CHRISTMAS

GERRI RUSSELL

Montlake
Romance

Text copyright © 2013 Gerri Russell

Printed in the United States of America.

Published by Montlake Romance, Seattle

www.apub.com

ISBN-13: 9781477808870
ISBN-10: 1477808876

Library of Congress Control Number: 2013906764

To Carrie Meredith Searing for her friendship and her bachelorette advice. I value both very much.

To my husband, Chuck, you are my hero, always.

Renfrewshire, Scotland

DECEMBER 12TH, 1679

"Y ou did what?" Lady Jane Josephina Catherine Lennox asked. The castle's library suddenly seemed cold, and sound echoed around the overly large space as Jane stared at her aunt Margaret, praying she had misheard.

"Something had to be done, Jane. I cannot sit around and watch you worry over who will attack us and when."

Jane tried to will away the headache that pulsed behind her eyes at the reminder of Lord Fairfield's arrival last week. He had come with only two men to support him, and yet he had demanded she turn over the castle and all the Lennox land to him. But that was not all he wanted. He had sidled up to her, and with a pinch to her bottom suggested she become his mistress as well.

Jane shivered at the remembered revulsion. She had never felt so alone or as fragile as she had at that moment. She was the mistress of Bellhaven Castle. That fact had not meant anything to Lord Fairfield, neither had it to the three other men who had come to her with similar offers. They jeered at her, citing her wanton reputation, her passionate nature, and all the other lies that had been spread about her in the last six months.

1

With the help of her servants, Ollie, Egan, and Angus, Jane had managed to send Lord Fairfield fleeing. But word was out that she was alone with very few men to guard her and Bellhaven. She felt again that fluttering of panic. How would she fight off the next man, or the man after that, if she had no army of her own?

And Margaret wanted to talk about suitors?

"I am only trying to help, Jane. To that end, I have sent for six men to apply for your hand in marriage. These men will demonstrate their skills in competition, but ultimately you will determine the winner." Margaret straightened and her face tightened with authority. Her aunt never looked like that. Usually her pleasant face was wreathed with a calm and serene smile, bringing out the tiny lines at the corners of her eyes. "I have only done what I had to in order to protect you from losing everything."

"I cannot lose anything if it is not mine," Jane said. "Father and Jacob—"

"They are not coming back. The conflict has been over for six months, yet they have not returned to the castle and neither have their men."

Jane focused on the task before her, studying a clans map her father had created years before. She had been trying to determine if her family's allies could help her now. She needed an army to defend Bellhaven Castle in her father's absence. "Father and Jacob are merely detained—"

"They are gone."

Jane's gaze snapped back to her aunt's. "No."

"Aye. And you, my dear child, will lose everything. You will lose your home and all the Lennox wealth to your cousin Bryce or some other challenger like Lord Fairfield if you do not find a groom. And fast."

Margaret reached for Jane's hands and clasped them tight. "You know your father's stipulation for you to inherit. You must be married to a man worthy of your love before Christmas Eve."

"I shall contest the will."

"There is no time." Aunt Margaret dropped her gaze to their linked hands. "I know this is unusual, but I could think of nothing else. Christmastide is in twelve days."

2

Jane pulled her hands from Margaret's. "You think the answer to our problem is for me to marry some stranger in less than a fortnight?"

"Aye."

Jane shook her head. "I only need a few more days. I am well on my way to raising an army. That will suffice."

"Who are these men, Jane? Who have you found? Mercenaries who you can trust no more than Lord Fairfield?"

Jane bristled. "They fight for money. They are Scottish. What other qualifications do they need?"

A twinge of irritation crept into Margaret's blue eyes. "In spite of the dreadful rumors circulating about you, you have no experience with the men of this world. Inviting strangers here could expose you to even more danger than you face at present. Or have you forgotten the odd accidents that keep occurring? Jane, I honestly think someone wants you dead."

A chill snaked across Jane's neck. "I need allies."

"What you need is a man you can trust to help you determine who is after you and why they are doing such horrible things."

Odd things had occurred. And Jane could not deny she was at risk without her father and brother to protect her. She bit down on her lip as her thoughts warred between finding her own army and her aunt's odd answer to her problem. Was marriage the solution? "And you think one of your suitors can keep Bellhaven safe?"

Margaret folded her arms in front of her. She looked at Jane hard. "Marriage is the answer. The only answer. Besides, it is already done. The invitations have been sent." She drew a breath and paused. "Consider this—these men will be your protectors as they vie for your hand in marriage."

Jane knew she was losing the battle with her aunt. She groaned. "But to marry in such a way . . . to a total stranger. . . ."

Margaret's face softened. "They are not all strangers, my dear."

Jane frowned. "Who did you send for?"

"Well, for one, Bryce, your cousin and my nephew."

"Bryce?"

3

"I had to ask him. That does not mean you have to choose him. Since he will inherit if you do not marry, we needed to involve him or he could contest your marriage to someone else. It was the only way to be certain you and your new husband would be safe."

New husband.

Jane could not deny that she was in danger, but to turn everything over to a husband? For a moment, she considered her options. The only advantage she could see was that a husband would not be able to turn on her. She stared back at her aunt. Perhaps she could turn the situation to her advantage—use the competitions, as her aunt had called them, to assess the men's ability to lead an army.

All that mattered was keeping her home.

Bellhaven was all she had left of the family she had once adored. Her mother had slipped away during the birth of her brother, Jacob. Jane had been only three years old at the time. Her father never recovered from the loss of his wife. He had distanced himself from his two children until only recently, when he had taken an interest in teaching Jacob how to use a sword to defend his country. If it had not been for their suddenly widowed Aunt Margaret, Jane and Jacob would have found themselves quite alone during that time. And now her father and Jacob were gone, too, off to fight the Covenanters.

Margaret smiled. "I only want what is best for you, my dear."

"I know that in my heart. It is my head that needs convincing." Jane straightened and with a sigh asked, "Who are the others?"

"Men from your past. Some of them are titled, others not. And one is a new friend I made last week who left an impression on me."

Jane could feel the hopefulness radiating from her aunt. Her cousin, acquaintances, and a total stranger would all vie for her hand in marriage. She forced her chin up. What other choice did she have if she wanted to protect Bellhaven and her people? "When do these men arrive?"

"In three days' time. I have sent Egan, Angus, and Ollie as messengers."

Jane drew a slow, deep breath. She had wanted an army to defend the castle in her father's absence. By her aunt's doing she would get her wish. An army of suitors would arrive in a matter of days.

4

The first invitation was received by Colin Taylor that same morning in the study of the palatial mansion he had built with his own hands and financed by the profits gained from the use of his sword. Colin schooled his features into that of reserve despite the flare of hope that surged inside him. He read the missive a second time, then set the paper down on the overly large desk that sat between him and the unusually large servant from Bellhaven Castle. "Why was this sent to me?"

The hulk of a man seemed entirely comfortable dressed in the traditional red-and-green livery of the Earl of Lennox despite the fact he was too large for the chair in which Colin had bid him sit. "The contents of the message are for yer eyes only. All I know is the Lady Margaret sent for ye. Do ye have a response I may carry back tae her?"

Lady Margaret had sent for him? He had met Lady Margaret only a fortnight before when she had been traveling through Renfrewshire and her carriage had thrown a wheel. He had come to her aid that day, and they had spent the better part of an afternoon together. She knew nothing more about

5

him than a few trivialities. Now she wanted him to "compete" for her niece's hand in marriage?

"Where are Lady Jane's father and brother?" Colin asked. "Do they not object to a competition of matrimony?"

The hulk of a man straightened and seemed to grow even larger, if it were possible. "They're no longer with us."

Colin frowned. "Dead?"

A look of regret shadowed the man's eyes. "It appears so."

The opulence of Colin's self-made home faded. No amount of money had ever purchased him what his heart truly wanted. Colin sat forward in his chair as a million questions raced through his mind. He studied the servant. "Who are the other competitors?"

"People from Lady Jane's past, friends, one relative. Ye are the only stranger . . ." The man paused, then cleared his throat. "Forgive me, ye are the only one who is unknown to our lady."

The only stranger. Colin was not offended by the word. He had been a stranger to most people his whole life. He was used to learning how to fit in by charming those around him. In fact, it was that skill that would help him now. If this was truly a competition of courtship, charm would be an asset. And perhaps it would help him achieve the one thing he wanted most—to settle down, which he had always denied himself while warring in lands far and near. It was time to grow roots and become a part of something. He might be the only stranger invited to this "competition," but being the only one without history might give him an added advantage.

Over the years, he had learned advantage was everything in battle. Colin tempered a smile as a surge of hope filled him. "Tell the lady I will arrive at Bellhaven in two days' time."

The man stood, bowed, then withdrew, leaving Colin alone with his thoughts.

Lady Jane Lennox could change everything for him—change everything for the better. He was a man with no past. At least not one he remembered. He was an orphan, the abandoned child of a nobleman. He was supposed to have traveled to England, to his guardian. He remembered the old nurse that took him to the orphans' home saying so. He remembered the feeling of her gnarled fingers wrapped around his wrist. He was six years old when she left him there on the doorstep in Scotland instead of his intended destination. His guardian had never been contacted. He had never come looking for Colin, either. And with the old woman's death, the knowledge of who his guardian was had died, along with Colin's dreams of being part of a family.

Colin shivered. There were so many things he had forgotten in the days after that time. All he remembered was the cold, the confusion, and the fear. All of it had blurred into a long, seemingly endless nightmare from which he had eventually escaped through his own cleverness and skill.

He was a soldier for hire, a self-made man. A man with a name he had borrowed from the town tailor and a dream of making a home with a woman who truly cared about him.

Was this that opportunity to become more than what life had offered him thus far? He clenched the invitation in his hand. It was a beginning. A beginning was all he needed.

"What is this you say? Lady Jane alone at the castle?" Sir David Buchanan tossed his invitation aside and unfolded himself from his chair near the hearth in the great hall. In a much-practiced motion, he grasped his sword and sheath, then lashed it to his side.

"Lady Jane is not precisely alone. Her aunt and the servants are with her," a young Bellhaven servant David knew as Egan explained. "All the servants are doing double duty. We've all done our best to protect our mistress. I might be a groom, but I'm also skilled with a sword."

"Her father is gone?" David asked, already calculating in his mind how many men he could spare from his own defenses to take with him to Bellhaven.

"Aye."

"Her brother is gone?"

"Aye, again."

"And the men? The castle's protection? They have not returned since the Battle of Bothwell Bridge?"

"Nay, sir."

He had been there at the battle himself. He had seen the carnage, the loss of life. He blocked the memory. War was war. Men fell. "We achieved our goal of victory over the Covenanters. And mark my words, there will be another battle, and soon. In the meanwhile, unrest in the country is the result. If anyone else discovers Lennox is dead, along with Jacob, Lady Jane will be at risk. There are men out there who would try to take her father's land and the lady herself by force."

The servant nodded. "They have already tried four times. And with me and two others gone to deliver these invitations, Lady Jane is more vulnerable than ever."

David frowned. "How many men are left at the castle?"

"Three."

"Three men cannot defend a castle," David said.

The servant straightened and a look of challenge entered his eyes. "For our lady, those who remain can try."

Despite the desperate situation, David could not help but smile. Jane did that to people. She endeared them to her with her gentle heart. Most of the men who had come to know her would do anything and everything to help her, protect her from harm. Especially himself.

"I will leave for Bellhaven immediately." David turned and strode toward the door, determined to gather a small retinue of men and leave within the hour. Jane needed him.

"Wait," Egan called, hurrying to keep up with David's long strides. "Have you forgotten about the gift?"

David stopped and turned back to the young servant. "A gift?"

"As the invitation explained, if you accept the challenge for Lady Jane's hand in marriage, you must bring a gift that expresses your devotion to her."

David tried to still his thoughts from those of men, weapons, and war. "I bring her troops and protection."

The young servant-turned-warrior frowned. "She is a woman. If you want to win the lady's hand, I would suggest something more feminine."

More feminine? David looked about his great hall, at the many hunting trophies—a boar's head, five deer, three bear, seven red fox. And those were just the ones he had had prepared and hung. Would she like one of them? His frown deepened. Probably not. Most of the ladies he had met were not fond of staring at the heads of woodland creatures. "I must bring her a gift?"

"Aye," Egan repeated with a slight smile. "By the look on your face I can see you are baffled by the thought. I will give you a hint. The simpler the better with Lady Jane." On those words the servant brushed past him and headed for the door. "I have another invitation to deliver if I am to return to the castle and my own role as a defender. Good luck to you, master. And I thank you for your haste in departing for Bellhaven Castle. Arriving before the others will serve you well."

Would his arrival be enough of a gift to her? Was that simple enough? Is that what the young man meant? David continued toward the door at a much slower pace than before as his thoughts spiraled from war to gifts, then the woman herself.

When the servant had arrived with the invitation and news, his first impulse had been to protect Jane. She needed him. Yet now that he had set those thoughts aside, he realized it was he who needed what the invitation offered— a wife, a partner, a mother to his children.

He put his hand against his right side, covering the healed wound he had incurred in the same battle in which Jane's father and brother had vanished. He had escaped with only a reminder that life was precious and tenuous. That wound had made him confront what was lacking in his life, what he tried to avoid with hunting and warring.

It was time for a wife, regardless if he loved the woman or not. He needed an heir. Love could come in time. He had lived alone for nearly ten years now. That was long enough. It was time for a change. A change that Jane now offered.

He pursed his lips as he headed for the door and the stable beyond. It was a change that all started with a gift.

He had to think of something.

The door to Jules MacIntyre's gaol cell opened. He was alone in his cell, as he had been for the majority of the past year, chained to the cold stone wall at his back. Heavy manacles circled his wrists. The false charge of murder hung over him, threatening him with his own death.

But today something was different. With cold anticipation, Jules rubbed his jaw against his shoulder. The pleasure of having a clean-shaven face once more was as heady a sensation as any he had known since his incarceration. He had been in prison sixteen months. Instead of beating him, the guard had tied him to a chair and shaved him. That was his first signal that something was about to change.

Light shone through the sliver of the open door. An overly large, polished boot stepped into his cell, followed by its mate. The boots were not those of the guards. Nay, these boots had never seen the mire and muck that was the gaol floor.

He felt a surge of bitterness. Was it his father after all this time? Had he finally come to retract his false accusations and pay for Jules's release?

The first three months Jules had been hopeful that his father would come. Yet as the months slid by, he had realized his mistake. There was no hope of that—instead a desire for revenge had taken hold. He had survived in this hellish place driven by a seething need to make his father pay for ignoring him yet again. As time went by, even that need had slipped away. Gaol had a way of stripping a man of all but his most basic drives. Eventually his pride had withered and died as he focused on the herculean task of staying alive until he could find some way to escape this hellhole.

The light at the doorway increased and Jules was forced to look away as his eyes adjusted to the brightness. Once the pain eased, he turned back to peer through the curious mix of light and gloom to see a dark figure standing in the doorway.

Something about the man was familiar.

Jules's attention sharpened as he watched the monolith step through the cell door. The time alone in silence had sharpened his senses. He heard the crisp rustle of finely starched linen as the man stepped toward him, his footfalls heavy but confident. He smelled the scent of roasted pork and rosemary mixed with horse and peat. The man, whoever he was, had taken a fine meal before coming to him on horseback.

A second figure appeared in the doorway. The guard. He followed close behind the large man. "Are you sure you want this one?"

"Absolutely," the man replied in a deep voice.

As Jules's eyes adjusted to the light, he could see the figure was clad in the red-and-green livery of the Earl of Lennox. A man who was not the earl looked at him, his eyes large and piercing. Eyes he remembered from his youth as a squire to Lord Lennox. "Angus?" The word came out as a croak. Jules swallowed, moistening his dry throat, and tried again. "Angus?"

"'Tis I." Angus drew nearer, then frowned as he stared into Jules's face. "Good God. Ye look like hell." He turned back to the guard. "He's too thin. Have ye not been feeding the man?"

The guard scuttled to his side. He picked up Jules's shackled left wrist and squeezed his biceps. "He's firm and vital and feisty as sin."

Angus grunted and handed the man a sheaf of papers. "These documents proclaim his innocence in the murder of Mary MacIntyre."

The man shoved the papers in his belt. "I cannot release him until his fines are paid."

Angus held out a heavy-looking black pouch. "He's mine now. His fines are paid."

Jules longed to ask if his father had finally sent for him, but the look in Angus's tired gray eyes told him the truth. His father had no part of what now transpired. He tucked away the hurt and lifted his chin, prepared for whatever came next.

Questions swirled through his brain, but he held his tongue, praying Angus would not change his mind before he was freed. He held his breath as the guard looped the long end of the pouch around his belt and fished for his keys. With a flick of his hand he opened the lock that held Jules manacled to the wall. "Shall I leave the chains?"

"He's a free man. Free men are not chained."

"As I said before, he's a wild one." The guard shrugged. "But he's all yours. Bought and paid for." He released the bindings at Jules's wrists and the chains clanked to the floor.

Jules could only stand where he was, allowing his body, his arms, to adjust to their sudden lightness. Taking his inaction for hesitation, the guard jerked Jules forward. At the rapid motion he nearly tumbled to the floor before Angus caught him. The big hands set Jules on his feet once more, then Angus shrugged off his cape and placed it around Jules's shoulders. "Come. We've a ways to travel."

Jules followed, forcing himself to keep up with the larger man's steps. He bit back the pain the movement caused and shuffled through the doorway after his benefactor. He did not know why Angus had come for him. He did not care as long as he would be free. They made their way down a low corridor toward a flight of stairs leading to the gaol's receiving yard. There, just outside the gate, waited two horses.

Outside, Jules lifted his face to the sky and sucked in a breath of sweet-smelling air. This was what freedom smelled like. He almost smiled, then caught himself. He still had no idea why Angus had come. He was certain there would be some way he would be made to pay for his release.

"Go ahead and mount, Master Jules." Angus's voice was surprisingly gentle as he led him to stand beside the smaller of the two horses.

Jules grasped the edge of the saddle and tried to pull himself up. He floundered, his legs too weak to push himself upward. His strength had deteriorated in the past sixteen months. He would have to do something about that, and quickly, if he were to survive and thrive in the world beyond the gaol walls. He clenched his teeth and tried once more to mount on his own. A heartbeat later, Angus's hands unceremoniously lifted him off the ground and settled him on the horse's back.

"You'll get yer strength back in time, son." Angus patted his leg before he moved to his own horse and settled onto the animal's back. With a soft cluck, he encouraged both beasts forward.

Silence hung between them as they made their way down the road, leaving the gaol behind. Only when they could no longer see the building did Angus stop. He turned to Jules. "No doubt yer wondering why I came for ye."

"You are about to tell me that." Instead of trepidation, excitement pulsed through his veins. Angus had had a purpose for releasing him. What would it be like to have purpose in his life again? Headiness almost made him dizzy. He clutched the reins more firmly. The horse beneath him responded with a sideways shuffle. Jules relaxed his grip and the horse settled once more.

"Aye. I am." Angus chuckled. "Yer freedom is yours whether ye agree to what I offer or not."

"What do you offer?"

"A competition."

Jules frowned. "I am in no shape currently for any type of sport."

Angus's gray eyes sparkled. "This sport ye have always excelled at."

Jules's frown deepened. "Please, Angus, speak plainly. My wit is not as sharp as it used to be."

Angus reached inside his tunic and withdrew a folded sheet of parchment. He extended the missive to Jules. "This will explain everything."

Jules broke the seal and unfolded the message. He read the words penned in ink, then read them again. "Whose hare-brained idea was this?"

"Lady Margaret's."

"Lady Jane is the prize?"

Angus nodded. "Will ye compete?"

A surge of strength infused Jules's tired body. He would do anything for Jane. He would regain his strength for her. He would compete for her. And if he won, he would release her from this crazy directive . . . if that was what the lady wanted.

13

Because while he had spent the last sixteen months in gaol, if it had not been for Jane, who had stood up for him when his own father would not, he would be dead.

"I will compete."

Angus smiled. "I'm pleased to hear that, son. Very pleased, indeed."

Jules swallowed hard, thinking. Angus might be happy at his decision, but the more important question was, would Jules's reappearance in her life please Jane?

Bryce MacCallister moved with the utmost care down the stone stairway. His head felt as though it had a heartbeat of its own. It pulsed with every step. He walked slowly, his muscles stiff, in an attempt to silence the relentless throbbing. That fifth tankard of ale had seemed like a good idea last night while he celebrated his narrow escape from the marriage knot. This morning he was not so certain. He released a groan. Then regretted it as his head thrummed all the harder.

As he neared the bottom of the stairs, he realized the thrumming in his head was actually a steady knock upon his door. "Mendleson," he called, and turned his head to look for his steward, then cursed softly as pain stabbed his temples and behind his eyes. Where was the man? And who could this be knocking on his door so early in the morning?

Bryce jerked the door open. "Stop that incessant noise!" Slanted rays of afternoon sunlight hit him squarely in the eyes. He squinted against the glare and recognized the hunched, familiar silhouette framed in the doorway. "Come in and shut the goddamn door," he said in a growl as he turned away from the light.

"My apologies, Sir Bryce." Ollie's voice was cheerful as he entered the foyer and shut the door. "You look like you've had a hard night, sir. My own experience has taught me that another tankard of ale with a raw egg mixed in will serve you well."

The thought of more ale turned Bryce's stomach. But he knew Ollie was right. Ollie was always right. "Have you traveled all this way to dispense your wisdom about drinking too much?"

"Nay, sir." Ollie's lips quirked as he shuffled past Bryce into the sitting room on the left. "You look as though you're going to fall over. Why don't we sit down while we discuss why I've come?"

Bryce had no choice but to walk slowly after the man. He gave Ollie a sour look as he dropped into the chair nearest the door. "Why are you here?" he asked flatly.

"I came to invite you to Bellhaven Castle." With gnarled fingers, Ollie thrust a folded missive at him. "This will explain everything."

"Read it to me." Bryce's stomach curled at the thought of reading anything. He drew a sharp breath, alleviating his nausea as he made a mental note to himself to never drink ale again in celebration or misery. Mary Thorne had lived up to her name. Despite the dowry she would have brought him, she had become a thorn in his side. Thank goodness he'd had the sense to cut his losses and leave when he did, or he would have made the foolish mistake of proposing. Then he would have been tied to that harridan forever.

While Ollie fumbled with the seal, Bryce closed his eyes and leaned his head back. An ache unfurled within him that had nothing to do with his overindulgence of the previous night. He wanted to belong somewhere, not just feel as though he waited for something that was never going to happen. He wanted to belong at Bellhaven. He wanted the castle, the land, and all the glory that came with the Lennox fortune. But Jacob and Jane stood in his way. And he was not the murdering type.

Although, he had considered such a dreadful deed in the dark hours of last night. . . . Poison would be the easiest way to rid himself of Jane and Jacob. Bryce gave a mental sigh. What was he thinking? He would never . . .

"You are invited . . ." Ollie's voice broke through his thoughts. "A competition . . ." The deep-throated voice droned on. "Lady Jane Lennox's hand in marriage . . ."

Bryce snapped his eyes open, ignoring the rush of dizziness that followed, and met Ollie's curious stare. "What did you say?"

Ollie set the invitation aside and leaned forward in his chair. "You have been invited to Bellhaven to compete for Lady Jane Lennox's hand in marriage."

"They are putting Lady Jane on the auction block?" Bryce pressed his fingers to his temples as he tried to make sense of Ollie's words. "Compete? Whatever for?"

"Both Lord Lennox and Master Jacob are missing. Presumed dead," Ollie said softly, all his good humor gone.

"I saw them at the Battle of Bothwell Bridge." Memories of the battle turned over in his mind. The battle had been a bloody one. So many Covenanters had died. Bryce frowned. "I saw them both before the conflict."

"They never returned."

"Never returned? That was six months ago." Bryce pressed his fingers to his temples again in hopes that the pressure would help him clear his thoughts. *Bellhaven.*

His breath stilled. A sense of disbelief tingled in his chest, radiating out to his hands and feet. Bryce knew the provisions of Lord Lennox's estate. With both of the male heirs to the Lennox fortune gone, Jane was the only obstacle left to conquer. If Jane were to inherit, she would have to marry before Christmastide began. If she did not, everything—the castle, the land, the fortune—would all become his. But if he married her, he would have the estate, the fortune, and Jane.

Bryce sat up, suddenly sober. They were trying to marry her off to someone other than him. Bryce muttered a low curse.

Ollie straightened, looking much younger suddenly than his seventy-one years. "I know what thoughts are going through that pickled brain of yours right now, sir. But the only way for you to get what you want is to compete with the others, fairly."

"I should not have to compete for what is mine."

"It's not yours. It's Lady Jane's until she fails to marry. And I suspect she will marry one of the other gentlemen who have been invited just to make certain that doesn't happen." Ollie got to his feet and headed for the door. "I need your response, Sir Bryce. You have just as good a chance of winning her hand as any of the others."

"God's Blood," Bryce muttered through clenched teeth.

Ollie nodded. "I'll take that as a *yes*." He placed the invitation on the seat of the chair he had just vacated. "I'm off to visit another suitor nearby. Read the invitation yourself after you have that morning ale. We look forward to your arrival at Bellhaven," he said as he left. A moment later Bryce heard the front door close.

He'd be damned if he would let Lady Jane Lennox marry another man. Entering this competition might make him a laughingstock among his peers, but what other choice did he have?

Poison. His earlier thought came back to him. He shook his head, then regretted the action. He clamped his head in his hands as he made his way to the kitchen. A glass of ale would help him think more clearly. Once the pounding in his head was gone, he had to figure out what he would do to keep what he so desperately wanted.

A chill that heralded snow filled the late afternoon air as Sir Nicholas Kincaid brought his horse to a stop outside his own stable. A man in a familiar livery waited for him there, standing at the arched doorway.

"Sir Nicholas." The man he once knew as the steward of Bellhaven Castle greeted him with a bow.

Nicholas jumped from his horse as a sense of unease filled him. "Ollie, what brings you here?" Why would Ollie come to him? He had not seen Jacob Lennox for the past two years, not since Jacob's father had come back into his friend's life.

"I have a message for you."

"From Jacob?"

"Nay." The old man's eyes filled with sorrow. "From Lady Margaret." Ollie extended a folded missive. "This will explain everything."

Nicholas did not reach for the missive. What could the Lennoxes want with him? His and Jacob's friendship had run its course. There was nothing left between them but painful memories of the last time Jacob had dismissed him from Jane's life.

"Sir Nicholas," Ollie said, taking the three steps that separated them. "The message from Lady Margaret is most urgent."

Nicholas reached awkwardly for the paper. The only reason Lady Margaret would contact him was if Jacob were dead. He shivered involuntarily as pain snagged his heart. He had always meant to return to Bellhaven one day and make amends with Jacob. Now it seemed he would never have that chance.

He read the missive and frowned. "This is not news of Jacob."

"Nay, sir, as I stated, it is from the Lady Margaret. She needs your assistance with a matter concerning Lady Jane Lennox."

Jane. Nicholas had wanted to pursue her. Jacob had let him know, in no uncertain terms, that Nicholas was not good enough for his sister. A mere "sir" with questionable heritage would never be a match for his precious sister.

Nicholas stared down at the note in his hands. Why did Jacob not object to *this?* If he had read the invitation correctly, it appeared that Lady Margaret was about to barter off Jacob's sister to the man who could pass a few feats of skill. Her hand in marriage would be essentially auctioned off to the man with the most resolve.

"Where is Jacob?" Nicholas asked.

Ollie's shoulders slumped. "It appears that he and his father were killed in the Battle of Bothwell Bridge. No bodies were ever recovered, but they left Bellhaven nearly six months ago and never returned."

"Lady Jane is alone?"

"Lady Margaret and I have been watching over her, but others are starting to deduce that the Lennox men are not returning. The ladies have been challenged four times already. Lady Jane fears a much larger attack is imminent. The land, the title—"

"Lady Jane."

"Aye, sir. The situation is tenuous." Ollie's brows drew together as he appraised Nicholas.

Nicholas could feel judgment radiating from Ollie. That was all he needed, another pair of accusing eyes, another person judging him by an invisible standard he had never understood. Nicholas shook off the thought, forcing himself to relax. Ollie was not his father.

"I remember you once had a fondness for our Jane. If you care at all about her still, you will come to Bellhaven and help her."

Nicholas squeezed his eyes shut, battling memories with everything inside him. There had been a time in his life when he had thought perhaps he had a chance with someone like Jane. The years he had spent in her presence were a time that stood apart in his mind—like a shining haven amidst the ruthless beatings from his own father, the dark holes he had lived in, the long nights without food, no security, and no hope. All he had to do was look into Jane's eyes, feel her hand tucked into his own, and his loneliness fled. She was a sliver of goodness in his life—something worth fighting for, something worth risking everything for. Until he had looked into Jacob's unrelenting eyes and had seen the truth. He never had a chance with Jane.

Nicholas rubbed his temples in an attempt to banish his memories. That was long ago. He straightened and opened his eyes. Life had been a cruel teacher, but Nicholas was a different man now. No longer was he anyone else's pawn. He had fame, riches, and independence. But no one else had ever filled that void in his heart like Jane.

He took a deep breath as hope began to unfurl. She was up for bid in a ridiculous contest of wit and skill. Without Jacob nearby to question his suitability, he just might stand a chance of winning her hand. "I accept," Nicholas said, his tone firm. "I will join Lady Jane at Bellhaven in two days' time."

In two days, he would change his life forever.

Hollister Cay, the Earl of Galloway, stood at the open window and stared to the south toward Renfrewshire. He could not see the object of his thoughts, but somehow it helped to look in her direction. Lady Jane Lennox. A thrill moved through him as he recalled the invitation he had accepted earlier that day. At thirty-six years of age he finally had what he had longed for, a new challenge, a potential conquest that suddenly left him feeling unsatisfied with all the women who had come before her. Even the one in his bed right now.

He looked back at the palatial bed in the center of the room, and the creamy skin of the woman he had only moments before enjoyed. He had taken her with the same bottomless hunger that stirred his blood each night. She had cried out beneath him with the greatest pleasure and yet he still felt nothing at all. Would Lady Jane touch his heart as no woman ever had before? He had heard the rumors circulating about Lady Jane in the past few months. *A passionate harlot. A seductress. A woman open to experience and desire.*

The claims had seemed so out of line with the young woman he had met on several occasions as she tended to her father's guests. But then again, people could change—loneliness could make a person do desperate things. And Lady Jane had been alone for the past six months.

"Hollister?"

"Hmmm?"

She smoothed the sheets with her fingers. "Come back to bed."

"I am restless tonight, my sweet." He turned back to look at her. Her ebony hair spilled across the pillow and she had tossed back the sheet, exposing her sultry body.

"Then come here and let me ease your restlessness."

Instead of renewed interest, a familiar coldness settled inside. "I must prepare to leave," he said on a sigh.

"Are you going to answer that absurd invitation and go to her?" she said, her voice sharp, then bit her lip, as though she knew she had overstepped her bounds. "You will be one of six men competing for her hand. You do not like competition." Shapely brows puckered into a scowl above her flashing brown eyes.

"It is a competition I intend to win."

She sat up and pulled the sheet over her body, shielding herself from his eyes. "And what happens if she does not want you? Or if you do conquer her only to be left unsatisfied, as your reputation claims? What then?"

Hollister turned back to stare out at the starry night. A lonely hoot of an owl echoed through the night and he felt an answering cry well up within him. He knew what loneliness felt like and what it did to one's soul.

The chill air touched his skin, raising gooseflesh on his bare torso but also his hopes. "Lady Jane will be different." The thought of her rumored seductive nature, her passionate reaction to his touch, hardened his body.

He had known Lady Jane for years as the daughter of his friend. With Henry gone, the way was clear for him to taste what he had always longed for. Then perhaps his insatiable desire would finally be quenched, his restlessness would end, and he would finally be at peace.

An odd sensation fluttered in his chest. Hollister nearly startled at the intensity of the feeling. How odd. It was not lust he felt. Nay, for the first time in ages, he actually felt hope. 'Twas a heady feeling, indeed.

Jane gathered her heavy cloak about her shoulders as she leaned against the cold stone of Bellhaven's north tower. She peered through the stone crenellations to the castle's approach. Snow had fallen last night, leaving a chill in the morning air and turning the landscape beyond into a blanket of white. Over the pristine whiteness paraded a column of men on horseback that stretched from the borders of Bellhaven to the lowered drawbridge below. Her army had arrived, an army made up of six men's retinues.

Six men.

Her suitors.

Jane released a ragged sigh. This was madness. She did not want to pick a husband from a group of men. Margaret had not elaborated on who the men were, other than her cousin, but they would be men she had met before. There was not a single male in her past she would consider marrying . . . except perhaps . . . Jane straightened. No, she would not consider such a thing.

There had to be a way out of this *arrangement* Margaret had concocted. Scottish law allowed for a woman to inherit her father's lands if there were no male heirs in the direct line. Her father might not deem her worthy, but she had run Bellhaven in part for many years, though fully over the last two while her father and brother had been too busy with their warring to care about the castle and its inhabitants.

In their absence, she had proven herself a capable heiress. But inheriting Bellhaven would not be any easier than living with her father had been. She knew the provisions he had left behind—a will specifically stating that if her father were declared dead, she must marry by Christmas Eve in order to inherit, or the land and title would go to her cousin Bryce.

The courts would see Bryce MacCallister as the indirect heir no matter if she contested his claim. Jane leaned her head back and closed her eyes. The only way for her to stay in her home and protect her people was to choose one of the other suitors Margaret had provided.

"There you are." Margaret's familiar voice sounded in the morning coolness.

"I needed some air." Jane opened her eyes, returning her gaze to the men below. "Do I truly have to pick a husband from these men?"

"There is no other way." Margaret brought her hand up to stroke Jane's cloak-covered shoulder. "The sooner you accept the need, my dear, and turn your mindset to one of pleasure and discovery, the better this competition will go for you."

Jane groaned. "I have so many other, bigger, problems at present."

"Such as?" Margaret asked lightly.

Jane frowned. How could the woman be so annoyingly happy when Jane's own world was about to end? "My need for an army."

Margaret waved a hand to the crowd below. "They are here. What other problems could you have?"

"Have you forgotten the rumors of my wanton reputation spread by—" Jane broke off as memories surged to the front of her mind, so powerful, they stole her breath. How could a man she had trusted with her whole heart and soul say such horrible things about her?

A look of understanding crossed Margaret's face. "I know what you are thinking," she said softly. "There has to be an explanation. Give him the chance to explain."

"Nicholas is here?"

Margaret nodded.

Jane tried to find words, any words, but all she had were memories and stark, sudden fear. Only moments ago she had wondered what it might be like to have him here, to see him again, but now in the face of that reality she trembled. "No, I cannot face him."

"Yes, Jane, you can. You are stronger than that."

In her mind she saw Nicholas as he had been when he had left her two years ago—the dark-haired handsome hero who had stolen her heart and kissed her for the very first time. Then came the hurtful memories, the ones that lingered long after he had gone. Jane forced those thoughts away and raised her chin. Nicholas was here. She would see him again, and she would show him that she was a woman now, not the girl he had left behind. "You are right, Margaret. I have learned to be strong in the past two years."

Margaret smiled. "Yes, you have."

Jane returned her gaze to the men below. "Nicholas and Bryce. Who are the others?"

"You will find out soon. But every one of those men arrived one day ahead of schedule." She winked. "They are eager for you as their prospective bride."

That left her ten days to choose one of them as her new husband. Jane tensed, angry that Margaret could talk about this with pleasure. She was angry at herself for not having another option. But she was angriest of all that she felt so terribly alone. She wished for a crazy, desperate minute that she had not been born as Lady Jane Lennox, subsequent heir to the Bellhaven fortune. These men were not eager for her. They wanted what she would bring to the winner.

Jane's throat thickened. She swallowed against it, finding no relief. Then again, who else would she be? And if she was not Lady Jane, she would not have Margaret in her life. Margaret was more than her aunt, she was her closest friend. And she needed a friend right now. Her aunt was only ten years her senior, yet she had taken on the role of mother after Jane's own mother had died. At times, Jane forgot how young Margaret truly was, but at the moment she was grateful for her aunt's friendship above all else.

Jane turned to her aunt with a tremulous smile. "Have I ever told you how grateful I am that you are in my life?"

"Many times." Margaret opened her arms, and Jane immediately went to her, folding herself into Margaret's strength and faith and love. Tears came to her eyes. "Oh, Margaret. . . ."

"I know, dear." Her aunt hugged her all the harder.

Jane knew Margaret understood what she did not say. Her aunt realized this moment was about more than just the suitors below. It was the first time Jane had cried over the loss of her father and brother. If she must be without them, then at least she was fully in charge of her own life. Whatever good or sorrow came to her from this point on would be a result of her own choices. The thought was a heady and terrifying mix.

"The six men below are a gift, one that will offer you a chance at happiness once more," Margaret said in a soothing tone.

Jane pulled back, her hands still resting on Margaret's waist. "Marriage does not necessarily bring happiness. You and I both know that all too well."

Margaret sighed. "Yes, but marriage can bring happiness, no matter how fleeting that emotion."

Jane knew her aunt referred to her own short marriage, but Jane's thoughts moved to her parents. "I am not sure my father was ever happy with his choice."

"You and I do not know what happened between your father and mother. However, you are in control of what happens to you, at least when it comes to choosing a partner for the rest of your days."

Jane bit down on her lip. "What if I do not want to marry any of them? Or what if none of them fancy me after they get to know me better?"

Margaret smiled and her eyes twinkled once more. "Now you are merely making up obstacles where none exist. These men all accepted the invitations. They like you, Jane, or they would not have come. You should be more worried about what you will do when they all fall in love with you. I have a feeling it will be you who will be breaking a few hearts before Christmas Eve."

Margaret took one of Jane's hands in her own. "Come now, my dear. Let us go below stairs and prepare to meet the men who will court you."

Jane's earlier trepidation was replaced with a small bubble of hope. Her aunt had said she would know most of the men below stairs, and they knew her. She should be thinking of this as more of a reunion than a sacrifice of the virgin bride. The thought pulled up the corner of Jane's mouth into a half smile. "Very well," she agreed. "They did travel all this way."

Margaret smiled. "That's the right spirit for this competition." She gestured toward the door and together they proceeded down the stairs, through the hallways of the castle, and finally to the stairway that led to the great hall.

Jane paused at the top of the stairwell. Sound roared around her as the men and their retinues talked to each other. The chamber vibrated with energy. There had not been this many visitors to Bellhaven Castle in many years. Jane took four steps down, then paused again as the room suddenly fell silent and all eyes turned toward her. Jane's heartbeat sped up as Margaret slid the heavy cloak from her shoulders, revealing her green linen dress beneath. She had not dressed with this occasion in mind this morning, yet she was grateful now that she had at least added the flare of her mother's gold and ruby girdle about her hips.

"You look beautiful, my dear," Margaret said quietly, as though understanding Jane's sudden insecurity. Margaret took Jane's arm and she gave her aunt a quick smile at the show of support. Together they continued down the stairs.

By the time Jane reached the room, her heart was beating wildly and there was a fine sheen of sweat on her palms. She took a deep breath and stepped toward the dais. She could feel the gazes of the men and their retinues watching her, appraising her. Margaret led her to her chair and she eased down into it, grateful for the support. Margaret set aside her cloak and Jane's, then remained standing beside her chair.

"Welcome, one and all, to Bellhaven Castle. We are pleased you could join us. As your first challenge, I would like you, one at a time, to come forward and present Lady Jane Josephina Catherine Lennox with your gift of welcome. Once you have all greeted Lady Jane, she will determine the winner of the first challenge. After that, you will be taken to your chambers." Margaret lifted her chin, and after a slight hesitation said, "I will call you forward in the order you arrived at the castle."

The silence of the room shattered into a hundred voices. "I arrived first," called out Hollister Cay, the Earl of Galloway. He strode forward with confidence. Jane had not seen him in many years. He had been a young friend of her father's, but she had never seen him this close before. He was older than many of the others in the chamber, but he wore his age well. Tall and slender and elegant were words she would use to describe him. His broad shoulders tapered to a trim waist, giving him an athletic look. Despite his age, he would be very competitive in the games ahead. She brought her gaze back to his face. His mouth seemed kind, but his eyes bored into hers. In their dark depths she read hunger, weariness, and strength.

"Lord Galloway," Jane acknowledged with a thickness in her voice. Men did not usually look at her in that way, or at least they did not until the rumors of her licentious nature had started.

Jane pressed back into her chair as she continued her visual exploration. His dark hair was neatly trimmed and his brows perfectly sculpted above his dark, searching eyes. He wore a coat of deep blue velvet with a white linen shirt beneath. Brussels lace fell gracefully over the knuckles of his long, lean fingers, and more lace cascaded from beneath his chin. His breeches were tight and made of tawny doeskin. His leather boots hugged his calves, climbed past his knees and were folded in cuffs over his muscular thighs.

The earl sketched an elegant bow. He straightened, then continued forward as his mouth stretched into a wide grin. It was a beautiful smile, easy and charming, and it brought shivers of excitement and discomfort. This man was both beautiful and dangerous. She had no idea why she thought that, but just looking at him made her feel as though she were entering some sort of

27

forbidden, enticing territory. She was afraid to step into the unknown with him. She was certain it would cost her a price she could not name, and yet something about him beckoned her to be reckless.

Jane shook off the unsettling sensation. "My lord, you have traveled a great distance. I thank you for that."

He stepped closer. "I would have traveled twice the distance and more to bring you this gift." He extended his hands and offered her a highly polished wooden box. "For you."

Jane accepted the box, but he did not release it. Instead, his fingers folded around hers. Sensation danced between them and her gaze moved back to his face.

"A beautiful woman deserves beautiful things. Open it." He released her hands.

Jane took a deep breath, suddenly unnerved by his gift—all the gifts she would receive this day as a means to garner her favor.

She slid back the wooden lid to reveal a long, lustrous strand of ivory pearls. She had never seen such plump pearls before. They shimmered as though they were freshly plucked from the sea.

She returned her gaze to Lord Galloway's. The dark centers of his eyes flared as his gaze flowed down her body and slowly, incrementally, roved back up her person, settling on the neckline of her gown with lazy regard. Her hand instinctively fluttered to her throat.

"Allow me to help you put them on?" He asked the question, but his fingers had already captured the strand and he lifted it over her head. He slid the cool orbs against her warmed flesh, then settled them in place with capable fingers. "Beautiful," he said, his voice deep, heavy, and smooth.

"Thank you," Jane replied, unsettled that his fingers still lingered against the pearls. These men would all try to win the competition with their gifts, their careful smiles, and knowing touches. Her gaze moved from Lord Galloway to the other men gathered at the base of the dais. These men were her suitors, and she would marry one of them.

"Lord Galloway, I thank you for the very thoughtful and very expensive gift of these pearls." She lifted his hand from where it rested on the pearls and gently set it free near his side. "I adore pearls."

Lord Galloway straightened and his mouth quirked as he turned back to face his competitors. "'Tis only the beginning of the gifts I intend to shower upon you, my lady," he said, then with a bow strode back to join the others.

Jane allowed her gaze to follow him and then to shift to the others gathered there. For the first time she had a clear view of the men her aunt had invited. Her heart leapt to her throat with a combination of fear and joy as her gaze moved over them. Jules MacIntyre, her cousin Bryce, David Buchanan, a man she did not recognize, and Nicholas Kincaid.

"Sir David Buchanan, come forward and greet Lady Jane," Margaret called out from beside Jane before she could even react to the tangle of emotions within her.

David came forward wearing leather armor. He knelt before her, his boiled leather creaking as he did. "Lady Jane, I am at your service. To protect you or marry you, whichever pleases you most."

Jane could feel heat come to her cheeks. "Sir David, please rise," she said when he remained on the ground before her, his head bowed.

"As you wish," he said, his deep voice moving through her. He stood and she suddenly remembered how tall he was. Well over six feet. He looked tough, dangerous, and as handsome as ever. Energy shimmered off him in waves as it always had. His brown hair was neatly trimmed around his ears, revealing high cheekbones in his angular face. Somehow she had also forgotten how broad his chest was, made more so by his leather and metal plating, and how the leather of his armor clung to muscular thighs. His arms hung at his sides and his deep brown eyes were fixed on her.

"You will not need your armor here, Sir David."

He looked back at his competition quickly, then returned his gaze to hers. "In that assessment, you may be wrong." His mouth tipped briefly to one side in a smile that lived and died in an instant. He moved closer until he was

29

no more than an arm's reach away. "I am here to protect you, from harm, from them, whatever is needed."

His voice was impossible to ignore, and his eyes swirled with power.

Yes, she was certain he would protect her from the others. "But who will protect me from you?" she whispered beneath her breath, but he must have heard because he moved even closer.

"There is no need for protection, Lady Jane, because I am already yours, and you are mine."

He was just so much of a male specimen, the woman in her had never been able to ignore him. Staring up into his deep brown eyes she wondered if he knew the effect he had on women.

"I am not yours. I am not anyone's. Not yet," she said as she straightened in her chair.

Again a brief smile came to his lips. "As you command, Lady Jane." He bowed once more. "May I offer you a gift, then, to truly get this competition started?"

She nodded.

He moved back to his men to gather something hidden beneath a muslin cloth, then approached her once more. "My gift to you, my lady." His words lingered on the word *my*.

Jane accepted the cloth-covered bundle. It moved and her pulse jumped. Her gaze shot to David's. "What is it?"

"There is only one way to find out."

Carefully she set the mass in her lap and pulled back the cloth to reveal a tiny black ball of fur. "It is a puppy?"

"An Aberdeen terrier," he said proudly. "She is a pup from my own Aberdennies Fala and Brock. And just like her mother and sire, she will be feisty and loyal. She will protect you with her life, if necessary."

The puppy wiggled free of the cloth, then reached up and chewed the pearls Lord Galloway had given her. The earl frowned. Jane chuckled. At that, the puppy stopped and looked at her with bright brown eyes. A moment later it settled back in her lap and nudged Jane's arm until it lay across the animal's small, furry body. She licked Jane's hand three times before closing her eyes, suddenly asleep. "She is adorable." Jane smiled up at David, feeling the happiest she had been in a long while. "Thank you so much for . . . Oh my, I will have to think of a name for this little girl."

"I am sure you will think of something fitting." With another bow, he stepped back into the line of suitors.

Jane was grateful for the diversion of the puppy as her aunt's voice called out once more. "Jules MacIntyre, please approach Lady Jane and present her with your gift."

As Jules stepped forward, Jane tried to keep the look of shock from her face. The Jules she remembered from sixteen months ago was gone. This Jules was pale and thin, and lines of weariness had settled around his eyes and his mouth. He looked sad and lost, not his usual dashing self at all. He was wearing a baggy black jerkin and black breeches. Even so, he was still tall with the potential for strength. His long blond hair hung loose about his shoulders as he stared at her with the most startling blue eyes she had ever seen.

"Lady Jane," he said, bowing deeply.

"It is so very good to see you," she said, meaning it. She had done the right thing, sending him to gaol instead of the noose. It had cost her every bit of jewelry she owned except her mother's girdle. He might not have enjoyed his time in gaol, but at least he was alive. Jane sat up in her chair, her spine stiff. Apparently because of this bizarre contest her aunt had devised, he had somehow been set free.

Who had gained his freedom?

Jane pushed the thought aside. It did not matter as long as Jules was safe and free once more. Today was the beginning of a new life for him. Was that new life with her? Did she owe him that for what he had had to endure over the past many months?

"My gift to you." He stepped forward and presented a parcel wrapped in cloth. "As you have restored something to me—" He stopped and brought his intense blue-eyed gaze back to hers. A rare smile came to his lips. "You have given me back my life. For that, it is time I returned something to you."

Whatever could he mean? Curious, Jane pulled the wrapping away from the object to reveal a small wooden figure.

"My doll," she whispered. "However did you find her?" She had lost Meriwether so long ago. Jane had shed many tears over the loss of her favorite toy.

A look of remorse settled over his features. "You did not lose her. We were playing a game of hide-and-go-seek, remember? Below stairs near the buttery, I found a priests' hole from bygone days and hid Meriwether there. I never went back to get her. I just forgot until . . ." He paused and his face became a blank slate. "I had time in gaol to remember all sorts of things."

Despite the mention of his suffering, Jane could not help the wistful feeling that came over her. She and Jules had become the best of friends after that day. But even as the softer emotions came over her, so too did a stab of old hurt. Jane forced it aside. Jules was the injured party here. She could not imagine all he had had to endure in gaol. He started to turn to leave, judging her silence as his signal to go.

She reached for his hand and held it. "Do not go just yet."

He stared down at her, long and hard, then quietly said, "Thank you for not letting them hang me that day."

She swallowed thickly. "I wish I could have—"

He reached toward her and pressed his finger to her lips. "You did more than anyone else, especially my father."

Jane nodded as he shifted his finger to smooth her hair away from her cheek. "You restored my life. I restored your doll. Are we even?" He gave her a soft smile that for a second transformed his weary face.

"Yes."

"A debt repaid," he said with a soft release of breath.

Jane startled at the sudden realization. He had not been the one to give her a gift this day. She had given him one. With her forgiveness she had put that familiar smile back onto his face. A welcome heat warmed her soul. She grinned at her old friend.

Jules MacIntyre was back.

"You two can reminisce later," Aunt Margaret interrupted, placing her hand over where the two of theirs were joined. Jules pulled his hand back, bowed, then returned to where the others stood waiting.

Jane's fingers felt cold at the loss of her friend's touch. She clamped her hands together, waiting for her next suitor to greet her.

"Bryce MacCallister, please approach Lady Jane." Her aunt's voice startled Jane back to the moment.

Her cousin Bryce came forward with his hand behind his back. Jane tensed, expecting the worst, but at that moment, the last rays of the morning sun came through the open doorway to the great hall and highlighted the shining darkness of his neatly barbered hair.

Had Bryce changed? Was that errant ray of light a signal from the universe that her cousin had left his anger at Jacob and herself behind him?

She offered Bryce a smile as he bowed. She searched his face, looking for more signs of transformation. His long sideburns accented the high cheekbones of his slightly elongated face, and the hollow line of his jaw and deeply bronzed skin. Compared to Jules's paleness, Bryce looked healthy and vital. His attire continued the impression—a waist-length dark blue tunic, a shirt of fine white muslin, and black breeches with polished black boots. He moved with a restless grace as if suppressing a powerful and volatile energy so similar to that of her father and brother. Perhaps her smile shrank a measure.

A shadow of stubble darkened his cheek and a cynical smile curved his lips. He brought his hand out from behind him to reveal a bouquet of tiny white snowdrops. Their heads drooped toward the ground and several petals fell onto Jane's lap to settle around the puppy as he pushed them toward her.

"Greetings, cousin. Please accept my gift."

Jane took the wilting flowers. Immediately, the puppy in her lap stirred and began chewing them, tossing the small white heads into the air until only one bent flower remained. Jane held the bruised stem out of the dog's reach.

"Thank you, Bryce. Very thoughtful."

He frowned. "I suppose I should thank you for including me among your many suitors." A hint of irritation lingered in his words. Perhaps he was not so changed after all.

"You are here at my invitation, Bryce," Aunt Margaret interrupted.

For an instant, venomous anger flickered in Bryce's eyes. He shot a glance at Margaret then turned back to Jane. "No matter who invited me, I am here."

Jane frowned. Nay, he had not changed at all.

His dark eyes fixed on her. "I intend to marry you and keep what should be mine."

"Nothing is certain, Bryce. I get to decide—"

His face hardened. "You brought me here. I must have just as great a chance of winning your hand as any of these fools." He stepped forward, intent, his concentration focused to a rapier sharpness. Jane pressed back against the chair until the wood bit into her back. He smiled, one side of his mouth turning up and carving a deep line beneath a high, broad cheek. A wicked smile. A devil's smile.

"Bryce, you will have to play by the rules. All of the rules," Jane breathed.

Bryce reached past her to place his hand on the back of the chair and lean in. His stance emphasized his much greater height. His gaze drifted down her face and throat and lingered where her breasts swelled in agitation above the low, square neckline of her dress. "Rules are meant to be broken."

Out of the corner of her eye she saw David tense. Lord Galloway's eyes darkened.

Jane shifted her attention back to the man before her. His gaze unsettled her. "Bryce, please . . ."

"Please what? Please myself?" He gave a humorless laugh and darkness flared in his eyes.

A sense of panic rose within her as he closed the short distance between their mouths. He crushed her lips. She fought against the intimacy, pushing him away. When pushing failed to remove him, she struck his chest with her fist.

The puppy in her lap growled. A heartbeat later Bryce was ripped away. Jules had him by one arm, David the other. Both men's faces were flushed and their eyes were wide with anger. "Are you all right?" Jules asked.

"I am unharmed," she said, dragging the back of her hand across her lips, her gaze fixed on Bryce. "Never kiss me without my permission." To hide the anger that made her fingers tremble, she turned her attention to the puppy in her lap, stroking the animal behind the ear. The pup immediately curled into a ball and settled in her lap once more as though nothing had transpired.

"You are done here," David snarled, as he pulled Bryce from the dais and returned him to his men below.

Jane pressed her bruised lips together, then released them. Quietly, to her aunt she said, "I am more determined than ever to continue the competition, because of Bryce and his antics."

"Then I suppose I should thank him for that," Aunt Margaret conceded in as hostile a whisper as Jane had ever heard from the woman. "He will never have the opportunity to treat you thusly again, especially in your own hall."

Jane straightened and abandoned the single flower bud on the arm of her chair. "I am ready to meet the next suitor."

"Very wise, my dear," Margaret said. She patted Jane's shoulder before returning to the edge of the dais. "I call forth Sir Nicholas Kincaid."

Jane looked up sharply. She longed to see Nicholas again—longed—but half dreaded, too.

He bowed, then came forward carrying a small parcel.

"I trust you to be a proper gentleman," Margaret said, her eyes narrowing sharply. "You are here by my good graces. Do not do anything, say anything, that might harm Jane any further than you already have."

Nicholas's brows drew together in confusion. "I would never hurt Lady Jane."

Oh, but he had. Jane had imagined this moment in her thoughts and her dreams for the last six months since the rumors had started to circulate. In those moments, she had wanted to act with cool reserve. She wanted to hurt him as much as he had injured her and her reputation. Instead, her body rebelled as the old attraction between them sparked, warming her cheeks.

"Thank you for inviting me here," he said with sincerity.

She had forgotten the sound of his voice, low-toned and warm like honey. Yet today, his tone carried a certain tension.

She drew in a tight breath. "There is no need to thank me," she answered, proud of the fact her voice sounded unaffected as she gazed into his familiar sherry-colored eyes.

"There is always a need."

They were speaking about common courtesy, and yet his words sounded like so much more. He offered her a half smile. It did little to soften the hard angles of his face, the edged cheekbones, the long planes of his cheeks, the austere set of his features—large sherry eyes set under a broad forehead, straight brown brows, surprisingly thick lashes, thin chiseled lips, and the strong prow of his nose. His square chiseled chin bore witness to the stubbornness he usually hid beneath a cloak of easy charm.

To Nicholas Kincaid, charm had always come easy, and its effect on her senses, even now, challenged her efforts to remain open to all her suitors. With a good four feet separating them, she could still feel her body responding to him. Her rib cage tightened and her breathing quickened. Her heart fluttered and her nerves tingled in telltale anticipation. She had not seen him for two long years.

She had changed in that time. No doubt he had as well. And yet . . . Jane pulled her gaze from Nicholas's. "The others are growing restless. Perhaps we should move our reunion along?"

Something changed in his face—a coolness slid into his expression. "I have not presented you with my gift." He moved closer and held out a small parcel wrapped in parchment. She accepted it. Immediately the puppy's eyes snapped open and she started sniffing the parcel.

"If I may," Nicholas said as he bent to pick up the puppy. He nestled the animal close to his chest, humming to the animal as he carried it toward the discarded cloth it had arrived in. Nicholas gathered the cloth into a small bundle then set the animal on top. The puppy immediately nestled into the folds and closed her eyes, once again asleep.

Nicholas straightened and came back to Jane's side just as she reached the contents inside the parchment. Several dark brown chunks of something she had never seen before lay against the honey-colored paper. Wordlessly, she looked back at Nicholas, hoping for an explanation.

"They are shavings," he explained.

"Of what?"

He picked a small piece up off the parchment. "Open your mouth to taste a new delight."

She eyed him with suspicion. "You are going to feed me?"

That charming smile of his returned. "Must you question everything?"

She obediently opened her mouth. He laid a small flake of what he termed a "delight" against her tongue.

"Let it melt, then press it to the roof of your mouth."

Bitter sweetness invaded her senses, as did Nicholas's masculine scent of cinnamon and bay leaves. She closed her eyes as the two scents mixed. She released a soft groan at the intensity of the sensation. The object in her mouth melted and intensified. "What is it?" she begged.

"Chocolate."

"Where?" she asked, unable to finish her sentence as the chocolate slid down her throat in a wave of ecstasy.

"I found it in a little shop in London called the Coffee Mill and Tobacco Roll. Chocolate is said to have rejuvenating properties and is a natural energizer. Do you like it?"

Enjoyment shuddered through Jane so intensely she could only nod her head in agreement. Just as strongly, so too, did the lies he had spread about her. *A passionate seductress.* Although, at the moment, she did not feel seductive, she felt seduced.

Nicholas brought his finger up to the corner of her mouth and touched the fullness of her lower lip. "Imagine a kiss on top of that sweetness . . ."

Margaret bristled.

Jane swallowed. She could imagine the sensation would be dangerous. Despite the years that had separated them, she could still remember the pleasure of his touch and his kisses. "Thank you, Nicholas. That was certainly a memorable gift."

He gave her one last heart-melting smile before he bowed and returned to the others.

Margaret relaxed as he moved away. "That looks unusual," she whispered from beside Jane.

"Have a taste." Jane offered the chocolate to her aunt.

Her aunt placed a small shaving on her tongue and groaned. Jane smiled as Margaret's reaction echoed her own. They both found the treat delicious.

Just like Nicholas. Everything about him was delicious, it always had been. But then again, she had had similar feelings about all the men who had come to greet her. All the men, that was, except Bryce. Suddenly the sweetness lingering in her mouth soured. Bryce was the fly in the ointment, for certain. He would try to stop her from choosing anyone else as her husband.

Jane's gaze fell to the shavings of chocolate that remained on the parchment. She folded the parcel back into its original form. Perhaps she would save these precious treats for the moments when she needed a bit of rejuvenation. The thought pulled up the corners of her lips as she straightened. She had five suitors to choose from and one suitor to send home. Bryce had no idea of her true mettle. But before this contest was through, he would.

"Are you ready to meet Colin?" Margaret asked. "I saved him for last. I found the young man to be quite pleasant. His quick thinking in the face of my accident saved my life."

Jane smiled. "Aye. I am so very grateful for your safety. Bring the man forward so I can thank him properly."

Margaret nodded. "It is with great pleasure that I call forth our final suitor, Colin Taylor."

As Jane watched the stranger approach, she could not stop a small shocked breath. She had imagined the man who had saved her aunt to be a simple countryman. There was nothing simple about Colin Taylor. He was sinfully male, with the sculpted physique of a warrior. He had wide shoulders, well-developed arms, and a tight, muscular chest that filled out his fine muslin shirt. Dark breeches were tucked into black boots. His dress was simple, yet the impression that he was lean and powerful was undeniable.

The man was nothing short of gorgeous. He would certainly leave an impression on her heart if she gave him a chance. He was the type of male women dreamed about in dark fantasies but knew did not really exist. Dark brown lashes swept his golden skin beneath arched brows and a silky fall of honey-colored hair. His jaw was angled and strong, with a slight cleft in his chin. Her heart raced and her palms felt clammy as she continued her visual exploration of his lips—pink and firm and sensually full. His eyes glittered like shards of silver, and his pupils were dilated with a touch of amusement and unmistakable masculine interest.

"Good morrow, Lady Jane," he said with a thick brogue that sounded roughened, as if by too much whiskey and peat smoke. "I am delighted to meet you and honored to be here among your guests."

Jane smiled. Handsome and polite. It was a good start. "I must first thank you for saving my aunt the other day."

He nodded.

Jane continued, "It is a pleasure to have you here."

"Nay, the pleasure has not yet started." He turned and signaled three men with instruments forward. They gathered in a half circle and the two men with a lute and a cittern tuned the strings a moment before they joined the flute and started playing. "The song is called 'The Outlandish Knight.' My gift to you is a dance." He extended his hand to her. "Dance with me, Lady Jane," he said, his voice smooth, compelling.

With a smile, she accepted his hand and he pulled her out of her chair to him, uncharacteristically close for such a dance. But before she could offer a suggestion for some distance, he carried her away with a light step. He sent her into a spin as though she were a butterfly suddenly released from its cocoon. She could not hold back a laugh of enjoyment.

Jane glimpsed each of her suitors as Colin twirled her like a feather dancing on the air. Each man wore an irritated frown.

Her gaze lit on Aunt Margaret, who nodded encouragement and clapped her hands in beat to the music. Jane's cheeks warmed. She had not danced in years. A feeling of euphoria came over her.

The room spun by in a whirl of colors. She closed her eyes and let the sensation of the air swirling past her face take over her senses. She felt the heat of Colin's presence as he took her arm in a promenade. It had been so long since she had known much else but loss and duty. Her life had become maintaining the estate whether her father was here or not. She let the rhythm of the music move through her swaying body. A swirl of air brushed against her fevered cheeks.

She opened her eyes as the music ended and Colin stopped. "Have you had your fill of dancing or should I have the musicians play another tune?" he asked, flashing a charming grin.

"It was a beautiful gift, Colin. I enjoyed myself very much." She dipped her head to avoid his gaze, remembering there was duty yet to serve. "I must make my decision now about who wins this competition."

He nodded, and with a hand on her arm led her back beside her aunt. He took her hand and brought it to his lips, offering her a salute. Heat tingled against her skin where his lips had so briefly touched. She fisted her hand at her side, fighting the sensation.

What was wrong with her to feel attraction for so many men? Aye, they were all handsome, including her cousin Bryce. All except Bryce had fearless hearts, courage, and compassion. And each wanted her to pick him as the winner of this first challenge. Jane stood beside the chair, unable to sit as tension filled her.

"Who will you choose?" Margaret asked, as though reading her thoughts.

At the words, the crowded room rumbled, the voices rising with curiosity. Jane drew in a measured breath. She did not know who had won. Her spirits had been lifted because of the dance. The weight of the pearls pressed against her flesh, and she tasted a lingering hint of chocolate in her mouth.

Her gaze moved to the single stem of snowdrop on the arm of her chair, then dipped to her doll, Meriwether, that she had set on the floor. Finally, her gaze shifted to the puppy asleep on the muslin cloth near her feet. She pressed her hands to her heated cheeks. They were lovely gifts, all.

Then she did what she had been avoiding. She shifted her gaze to the men before her. Each met her gaze in turn. Blood roared in her ears, but she pushed the sensation aside. This was simply a choice. It was not life or death. There would be other opportunities for each of the men to win that had nothing to do with her choice now. And yet, choosing one now over the others would hurt them. It would disappoint each of them in a different way, but the pain would be there, even if it only wounded their pride. Except . . . a thought emerged from the chaos of her emotions. If she picked Colin, no one would blame her. He was new to her. They had no history. She slid her gaze to him. He seemed nice enough. At least she hoped so.

"I choose Colin Taylor as the winner of this challenge. His dance was refreshing and invigorating. Exactly what I needed."

Colin broke from the group and came toward her. His silver-gray eyes sparkled with proprietorship.

Nicholas's eyes were shuttered. Jules's bore disappointment. Lord Galloway frowned. David's face was a blank slate, but the sudden twitch of his hand spoke volumes. Bryce's gaze was as sharp as an ice shard.

Oblivious to the men's reactions, Margaret beamed. "Excellent. The rest of you will be shown to your chambers. Colin, you will escort Jane through the gardens alone until our midday meal. At that time, we will all reconvene in the great hall for the details of the next challenge."

"Jane?" Colin's voice sounded beside her and she turned toward him. A heartbeat later, she saw a silver gleam, then heard a *thunk*. Her heart pulsed as she wheeled about. The heat in her cheeks faded to ice. A dagger vibrated in the wood paneling of the wall behind her.

Exactly where she had been standing.

David startled at the sight of the blade so close to Jane. Her face went pale as she stared at the still-quivering blade. Lady Margaret gasped, and at the sound many voices rumbled through the chamber. David surged toward the dais and was momentarily pleased when Colin instinctively drew Jane behind him, protecting her from further attack. David spun back toward the chamber, seeking the villain who had thrown the dagger.

All eyes turned to Bryce. His face was a mask, giving no sign of his guilt or innocence. David looked beyond Jane's cousin and hunted through the assembled crowd, searching for a sign, any sign of the villain who had thrown that knife. Had they all missed whoever had thrown the dagger because each man in the room immediately suspected Bryce? "Did anyone see anything?" David shouted above the noise.

The noise in the room died down and one of his own men, Curtis, from the left-hand side of the chamber said, "Out of the corner of my eye I saw an overhand motion. Before I turned that direction, the assailant was gone."

If Jane had not moved—David squelched the thought.

David balled his hands at his sides. His worst fear was coming true. Jane was not safe in her own home and she would not be until she married and news that another male had taken charge of the castle spread across the land.

Lord Galloway hastened to David's side. "You are the best hunter of all of us," his long-time friend said. "Your skills are best suited to find the villain. How can I help?"

Tracking people was not his specialty, but he accepted the role as leader. "Keep your eyes sharp for anyone or anything out of the ordinary."

"They all look innocent, like helpless lambs, watching the entertainment that is all of us," Lord Galloway said with an attempt at a laugh.

"They might look like lambs, but there is a wolf among them. That blade impaled the wood near Jane at chest level. The assailant was aiming for her heart, and would have succeeded, too, had she not moved at the last instant. Someone in this room hurled that blade with speed and precision. It is up to us to determine who."

Lord Galloway forced a smile. "Then it is a good thing neither of us won this competition. While Colin Taylor escorts Jane to the gardens for his time alone with her, we will be searching the dark halls of the castle for a 'wolf.'"

"Agreed," said David, as he and Lord Galloway joined the others.

Bryce hung back. No doubt they all assumed the attack on Jane was his doing. He searched the other men's faces. Not one of them looked at him after their initial suspicion of him. Now, they were all busy, with their heads together, trying to determine how to help Jane. Perhaps that is what he should do as well, show them he was not as cold-hearted as they imagined.

He simply wanted what should be his. Women did not need to inherit things they could not manage or protect. Bellhaven, and all her people, would be better off under his care.

Bryce straightened. Perhaps he had better start showing them that fact instead of trying to force his way into Jane's affections. He had no doubt he was only here, and involved in the competition, so that he could not object to her marriage in the end. She had no intention of considering him as her husband.

His tactic for the competition would have to change. Instead of forcing her to choose him, he would see to it she did not choose any of them. No doubt they all had dark secrets they wished kept from Jane. Bryce smiled. He would find out what those secrets were and use them for his own purposes.

By the time he was through, Jane would have to choose between him as her husband, or no one.

Bellhaven would be his either way.

Bryce allowed his gaze to settle on Jane, with her new puppy in her arms and the golden-haired god who hovered near her side. All his earlier pleasure vanished. He would begin his attack on the golden boy first. Behind all that muscle no doubt were a few secrets the man wished no one else would discover.

Bryce needed to know more about Colin Taylor. And there was no time like the crisis-filled present. Before the day was through, he would set that plan in motion.

Feeling once more in control of the situation, Bryce headed for the dais, Jane, and his newfound target.

Nicholas moved to Jules's side. "Come," he said. "Let us talk to the men that make up the retinues. You take the left side of the chamber. I will take the right. Anyone who is the least bit suspicious, pull them aside for further questioning. Whoever threw that knife has to be here. No one can simply vanish like that."

Jules nodded and headed off to interview the men. Two hours and nearly sixty men later, Jules and Nicholas came back together. "Did you find anything?" Jules asked.

"Nothing." Nicholas exhaled in frustration. "They all seemed as baffled as we are by the attack."

Jules fell silent. He swayed on his feet.

Nicholas reached out to steady him. "Are you well?"

"Tired. My entrance back into the world has been rather sudden. I am still trying to adjust."

Nicholas nodded. "I think we can leave Sir David and Lord Galloway in charge here. "Want to help me with something else?"

He nodded.

Nicholas clapped his one-time friend on the back as they turned toward the doorway.

Jules stumbled, then caught himself.

Nicholas frowned. Jules might be tired, but he was not as healthy as he appeared if a swift clap on the back could set him off balance. Gaol had taken its toll on him. "You are certain all is well with you, my friend?"

A look of challenge came into Jules's eyes as he tried to appear casual and easy. "I told you. I am tired from travel."

He lied. His flesh had turned gray. "Come along," Nicholas said. "There is one more security measure I would like to take. Then, I know just the thing to help you get your strength back."

Jules nodded and together they walked out of the great hall toward the outer bailey. At the main gate, Nicholas signaled the guard to lower the gate and raise the drawbridge.

"What are you doing?" Jules asked, his face reddening in anger. "You are locking the would-be assassin inside the castle."

"Aye," Nicholas replied. "We are also locking accomplices out."

"I see the sense in that," Jules said after a moment, then nodded his approval.

Nicholas ordered that nobody be let in or out "In your lady's name." After the guards nodded in compliance, he turned to Jules. "Come," Nicholas said, angling his head toward the gate to the inner bailey. "We need to stop at the kitchen before we get back to the others."

Inside the kitchen, four women shuffled back and forth from the hearth to the long table in the center of the stone building. Standing at the edge of the enormous hearth, Marthe the cook hummed a lilting tune as she stirred what was most likely their midday meal in the cauldron set over the fire. At their entrance, the women paused in their duties and all eyes turned toward the two invaders of the female sanctuary.

As though sensing the sudden tension in the chamber, Marthe turned around. Her mouth was an irritated slash when her gaze lit on Nicholas. When she saw Jules, she smiled.

"Saints be praised. Do my eyes deceive, or could it possibly be Master Jules here in my domain again? You rapscallion, you haven't come lookin' for scraps from me for years." She set down her spoon and bustled to greet them. She took Jules's hands in hers. "You're a sight for sore eyes—" She stopped speaking as she sized Jules up, her smile slipping. "You don't look so well, young man."

"That's why we are here, Marthe," Nicholas said, bringing her gaze back to him. "We need one of your special tisanes to help Jules recover his strength."

She frowned at Jules and dropped his hands. "He looks like he needs more than that. Both of you, sit down before he falls down from exhaustion." She strode toward the far wall where she kept a full pantry of herbs and what Nicholas had always termed her "potions." The woman had a gift for knowing how to treat any ailment as well as how to season food.

Nicholas directed Jules to the small table in the corner of the room. "Thank you, Marthe."

"I am not doing this for you, Nicholas Kincaid," she said while she studied her shelf. "You have some nerve comin' here after all you put our mistress through."

Nicholas frowned. Lady Margaret's cool greeting he had understood. She and Jane were close and no doubt talked about his dismissal from her life two years ago. But Marthe? The cook had always loved him. "What have I done to deserve such a chilly reception from my favorite cook?"

She turned around and fixed him with a chilling stare. "Anyone who hurts our lady hurts us all."

Nicholas pressed his lips together. He wanted to deny the accusation, to proclaim his innocence, to tell her that it was Jacob who had sent him away, but he remained quiet. He had hurt Jane. There was no denying that. "I never should have left her."

Marthe's gaze warmed somewhat. "You did more than leave her, Nicky." She sighed. "You hurt her somethin' fierce."

He could only nod, uncertain to what she referred, but he intended to find out. And soon.

"Regardless of your feelings for me, I thank you for helping Jules."

She waved a hand in the air. "Don't thank me yet, but when Jules is back to himself, he can come back here and thank me properly." She busied herself with her jars and bags, tossing a bit of this and that into a small basket before she scurried to the hearth and dumped the herbs into a kettle already heating over the flames.

She glanced up from her kettle at Nicholas. "Darn you, Nicholas Kincaid. I want to be mad at you, but seein' you again in my kitchen . . ." She stirred the contents of the kettle. "Promise me you won't tarnish our lady's reputation any further."

"I would never—"

"That's right. Never is the right word. And if you do," she said narrowing her gaze once more, "you'll have to answer to me."

Nicholas could only stare. He did not know what to think or what to feel. *Tarnish her reputation?* he repeated in his mind, trying to let the words sink in. He closed his eyes and concentrated on his breathing. Was that why Lady Margaret had treated him that way? Why Jane had been distant? Had he wronged her in some way he was not aware of?

Then very slowly he opened his eyes. "I will set things right."

"You do that," she said with a nod. Moments later she returned to them with the kettle and a cup. "As for payment for my tisane, a kiss on the cheek should get my heart pumpin' . . . that would be reward enough." She smiled again at the two of them and an impish sparkle came into her eyes. "Better make that a kiss from each of you. One for each cheek."

"Done," Nicholas said, grateful the cook had warmed up to him once more.

Jules smiled. "'Twould be an honor."

She released a girlish giggle as she poured the steaming brew into the cup and slid it toward Jules. "Drink all of it. It'll be a bit bitter. That's the burdock root, but you'll be right as rain soon after drinkin' this."

"My thanks," Jules said as he took his first sip.

Marthe watched him for a moment then moved back to the hearth. "One more thing," she said as she reached for a knife and sawed thin slices of meat from the boar roasting on a spit over the flames. She returned with two plates of shaved meat and set them before the two men with a triumphant smile. "'Tis just like old times, feeding you both here in the kitchen. I have missed you both," she said, her voice soft. A faraway look came into her tired gray eyes.

"We missed you, too," Nicholas said, patting her time-weathered hands.

"I'm pleased you both responded to Lady Margaret's plea for help. Lady Jane needs you both."

Jules finished the cup and set it down on the table with a soft thud. "She can only choose one of us as her husband."

Marthe slid the plate of meat and a two-pronged fork closer to Jules as she nodded. "That is true, but there are no limits on friendship. And she needs friends now more than ever."

Nicholas frowned. "What do you mean?" He took a bite of the meat. Jules ate his eagerly.

She looked past the two men at the wall behind their shoulders, her eyes shadowed. "The accidents. They seemed only to be small mishaps at first, but they are becomin' more frequent and more disturbin'."

"What manner of accidents?" Jules and Nicholas said together as they shared a look of concern.

"Jane fell when a wooden stair collapsed beneath her. The week before that there was a piece of the castle wall that fell from the tower. It landed where Jane had been standin' moments earlier. And Lady Margaret was badly shaken when the wheel of her carriage broke and nearly sent the vehicle with her inside into a nearby stream."

"And today, someone threw a dagger at Jane in the great hall," Nicholas said, pushing the remainder of his meat aside as his appetite faded.

Marthe gasped. "Nay."

"Jane is well, but you have convinced me that someone wishes her ill." Jules finished his meat and set the plate aside.

Nicholas could feel the muscles of his neck tighten as fear for Jane's well-being overtook him. "I agree. All these events were no mere accidents. Someone is trying to harm Jane, and perhaps Lady Margaret as well. The question is who?"

"Some say it's the ghost of her mother," Marthe said in a whisper-soft voice.

"Her mother?" Jules asked with a frown.

Marthe shivered and crossed herself. "She's been sighted on many occasions lately roamin' the north hallway of the castle as well as the north tower."

Nicholas met Jules's frown with his own. Lady Angelina Moriah Lennox had come back as a ghost? "She has been dead for nineteen years. Why come back to haunt her home now?"

"Perhaps she's come to take her daughter with her into the afterlife," Marthe said as she crossed herself again.

Nicholas stood. "Nay. A mother who gave up her life at birth so her son could live would never hurt her daughter. I would venture to guess Lady Lennox's reappearance has more to do with protection than harm."

Jules stood as well. "Thank you for your healing tea and the savory meat. I feel stronger already."

"You come back here tomorrow for another cup of my tea, you hear me? And give me the chance to put more meat on your bones as well." Marthe gave them each a soft smile.

Nicholas stepped toward the cook and placed a swift kiss on her left cheek. Jules placed a kiss on her right.

Color flooded Marthe's face as she brought her hands up to cover her cheeks. "Thank you, you scoundrels. Now get back out there and protect our girl."

"With pleasure," Nicholas said with a bow.

"Indeed," Jules replied as he, too, offered the cook a bow. Together they left the kitchen, heading back toward the keep. "I want to thank you also, Nicholas. I feel stronger than I have in months."

"Gaol could not have been easy," Nicholas said as guilt assailed him. Why had he not tried harder to set his friend free?

"I am free now," Jules said as though reading his thoughts. In silence they walked to the stairs leading to the great hall.

Nicholas stopped at the sight of the fresh wood that had been cut to rebuild the collapsed part of the stairs—second one from the top. He turned and looked back down the stairway.

"Jane fell quite a distance. It is a wonder she did not hurt herself."

Jules inspected the stair, testing it with his foot. "That is three, possibly four attempts on her life if the carriage accident was truly meant for Jane." He frowned. "Do you think Bryce is behind it all? He stands the most to gain from Jane's death."

"Perhaps," Nicholas mused. "But the events started happening well before Lady Margaret announced the competition that brought Bryce back here."

"Still, we had best keep a close eye on Jane's cousin."

Nicholas and Jules continued into the great hall. "We will keep a close eye on everyone. No one is above reproach at this point," Nicholas said.

"Not even us?" Jules asked with a lift of his brow.

"You, I trust," Nicholas replied. "Besides, you have been in gaol until two days ago. You cannot be in two places at once unless you are a spirit like the supposed ghost of Lady Lennox."

"Do you truly think it is her ghost?"

"Nay, I do not believe in such things. There is a rational explanation for everything that is going on in this castle. And you and I are going to figure out exactly what that is."

"No villain or specter will get the best of us," Jules said as they moved to join the other suitors, who must have reconvened in the hall after their various searches for the villain.

"Where have you two been?" Bryce's eyes narrowed suspiciously.

"We made certain no one could get in or out of the castle," Jules said tersely. Jules and Bryce had known each other for years, from when Jules had served as Lord Lennox's squire. They had been antagonistic as young men. It appeared nothing had changed between them.

"Just freed from gaol and protecting the lot of us, are you?" Bryce sniped.

Lord Galloway put a hand on Bryce's shoulder. "Leave him be."

Bryce shrugged off his hand and a spark of malice flared in his eyes.

Ignoring him, David nodded at Nicholas. "Glad you remembered to seal the gates. Now, what we need to determine together is how to proceed. Do we cancel the competition?"

"We continue with the challenges," Jane said, returning to the chamber.

Nicholas's heart skipped a beat as Jane approached with Colin on one side and Lady Margaret on the other. Jane's face was marble-pale in the filtered light of the great hall—so different from her normal vivacious self. She needed to be outside in the fresh air, where the sunshine could touch her cheeks and bring them back to their natural rosy color.

"Nothing changes," Jane continued. "Colin and I will have our courtship time, as planned."

Colin offered Jane his arm, and she placed her fingers on it. "My lady," he said with a smile. Jane smiled in return.

Nicholas balled his fists at his sides. He so desperately wanted it to be he who touched her, comforted her, but all he could do was remain where he was. It would do him no good to reveal his emotions. What mattered was keeping Jane safe.

"She could be in more danger outside," Lord Galloway argued.

Colin gripped the hilt of his sword without removing the weapon from its sheath. "She will be safe in my care. I promise you."

Nicholas clenched his hands all the harder. "She had better be."

"She should be under constant surveillance," David added. "At least until the villain is—"

"Quiet, all of you," Jane said with a touch of irritation. "I can take care of myself." She reached beneath her skirt in the direction of her calf. "I have my own blade." She withdrew a dagger and held it out to them, the point sharp. "I honed the blade this morning."

After grabbing cloaks to protect them from the weather and making certain Jane's footwear was appropriate for the outdoors, Colin escorted her to what others had called the garden on the east side of the castle, tucked between the walls of the outer and inner bailey. He had seen the tranquil location as they had ridden through the bailey gates upon their arrival.

The snow in this area of the castle was still undisturbed. As they walked, they left a trail of impressions in the two-inch deep snow. Colin smiled. His breath curled in the chill air, floating toward the heavens. He loved the snow, and he could definitely become accustomed to the lovely Lady Jane Lennox at his side.

He had won the first competition with his spirited dance. Now he had to woo her with talk as he had for the past two hours in Lady Margaret's presence. That first test had gone well, and had won him this time alone in the garden with Jane where they could talk in private. Colin swallowed roughly. Discussions with ladies were not his strong suit, especially ladies who looked like Jane. Her unbound, shining golden hair fell in a luxurious tumble over her shoulders and back. Her tresses framed a face of striking beauty. Her finely molded cheekbones were high, her skin creamy and glowing, her lips generous and soft. But it was her eyes that drew his attention. Beneath delicately arched brows, long curly lashes fringed eyes that were a vivid, startling violet.

They walked in silence until they reached a half wall that separated the farmed part of the garden from the fruit trees. "May we walk among the trees?" he asked.

"I played there as a young girl. The gate is ahead," she said, stopping her progress along the snowy path.

"We need not enter through the gate." He dusted the snow off the top of the fence before he brought his hands to her waist and lifted her onto the ledge.

"Oh," she breathed, startled, and her cheeks flushed.

"Remain there a moment." In his eagerness to help her down, he vaulted over the divider as though it were nothing. She was taller than most women and voluptuously curved. He placed his hands on her waist once more and lifted her down. He did not set her on her feet right away, but gazed into her beautiful eyes as he slid her down his body, enjoying the feel of her softness against his hard chest. The friction between them was delicious, and he felt her knees wobble for a moment before she found her stance on the snow-covered ground.

"Now we will not be interrupted," Colin said, then drew a deep breath of fresh, cold air before they started walking through the snow once more. "Might I ask you a question, Lady Jane? Why did you choose me for this first round? You already know so many of the others."

"Honestly?" she asked, peering at him from beneath her lashes.

"Of course. I am a warrior. Nothing you say will hurt me."

A hint of an apology lingered in her eyes. "It was easier to choose you, a stranger, than to pick one of them."

He was wrong. That hurt, just a little. "I understand," he said, feeling slightly deflated about his time alone with her before he caught himself. It did not matter how he had gained this time. It was up to him to use it well.

He took her hand in his. They walked along an open area Colin could only assume was a path beneath the snow. He helped her toward a swing that hung from a stout branch of an apple tree. "If I'd had more time to prepare, I would have arranged a meal for us to eat beneath the boughs of this leafless tree."

"A meal out in the snow?" Jane asked with a chuckle.

"At the moment, I would like nothing better," he said with a smile.

Jane felt his smile all the way to her toes. Her pulse raced as she tried to ignore the tug of his eyes and voice. She had seen that momentary hurt in his eyes when she had told him the truth. The honest truth about the competition was she was not sure how she would choose any one among the others. Perhaps she should insist the next competition be the drawing of sticks. The suitor with the shortest stick would win her hand, sparing their feelings and her heart.

Colin stopped before the swing and released her hand. He gave the thick ropes a swift tug. "The ropes seem sound. Would you grant me the honor of pushing you on the swing?"

"In the snow?"

He brushed the snow from the wood with his bare hand. "Why not?"

"Very well," she said, and sat on the base. In an instant the tension in his shoulders relaxed and a warm, intimate look settled in his keen silver-gray eyes. He moved behind her, lifted her, and sent her soaring into the air.

The wind rushed past her cheeks and tossed her hair wildly about her face. Another push and she picked up speed, feeling vibrant and alarmingly alive. She did not know this man at all, but in the first few minutes of being in his company she found herself relaxing. He pushed her into the air for several minutes until suddenly she wanted to know more about the man behind her. All she knew up to now was that he was gorgeous, a good dancer, seemingly kind, gentle, and polite.

She twisted backward. "Colin, may we talk?"

He pulled her to a stop. "Always."

She shifted around, still feeling the rush of the wind where it had no doubt pinkened her cheeks.

He watched her with a gaze that was both personal and possessive. "What would you like to discuss?"

"Tell me something about yourself."

"Anything in particular?" His eyes narrowed playfully as he flashed a devastating smile. He leaned against the trunk of the tree and watched her intently.

"Very well, let us begin with why you came here? You do not know me at all."

"Are we sticking with the theme of honesty?" he asked.

"Please," she replied, searching his face as a mixture of amusement and hope welled inside her. Her aunt had been right about including Colin among her suitors. He was a refreshing change from those with whom she had a history. He was a mystery for her to solve.

He held her gaze. "I came because marrying you would give me something I have sought for many years and never found."

She frowned. "What is that?"

"A family," Colin said.

"You have no family?" she asked sympathetically. "Have they all passed on?"

"No. I do not know," he admitted with a shrug. "I was abandoned as a child with only a nurse to care for me. I only have hints as to who I am, but no solid proof."

"That must be terribly hard for you."

He shrugged again. "I have become accustomed to the fact that I might be someone's illegitimate son and unwanted."

She hopped off the swing and closed the short distance between them, placing her hand on his arm. "I am sure you were wanted. I for one am glad you are here."

In a heartbeat his gaze turned warm and sensual. "My past, or lack thereof, has haunted me for years, Lady Jane," he said with a slight brogue in his voice. "But in this moment it does not seem such a desperate thing. The future is what really matters. If you want the truth, I want a wife and a family."

He closed his eyes briefly, as though gathering his thoughts, before opening them again. "I am not looking for a conventional woman. I long for a woman who is curious about the world around her. A woman who wants children and would love them no matter what or who they are. My woman would have a fearless heart, a courageous soul, and endless compassion."

Something inside Jane melted as he spoke from his heart, his voice deepening as he continued. "I want a companion who would talk with me about anything and everything into the small hours of the night. A woman who is my friend, my lover, my cherished wife."

Jane drew a shattered breath as he took her chin between his thumb and forefinger and lifted it, forcing her to meet his steady gaze as he quietly asked, "Are you that person?"

Jane looked at his mouth.

He released a soft groan. "I had meant to be a gentleman with you." His lips descended to hers, just shy of touching.

She sought to forestall what was inevitable by saying, "For all you have been through, you deserve someone wonderful."

"You are quickly becoming the most wonderful woman I have ever known," he murmured huskily. His cool lips covered hers. The kiss was soft and sweet at first, then grew bolder and filled with yearning.

He is a stranger, her mind cautioned. *You do not know this man.* She might not know him, she countered, but he had given her a glimpse of his heart.

As if sensing her hesitation, he pulled his mouth from hers and stepped back. He lifted his hand to her hair, gently brushing a golden lock off her cheek. He tried to smile. "I was swept away," he said in a husky voice. "I knew this might be my only time alone with you, and when your gaze lit on my lips, I could not help myself."

At the mention of his lips, her gaze returned there.

"You had best look elsewhere unless you want me to continue," he whispered.

Stunned into stillness, Jane shifted her gaze to his eyes—eyes that were warm and sensual and filled with raw need. He was still a mysterious stranger, but what they had shared had been volatile and passionate. He would definitely challenge a wife physically as a husband. But in the end, would he be hers or someone else's?

At the thought, she drew in a long, shaky breath. Her passion faded and fear took its place. Would she feel this way with all her suitors, except her cousin? A moment of anguished shame took hold. Jane knew she had a sensual nature. She experienced emotion, whether carnal or fearful, to her core, deeper than her own aunt ever did. She tried to repress her base instincts, had spent hours on her knees in the confessional trying to change and to make decisions with her head, not her heart. Yet time and again, her passions won out.

She returned her gaze to Colin. This competition would truly be a challenge for her if she found herself attracted to more than one man.

She straightened as her thoughts moved to the rumors that had been spread about her passionate nature. The rumors were unfounded—but unfortunately, they did have some foundation in the truth. She was a passionate person. Did that make her unsuitable as a bride? Should she end the competition now before emotions, hers and her suitors', progressed any further?

Colin settled his hands gently on her shoulders. "Lady Jane, do not be afraid of your passion," he said, as though reading her thoughts. "Any one of your suitors would see it as the greatest asset in a wife. I especially would."

Jane drew back. A shiver of fear worked its way down her spine. "You have heard the rumors, then?"

At what must have been a horrified look on her face, he reached up again and smoothed his finger across her cheek. "I care nothing about what others say. I judge for myself. I can clearly see now that the rumors were untrue. You should not care so much about gossip."

"That is easier for a man than a woman to accomplish."

"You may be right, but it has been my experience that others will hold you back from achieving your dreams only if you let them." He smiled. "Come, let me take you back to the castle." He took her fingers in his and guided her back down the path of their footprints.

"Your fingers are cold," she said, realizing how silly the words sounded in light of what had just passed between them.

He stopped and took both her hands in his. "My heart is warm and that is what matters. Thank you, Lady Jane, for these first moments alone with you. I am so honored that you chose me, no matter the reason." A heartbeat later, his words faded and his features hardened.

"Colin?"

"There are three sets of footprints," he said softly. "There were no others besides ours when we first entered the garden."

As a shiver of alarm raced down her spine, Jane allowed Colin to pull her close against his side.

His gaze narrowed on the nearby trees. "Come, we must hurry back inside where you will be less of a target."

"Why did we not notice someone else in the garden?"

His face softened. "The kiss."

Jane felt her cheeks warm.

He curled his arm around her waist and matched his steps to hers. "I should not have brought you out here."

"The location does not seem to matter," Jane said, trying to make him feel better.

He frowned. "What do you mean?"

"After the dagger in the great hall, I have come to realize that all the accidents over the last few weeks were not 'accidents.'"

"You mean your aunt's carriage wheel?"

"That and a falling stone and a collapsing stair."

Colin drew her even closer against him, nearly carrying her along with his steps. When they reached the half wall, he had her up and over before she could even assist him. Finally, when they reached the keep, he drew away and his gaze met hers. "I will not let whoever it is hurt you."

Before she could comment, her Aunt Margaret hurried toward her, followed by David, Nicholas, Jules, Lord Galloway, and Bryce, their faces a mixture of concern and anger.

"Back so soon?" David asked as his eyes narrowed with suspicion on Colin.

"Someone followed us to the garden," Colin stated.

"Did you find the person?" Lord Galloway asked.

"Not yet. I thought it best to return Lady Jane to safety before I went in pursuit."

Colin signaled two of his men forward. They hastened to his side. "Stand guard over Lady Jane."

Jane stared at the two big warriors. Each carried a sword and looked quite capable of protecting her, but this was not what she wanted. For a brief moment her gaze shifted to Jules, then back to the warriors. "I will not be a prisoner in my own home."

"Your safety is at stake." Concern flared in David's eyes.

"I will not walk around Bellhaven in fear," Jane said, suddenly feeling dwarfed as her suitors gathered around her. She straightened. "Lord Galloway, you mentioned Sir David's skill as a hunter before. Perhaps it is time to use his knowledge to aid us."

"How?" Lord Galloway asked.

"By setting a trap, with me as the bait."

"No." Colin's features darkened. "That is unnecessary."

Jane ignored his and all the other dissenting comments the men tossed her way. "Tomorrow you shall compete in a fox hunt. We have until then to come up with a plan to draw out whoever is trying to harm me and Aunt Margaret."

"Not outside of the castle. It is too dangerous," Nicholas argued.

"A hunt inside the castle walls would be no test of your skill at all," Jane countered with a smile.

The smile did not have the effect she had hoped for as David's frown deepened. "I agree with Nicholas. You will be too exposed outside the castle gates."

"What better way to force our villain to show himself," Jane replied with a false sense of bravado. Inside, she shook. If she were honest, that dagger had unsettled her more than any of her other accidents. A fall, or a loose stone, even a loose carriage wheel she could rationalize away. A dagger thrown at her—that was a message even she could not avoid.

Her aunt worked her way to Jane's side. "Allow me to dress in your clothing and cover my face with a veil."

"No," Jane said emphatically. "I will not put you or anyone else in danger." She looked at each man gathered around her. Jules looked at her with sadness. David's face was pensive. Lord Galloway shook his head in disagreement. Nicholas's dark eyes smoldered as though pleading with her to change her mind. Bryce shrugged.

Colin's features were hardened with concern. "I still do not like the fact that you will be in harm's way, but such a ruse just might work."

"Fear not. I have no intention of dying today or any day soon," Jane said. "I have six worthy protectors. What could go wrong?"

6

Up in her chamber later that evening, Jane sat in a chair near the hearth and mindlessly brushed out her hair. For her suitors she had dismissed tonight's attempt on her life and the extra set of footsteps in the garden, but both events had rattled her to the core.

Even now, her hand shook as she brushed, for the hundredth time, her long, golden hair. It was dangerous to be anywhere near her at the moment. Could she willingly endanger the lives of the brave men who had responded to Margaret's invitation for her own gain? Bellhaven was all she had left, but to allow anyone to be harmed in order for her to keep her home seemed so very wrong.

The door on the opposite side of the room opened softly and Margaret slipped inside the room. "I was wondering where you had gone," she said approaching Jane. She held out her hand. "Here, let me do that for you."

Margaret used to brush her hair every night after her mother died. It had helped to calm Jane enough so that she could sleep. Perhaps her efforts would have the same effect now.

"Are you truly recovered from the incident in the great hall?" Margaret asked, studying Jane's face.

"These accidents are becoming a regular part of our lives. Are they not?" Jane replied with a forced laugh.

Margaret paled. "This is a serious matter, Jane. One of these times, whoever is behind the attempts will hit their mark."

Jane reached for the small dagger she had set on the table before her. The weapon had once belonged to her mother. Jane had spent the last hour sharpening the blade to a lethal point. "I am prepared."

Margaret frowned as she began to smooth Jane's hair. "That dagger will only stop so much."

"I know," Jane replied, her voice tightening with emotion. She forced back sudden tears. She would not cry. There was no reason other than the fact that someone wanted her dead, her whole life was about to change, and she could do nothing about either.

Not noticing Jane's emotional state, Margaret continued to brush Jane's hair. "All of the men are rather handsome, would you not agree, Jane?" She did not wait for a reply. "Colin seems quite taken with you. He is rather handsome, in a rugged, debonair way. He would make you a fine husband."

Margaret frowned for a moment, then continued without a response from Jane. "Then again, David has changed much since you have last seen him. He is more confident now. His manner seems more refined as well."

Her aunt sighed. "Then there is Lord Galloway. That man is too handsome by far."

Margaret continued to brush, but the brushing had no calming effect on Jane's nerves this time.

"Jules is too thin, by far. Would it be wrong of me to ask Doctor Samuelson to come look him over?"

This time she waited for Jane's response. "It depends. Do you want him examined because you think he is ill or because you wish to identify any impediment to his marrying me?"

Margaret forced a smile. "Both, I suppose. I merely do not want you to suffer as I . . ."

When she did not continue, Jane added the words Margaret did not say, "As you have suffered?"

She nodded. "I was married for three days, Jane. Three whole days before Thomas was gone."

Jane did not know much about Margaret's history with her husband; she had been only an infant when Thomas had died. "Did you love him so very much?"

Margaret stopped brushing. "Love him? I hardly knew him."

Jane turned to face her aunt. "What?"

"Our marriage was arranged by the king. Sir Thomas Avery and Lady Margaret Lennox. Everyone thought it was a perfect match. That was until Thomas fell dead."

Jane knew the man had died young, but she had never asked about the details. Did Margaret wish to talk about her husband now? "How did he die?" Jane asked gently.

Margaret blushed. "It was terrible, really." Her blush deepened. "Since you are about to marry yourself I might as well tell you. We were coupling. It was that moment—and he just died."

Jane had no idea what "that moment" meant, but she could imagine by the tone of Margaret's voice that it was something special. "I am so sorry," Jane said, meaning it, yet not knowing what else to say.

Margaret shook herself. "That is in the past. I do not regret a moment of what happened after that. Before the king could arrange yet another marriage for me, my good brother called me here to care for you and your brother. I was pleased by the outcome."

Jane took Margaret's hand in hers and squeezed it gently. "You were a blessing then as you are now."

Margaret's smile returned. "In order not to repeat the past, we need to find you a husband who has good health and stamina. And I am not certain Jules is that man."

"Jules will be well." He had to be. She would move heaven and earth to see he fully recovered. Yet Margaret had a point. Jules was not nearly as healthy as she had hoped he would be despite the coins she had slipped to the guard to make certain he was cared for. "It might be a good idea to send for Doctor Samuelson, but only if Jules agrees."

Margaret nodded and continued her brushing. "What about Nicholas?"

Just hearing his name sent an odd combination of warmth and pain straight to her heart. She drew a sharp breath. "I cannot honestly say I have given him much thought," she lied.

"How does it feel to see him again? You parted so suddenly."

The memory of that day stabbed her with the agony of a knife. All the emotions of the day must have breached the wall she had erected between herself and Nicholas. Her heart raced and her pain was palpable. With her emotions so raw, she felt stripped bare and more vulnerable than she liked. She stared blandly back at Margaret.

"Nicholas was once very dear to you," Margaret said, watching her reaction with caution.

Jane stood and moved to the opposite side of the room, leaving Margaret holding the brush in empty air. She needed distance, but there was no distancing herself from the memories and emotions now pouring through her mind. She needed to close herself off again, pull that wall back around her. Her brother had sent Nicholas away, and Nicholas had left without a fight. But it was what happened after that tightened her rib cage and made it hard to breathe.

Margaret caught her gaze and in it read her anxiety and her pain. "Oh, Jane. I understand what his words have done to you more than anyone else. I was furious with him for a time, however, with time and distance, I cannot help but wonder if he was tricked into saying such things about you. The Nicholas I knew would never have hurt you in such a horrible way."

Jane did not know what to think. A part of her had hoped it was all a mistake, but the men whose jeers she had had to endure for the last six months were no fantasy. Jane swallowed hard. Could she ever forgive him for the pain he had caused her? Could she ever trust his love again?

"I need time to think about Nicholas, about them all," Jane finally replied when she could do so in a steady tone. Her back was to a wall. She had to choose one of them if she wanted to keep her home. She let loose a hitched breath. It was more than that—she would lose so much more than her home. But asking one of them to join with her might also end their very lives, and in a much more violent way than Margaret's husband met his end.

Jane had been so deep in her own thoughts that she had not noticed Margaret approach. Margaret reached for Jane's hand. "I know the fear you carry in your heart. But trust in these men to protect you and love you as you deserve. You must choose one of them. Marry for love, Jane, if at all possible, and let the rest take care of itself."

That would mean trusting in someone else again—something she had not done in a very long time. There was no one else to help her and Margaret but the six men and their men-at-arms, who were below stairs settling in for the night. Jane fully grasped the danger they faced. She had to marry to get the army she needed and to mend her tarnished reputation.

Jane brought her gaze to Margaret's, saw the earnest expression there, and against all rationality, made a decision with her heart. "I will keep myself open to possibility, Aunt Margaret. Love is a stretch, but I will not close myself off to their affections over the next few days." She drew a sharp breath. "I will let destiny take me where it will with any one of these men."

The next morning was crisp and a new layer of snowfall covered the ground as Jane rode her gray mare from the stable to where her suitors had gathered in preparation for the hunt. For a moment she signaled her horse to stop. The hunt would be the second competition between her suitors. Her bold statement last night to keep herself open came back to her and her stomach knotted as six gentlemen turned her way. Of all the six, it was Nicholas her gaze moved to.

A familiar warmth simmered in his sherry-colored eyes and a sudden thrill echoed inside her. She smiled at him, but that smile died a heartbeat later as he turned away.

"A beautiful day for a hunt, wouldn't you say?" Lord Galloway asked as she neared. His breath rose in a warm, thin coil matched only by his gaze as it lingered on the slight glimpse of her leather boot peeking out from beneath her riding habit.

Heat flooded Jane's cheeks. She shifted the corner of her woolen skirt to cover herself more fully. Jane had enjoyed it when Nicholas had looked at her that way. With Lord Galloway, she felt bared and uncomfortable.

An amused smile lifted the corner of Lord Galloway's lips.

"Indeed," Jane replied in a tight voice, shifting her gaze from him to the chaos around her. David was dressed in the traditional scarlet coat and white breeches. He would act as the master of the hunt and guide the pack of twenty dogs through the competition. The dogs danced in the excited knowledge that they would be dashing across the pristine snow cover any moment in search of the scent David would offer them on a coiled piece of cloth. Baying filled the air as the dogs scratched at the frosty earth and frolicked with each other. The horses danced with as much anticipation as the dogs.

Jane held her reins loose, but signaled her horse to remain still with her knees. Lord Galloway, Jules, Bryce, Colin, and Nicholas all wore black coats, buff-colored breeches, and shiny black boots. Of all the men, only David looked entirely comfortable in the clothing of the hunt. Colin looked entirely uncomfortable as he fidgeted with his white cravat. As he noticed Jane's glance, he offered her a smile and brought his horse alongside hers.

"Judging by the way you sit your horse, you appear to be a skilled rider," Colin commented.

"I am no stranger to this horse or the hunt."

Colin smiled. As his features brightened, Jane's pulse leapt. The man was devastatingly handsome when he smiled.

"Are we to hunt a red fox?" he asked Jane.

She nodded. "How else are we to determine a winner of this competition if not for the fox?"

Bryce frowned and his eyes narrowed at the two of them. "As I am most familiar with the woodlands, I will win this farce before any of you or your dogs have caught the scent."

"We will see about that," Colin replied with confidence.

Jane turned her horse away from the two men beside her to seek out Nicholas and Jules. They hung back from the others, gazing off into the distance, searching the woodlands beyond.

A shiver danced across Jane's neck. She forced it away. The accidents of the past few weeks would not touch her here, with so many protectors nearby. David blew a horn, indicating the hunt was about to begin. At the call of the horn and the barking of the racing dogs, Jane gave her horse a thump of her heels and urged herself forward into the fray. Careful to keep her distance, Jane surged into the woodlands behind her six suitors. David was in the lead, followed by Bryce and Nicholas. Lord Galloway rode more carefully alongside Jules, and Colin brought up the rear, almost as if he were hanging back in order to keep an eye on her. As the forest became dense with foliage, Jane soared over a fallen tree that lay across the path and came to earth again. The rushing wind tugged at her hat, but it remained in place as they zigzagged from the woodlands to an open field.

"Well done, milady," Colin shouted, sending her one of his devastating smiles.

The smile distracted Jane. She startled at the sudden movement of a deer darting back to the safety of the trees.

Instantly Nicholas was beside her. He said nothing, but his gaze spoke volumes as he first assessed her then the surrounding area for signs of danger.

Egan, the one servant who had come along with them, corralled the dogs with the crack of a whip and kept them on the scent of the fox. The open field was cloaked with drifting shreds of fog that dispersed briefly as the horses pelted across the sleepy earth. A glance back over her shoulder showed the fog settling again as though undisturbed. The echo of hoofbeats sounded in the morning air.

Colin, sensing his private moment was over, moved ahead with the others, but another rider remained.

"You will not win this competition if you hang back here with me, Sir Nicholas."

"You know I do not care one whit for winning if it means you come to harm," Nicholas replied without looking at her. His shoulders were tense.

"Relax. What could happen out here while we are moving?"

His lips tightened, but he said quietly, "Anything."

Jane was about to laugh when her horse suddenly pitched forward, in but a moment hitting the ground with an audible thud. She released the reins and rolled away from the beast as the ground slammed up to meet her. She gasped at the shock of pain that radiated through her side.

Before she could even orient herself to the situation, Nicholas was beside her. Instead of scooping her into his arms as she expected, he pulled her gently behind the fallen horse, using the animal as a shield as he peered out over the meadow.

All was quiet except for the retreating hoofbeats from the riders who had not seen what had happened. A moment later, she and Nicholas were alone in the open space. His horse pranced while hers whinnied, frightened in her entangled state.

"Are you hurt?" Nicholas said, hovering over her. The concern in his eyes nearly brought tears to her own. A warm sensation moved through her, dispelling the remnants of pain. "Only my pride."

He reached out and touched her cheek with one finger. "I could not bear it if something happened to you." A heartbeat later his finger was gone and he reached for his boot, withdrawing a small dagger.

"Stay low," he warned as he stroked the neck of her horse, then reached over the animal to slice through the rope that entangled her feet. The horse kicked until her feet were free.

"Get ready to move," he warned as the horse rocked back and forth a moment before gaining its feet. Once the horse was in motion, so were they. Jane got to her feet, but then she found herself lifted as Nicholas ran for his own mount, set her on its back, then joined her. With a click of sound he guided the horse back toward the castle at breakneck speed. Her own horse followed. She was pleased to see her gait steady and strong as the scared animal hung close to Nicholas's mount. Jane was scared, too, as she clung to the horse's mane and took comfort from the solid wall of muscle at her back.

"I need to stay with the hunt." The masculine scent that was Nicholas's own spun Jane's head so thoroughly she could barely think straight.

"No." The harsh sound brought her gaze to his. Anger and frustration darkened his eyes.

"But the competition—"

"There will be no need of a competition if you are dead." The words were rough, crisp, and true.

Jane turned back around as a frisson of fear tingled across her flesh. There could be no more denying that she was the target of the so-called accidents that had occurred over the past several weeks. Someone wanted her dead. Bryce? Or someone else? Bryce could not have orchestrated this attack. He was hunting with the rest of her suitors. She had seen him only moments before the attack, riding beside David for the lead.

Then who? Jane shook off her thoughts and looked about her. Nicholas had changed his course while she was lost in thought, no longer heading toward the castle. Instead, he came to a halt outside the vacant woodcutter's cottage on the eastern side of Bellhaven's land. He slid down from the horse then, gripped her waist, and lifted her down beside him. He did not linger beside her. He grabbed his satchel and headed for the door.

Jane halted in the doorway of the musty cabin, waiting for him to locate a candle or lantern. "Why are we here? I thought it was protection you sought?"

"I am adequate protection for you right now." He shuffled in the darkness until a flare of light suddenly lit the small room. He set the candle on the rickety table. "We cannot give ourselves away with a fire," he said as the small flame sputtered in the chill air.

Jane shut the door, then unfastened her crushed hat and set it on the rough-cut table two paces from him. Her heart hammered at the sight of his lean power and strength. His dark gaze fixed on her. The raw hunger in them made her hot and shivery.

Jane broke her gaze and turned away even as a shiver that had nothing to do with the chill air slipped down her spine.

Nicholas moved to the closed doorway. A heartbeat later, Jane heard someone walking around outside. Nicholas stepped back from the doorway, swept Jane into his arms and pulled her behind him into the shadows while they listened.

Jane went stock-still as her chest connected fully with his back and a wave of familiarity and desire tore through her. The heat of him warmed her and his raw masculine power overwhelmed her. Even more disturbing was the fact that she closed her eyes and drew in the scent of leather and sandalwood. Nicholas's scent. She had never forgotten it. But she also had never forgotten the way he had left her behind. Her brother had demanded Nicholas leave her, accusing him of only wanting her title and land. Instead of fighting for her and what they had once shared, he vanished from her life.

It had taken her months to get over his betrayal and to feel as though her life was not fracturing into a million little pieces. Jane opened her eyes. Her body still remembered his and mourned his loss, but she was older, wiser, and would never allow him to hurt her that way again. She clenched her fingers at her side, fighting for control as the sound of boot heels stopped right in front of the door.

Nicholas could not breathe with Jane so close to him. He had always been highly tuned to Jane's senses, and with her this close, the torture was all too real. He felt her all the way through his body. He flexed his hand at his side, fighting the desire that had been theirs so long ago. They had only ever shared passionate kisses, but the memory of her touch, her softness, haunted him now.

He had brought her into the cottage because he knew they were being followed. He had heard the telltale sounds of one set of hoofbeats behind them and he had wanted to confront the enemy at a point of his own choosing. Had they returned to the castle, it would have been too easy for the villain to blend in with everyone else, as he had before, bringing them no closer to finding who was threatening Jane. He could protect her from harm here with a face-to-face confrontation.

There was a shuffle just outside the door; the latch raised.

Nicholas tensed and soundlessly moved with Jane further into the shadows, out of harm's way. The door creaked open, and a sliver of daylight seeped into the cottage. With only a rush of air to be heard, Nicholas drew his sword. A foot appeared, then the full skirts of a woman. A young woman?

"Who's there?" the woman asked, peering inside the cottage.

Nicholas did not lower his weapon as he stepped out of the shadows. "The better question is who are you?"

She fumbled with her skirts as she stepped back outside. "I came to meet my brother, the woodcutter. He lives here. I saw the horses and worried he might be in trouble."

Nicholas kept his grip firm on his sword, still uncertain about the woman or her purpose in the woods. "Who is your brother?" Nicholas asked, watching her response.

The girl paled. "I told you. He is the woodcutter here."

"His name." Nicholas stepped toward the intruder. "If he was your brother, then what was his name?"

"P-Peter," she said with a hint of triumph in her voice.

"And your name?"

"Clara-Clarisa. Clarisa."

Nicholas's instincts warned him that all was not right with this girl. But he honestly could not tell if the girl had a simple nature, or if she were having a difficult time recalling her brother and her own name. She appeared harmless enough.

"Where is my brother?" she asked again.

"He is not here." Nicholas eased his grip on his sword.

Her eyes narrowed. "Then what are you doing here?"

Nicholas studied the woman. Was she the one who had attacked Jane that morning? A thin serving girl? She appeared too slight and inexperienced to launch the weapon that had taken down Jane's horse. "We needed to rest before we returned to the castle."

Nicholas sheathed his sword, but his senses remained on alert. He moved back toward Jane as his protective instincts heightened. Never would he take chances with Jane's life. If the girl were involved in Jane's accident, she had to be working with someone else.

The girl scowled. "You're from the castle? I have never seen you before."

Jane stepped around him. "Perhaps not, but I am from Bellhaven."

At the sight of Jane, the young woman's eyes widened. She dropped into a curtsey, bowing her head, or blocking her face from full view. Nicholas was not certain which. "Milady, I had no idea 'twas you."

By the inflection in her voice, the girl sounded genuinely surprised at Jane's presence. As the young girl straightened, Nicholas turned his attention to Jane. Her face was calm, but a slight crease settled across her forehead as she studied the young, flaxen-haired woman. Neither woman spoke as they sized up each other. Finally, Jane turned back to him. "We all need to return to the castle. At least there we are safe."

Jane's last word trailed off and Nicholas knew she was thinking about the times at the castle when someone had threatened her life. She was not safe, neither in nor out of the castle. Was she even safe in the presence of her suitors? The thought made Nicholas uneasy, for he knew he could not have exclusive rights to Jane. Not while this ridiculous competition was underway. Something inside him twisted at the thought, but he forced it away. He needed to remind Jane of what they once shared and let the memories bring her back to him.

Wasting precious moments in the cottage would not serve him there. He gently took Jane's hand in his. "Come, let us return to the castle."

Jane started at the touch of his hand, almost as though the feel of his roughness against her softness were a foreign kindness. She tightened her fingers around his and scorched him all the way to his heart. He swallowed, then stiffened as he led Jane outside.

Nicholas made certain at all times that the flaxen-haired girl was in front of them. He watched her mount the horse she had taken from Bellhaven before he set Jane upon his horse. They would once again share an animal since Jane's horse was no longer in sight. Presumably instinct had sent the injured animal back to the castle. He would make certain to find the beast when they returned and treat any possible wounds.

"After you," Nicholas said to the girl, waving her in front of them. He had no intention of giving her access to Jane or a chance to run away. He had more questions for her when they returned.

As they plodded through the snow, Nicholas was keenly aware of Jane's nearness. The feel of her back against his chest did something to him that he could not define. Nicholas breathed in her sweet, feminine scent as his body throbbed and ached for her with a primitive need. Was there anything he could do or say that would help her remember what they had once shared? Did he have a chance of winning at all when compared to the physical perfection of Colin Taylor?

Plagued by the disquieting thought, Nicholas turned his attention back to Jane. Despite the incident this morning, she sat tall and proud upon the horse. Her chin was tilted slightly, and a look of determination settled across her face.

Instantly, he remembered what it was about Jane that had captivated him long ago. It was not her beauty; it was her indomitable will. There was a strength in Jane he had rarely seen in other women. She spoke her mind. And as she spoke, it was hard not to see that her soul was filled with fire and vitality. An irresistible combination.

Nicholas frowned. Did the others see what he saw in Jane? If so, this competition could become ruthless, for Nicholas did not intend to lose what was once so precious to him.

With the reins in one hand, he brought his other hand up to pluck a leaf from the escaping hair of Jane's tight plait. He should have pulled back when the leaf was gone, yet he could not resist coiling his finger in the wisp at her nape. Her glorious thick hair had always intrigued him. In the weak winter sun, her hair was like golden sunshine and warm silk against his flesh.

At this touch, she did not pull away. He saw her smile. Sensual and knowing and devastating. The amused gleam in her eyes was breathtaking, and her features softened with the charm that had always been his undoing. She would melt their hearts, all six of her suitors.

Nicholas suddenly needed to ask the question burning in his mind. "Why have this competition, Jane? Why not choose your champion and be done with it?"

"The competition was Aunt Margaret's idea."

"You seem perfectly happy to participate," Nicholas replied with an edge to his words.

Jane's smile faded. "I have no other choice. If I want to keep the castle, I must marry. Father's will allows me no other option."

"You are certain your kin are dead?"

"It has been six months." Her voice rose. The girl on the horse in front of them turned back to stare. "Why do they not return if they are alive?" Jane asked in a softer voice as her brow knit. "I know it sounds terrible, but I almost hope they are being held prisoner somewhere. Better a prisoner than dead."

"If they were being held hostage, would not their keepers send word for ransom?" Nicholas lowered his voice. "I am sorry, Jane. Losing your father would be difficult. Losing both your father and brother must be unbearable." He smoothed her arm atop her cloak, not knowing how else to comfort her.

"The odd thing is—they left with a company of men." She twisted to look him in the eyes. "Not a one of them returned." She paused and drew a sharp breath before continuing. "How can all those men vanish, every single one of them? Not even a horse returned home to us."

She swallowed hard, saying nothing, and he knew the turmoil of emotion that must tie her in knots every night. He had felt that kind of loss before when his own mother had died. It was not the loss of her that had hurt so much, though he did miss her every day. It was the monster her loss had unleashed in his father. Nicholas had been forced to endure that pain for years.

To counter the emptiness inside him, Nicholas had become ferocious and reckless, hiding his pain and desolation. He had thought himself jaded to all humanity before he had met Jane. Somehow she had managed to touch something soft in him, and from that day forth he had been a different person. He had come back to life because of Jane and her brother Jacob. Only when he had befriended them and escaped the horrors of his own home had the endless twisting in his gut disappeared.

A chill breeze teased the end of Jane's hair against her neck, the same wind that caused his hair to ruffle against his forehead. He became acutely aware of the crisp scent of the forest they had left behind, the rhythmic sound of the wind in the grass, the bitter cold as it brushed his cheeks. The air seemed suddenly thick and hard to breathe.

"Jane," he said, forcing her name past the roughness in his throat. "I will make inquiries. I am well connected. Someone had to see them during the battle or after."

He did not say the word "dead." He would find her something of the truth—give her some way to accept what had happened. He owed her that much, and more.

"Thank you, Nicholas, for giving me something to hope for."

He smiled. "'Tis the season of hope. All things are possible at Christmastide."

She tipped her face up to greet the wind, and tendrils of hair brushed her temples and cheeks. "I keep forgetting it is the holiday season."

"I will see what I can do to help you remember that fact each and every day until Epiphany."

She smiled, a true smile this time. "I used to love this time of year."

"You will again," he said, as they reached the approach to the castle.

The drawbridge was down and the gates stood open. Why had they not closed the gates when the hunters left? Nicholas frowned. He would have to speak with the guardsmen about security. They could not afford any more vulnerability than they already had.

They rode the rest of the distance in silence. The outer bailey was silent, eerily so. It was not until they entered the inner bailey that activity resumed. Six warriors stood next to their horses while others from the castle gathered around. As Nicholas and his party approached, all eyes turned toward them. A cry rose from the crowd and Margaret rushed toward them. Nicholas dismounted and assisted Jane, holding her close for one final moment before he set her on the ground. He kept hold of her hand as he led her from the horse toward her aunt.

"Merciful heavens. What has happened?" Margaret asked, stopping before them. Her cheeks were flushed, her eyes concerned as she studied the two of them from head to toe.

"Jane was attacked during the hunt," Nicholas said, releasing Jane's hand.

Nicholas's gaze shifted to the unidentified warriors. Why were they not wearing their colors? Was it a mere coincidence that these men had arrived on Jane's estate very shortly after she was attacked? Were these men responsible? He had an easier time believing these men were Jane's attackers rather than the slip of a girl they had met in the woods. Nicholas gripped the hilt of his sword, ready to draw if necessary. The odds were against him should they attack, but he would not make their task easy.

"We knew something was amiss when Jane's horse returned on its own. I was preparing a party to go search just as these warriors arrived." Margaret picked up Jane's hands and intensely scrutinized her niece. "Are you hurt?"

"I am well," Jane reassured. "How is my horse?"

Her aunt sighed. "She is in the stable with Ollie."

Nicholas maneuvered so that he was between the women and the men. His gaze fixed on a blond-haired man about his same age. The man's gaze held anger, then resentment, as he studied Jane. Nicholas's frown deepened. He tightened his grip on his sword. Was the warrior disappointed not to be among those invited to compete for Jane's hand in marriage? Or was there something more at play here?

Nicholas ran his gaze over the others, watching for any aggressive movement toward their swords. It was not until Nicholas sized up the oldest member of the group that recognition flared. Seamus MacGuire, one of his late father's friends.

The way the other men stood behind the patriarch, Nicholas assumed the others to be members of that clan as well. Something inside Nicholas tightened. Seamus MacGuire had been as mean-spirited as his own father and not known for his diplomacy. Quite the opposite. The man and his clan were far more likely to draw their swords than ask questions of their neighbors.

Nicholas was about to draw his sword when he saw Ollie and Angus approach. He did not relax his grip on his sword, but his tension eased as he asked, "Why are the MacGuires here?"

Margaret's eyes clouded with tears. "They have something to present to you, my dear," she said to Jane, guiding her closer to Seamus.

Nicholas spared a glance back at the girl they had discovered in the woods, only to find her gone. Her horse remained beside his, but there was no sign of the young woman. His irritation spiked. He had had several questions for her. No matter. He would find her later. At the moment, whatever the MacGuire clan wanted with Jane was far more urgent.

Jane's expression was nervous and intense as she approached the men. Seamus stepped forward, bowed, then offered Jane a folded piece of cloth. "We felt it necessary tae return this tae ye. We found it after the Battle of Bothwell Bridge. We thought ye might like the remembrance of yer father and brother."

Nicholas stiffened as she unfolded the standard bearing the Lennox crest of two broadswords in saltire behind an imperial crown. Jane's face paled.

"We also retrieved this." The man held out a white piece of linen. When Jane simply stared at the cloth, Seamus unwrapped the object within, revealing a broadsword.

A chill air rushed past Nicholas. "Your father's sword."

Jane paled even more.

"Where did you get these?" Nicholas asked, stepping closer to Jane. He pressed close to her side, offering support with his presence.

The wiry-haired leader straightened. "We found them among the carnage."

"And the bodies?" Nicholas prompted.

"The man we found these items near was unrecognizable as his head was cleaved—"

Margaret gasped.

"Enough," Nicholas interrupted as Jane's pallor turned unearthly white.

Jane swayed on her feet a moment before Nicholas put his arm about her waist, supporting her weight. He removed the standard from her fingers and handed it to Margaret. "We need to get you inside," he whispered softly to Jane.

She gave a wooden nod and took one step only to have her legs fail her. Nicholas scooped her up into his arms. "Thank you, gentlemen, for bringing Lady Jane news of her father. The guards will escort you to the gate."

Seamus startled. "We've traveled far—"

Nicholas would add no more danger to Jane's welfare in the castle this eve or any eve, until they determined who was trying so desperately to harm her. Visitors other than those who were invited by Margaret would not be allowed. "I would advise you to leave."

At Nicholas's frosty gaze, Seamus retreated toward the rest of his men. "Perhaps that would be best."

Nicholas's gaze moved past Seamus. The young man who had been appraising Jane was not focused on her any longer. Instead, his back was turned as he studied the inner courtyard. Why?

Nicholas's anger spiked as he hugged Jane closer against his chest. "Shall I escort you out?"

The young man flinched at the look on Nicholas's face. "Nay, we can escort ourselves to the gate."

"Margaret, make certain the gates are closed when these men leave," Nicholas demanded once the men had mounted and were headed in the direction of the gates.

"But the other hunters?" she asked

"We can open the gates when they return."

"What of Jane?" Margaret asked as her gaze shifted to the standard in her hands.

"I will see to her needs."

"Aye." The fear left Margaret's eyes as she straightened. "Gentlemen," she called to the men in a militaristic clip. "If you will follow me." She marched toward the gate. "We thank you for your courtesy in returning these items, but now Lady Jane must come to terms with their meaning . . . alone."

"Close your eyes," Nicholas said as he leaned in toward Jane and pressed a kiss to her forehead as he had done a hundred times in the past. "I will see you safely to your chamber."

As if no time had ever separated them, she buried her face against his chest. "I cannot close my eyes. All I envision is my father with his head disfigured and his eyes staring up at me, empty and lifeless."

Nicholas whisked Jane into the keep, through the great hall and up the stairs leading to her chamber. "Think of a time when you were here at the castle with your father and brother. Focus on the good memories." That was what he did every time the shadows started creeping into his mind again.

Jane nodded, but Nicholas could still see the pain of loss in her eyes. He continued steadily up the stairs until he paused at her closed door. He had been in her chamber before, briefly, along with her brother, Jacob, while they had still been friends.

A vivid memory of when they had first met swam across his mind as he entered the chamber. She had been barely seventeen. He had been nineteen. They had met after one of his and Jacob's wild riding jaunts through the countryside. Jane had been out riding that day as well. When they all had gathered outside the stable, he and Jane had seen each other over the back of Jacob's horse. Their eyes had met—and that had been that.

Jane had been a beauty even at seventeen. Seeing her sitting atop her horse, the wind ruffling her long, golden hair, her eyes filled with intelligence and curiosity, and he had been lost.

For him, however, looking had never been enough.

It had not been for Jane either.

Over the course of a few days, they had become acquaintances, then friends, then sweethearts. They spent every moment of every day together. Laughing and touching had led to kissing, and their connection to each other only grew stronger. Despite the link between them, they never became lovers. Before they took their relationship further, Nicholas had every intention of marrying Jane.

One day, he asked Jacob's advice about how to approach Lord Lennox. That was the day Jacob had sent Nicholas away, banishing him from his sister and Bellhaven Castle. He shuddered. Despite the years, the wound was raw—it still bled.

Holding Jane in his arms now, he remembered how desperately in love with her he had been. But they were older now. And time had a funny way of changing a person's heart. Drawing a deep breath, he looked down at Jane, almost afraid to see what was reflected there.

Her violet eyes were locked on his. "You can put me down."

"I could." His nerves flickered as the scent of roses teased his senses.

"Will you?" she asked with a quip of a smile.

"I like you here, docile and helpless in my arms." He let his gaze drop to her lips. He wondered how her lips would taste after all this time. . . . A lick of desire slid down his spine.

Her lids lowered, but then she forced them up and locked her gaze on his. "I have two legs that are perfectly capable of holding me up."

"You have recovered from your shock, then?" His gaze drifted to her lips again.

She released her hold on his neck and pushed gently against his shoulders. "I may never cleanse that image of my father from my mind, but I am well enough to move forward."

He set her down and she immediately moved to the cold hearth a few paces from him. In the luxury of her chamber, the hearth seemed out of place. Yellow, gold, and green tapestries covered the walls, and gold linens hung from the bed, giving the room a warm and opulent feel. Despite her familiar surroundings, Jane simply stood in front of the hearth, studying the ashes. "My father is truly dead."

"Perhaps. Without a true identification, you will not know that for certain."

She looked up at him, her eyes stormy and confused. "But the standard and his sword?"

Nicholas shrugged. "Artifacts from a battlefield are not indisputable," he said gently.

"It changes nothing, though."

He stepped closer. "Your need to marry in order to inherit?"

Jane's eyes widened, whether at his statement or at his nearness he was not certain, until warmth flared in them. "Yes. There is no escaping that fate, especially now that the MacGuires have offered even circumstantial proof of my father's death. He will be declared dead and the estate will be in jeopardy."

"That is why we are all here." He held her violet gaze, unable to let her retreat this time. Once again they were close; excruciating awareness arced between them. The past seemed tangible, and a web of feeling threatened to snare them anew. He could not resist the urge to raise his hand and brush a finger against her still-pale cheek.

"Yes," she breathed. "I must decide which of you I will spend the rest of my life with—however long or short that might be."

"I will not let anything happen to you, Jane." He took another step closer, his gaze fixed on her lips, when a scuffle at the door startled them both. Nicholas stepped back, turning to see David filling the doorway. Behind him stood Jules, Colin, Lord Galloway, and Bryce.

"Lady Jane, are you well?" David asked, coming into the chamber.

"Lady Margaret told us about the attack." Jules followed.

Jane looked at Nicholas, held his gaze for an instant, then moved to greet the others. "I am unharmed, but yes. Someone did attack my horse during the hunt. Nicholas was kind enough to see me safely home."

"We would have canceled the hunt had we known." Lord Galloway pushed his way forward and took Jane's hand. He searched her from head to toe. "Are you certain nothing harmed you this day?" he asked, shifting his gaze to Nicholas.

"All is well." Jane forced a laugh. "Let us go below stairs and you can tell me about the hunt." She pulled her hand out of the man's grip as she took a step toward the door, most likely hoping all the others would join her. "Who won the competition?"

"David," Bryce said with a sneer. "Although technically he did not win, because he was on the pest moments before he went to ground and escaped."

"Besides, at that moment we all suddenly realized Nicholas and Jane were missing from the group. We came back to find you," Colin explained.

"My heroes," Jane said, again keeping her voice light, although the storm in her eyes spoke of some deeper emotion. "Since David is the winner of this competition, then he and I will have our shared time alone this evening." She turned to David. "Unless you would prefer to wait until morning?"

He smiled. "I could not wait until morning."

As the others left the chamber, Nicholas transferred his gaze back to the cold hearth and leaned against it. He ran his hand through his hair. His temper cooled. His arousal was less forgiving. Unexpectedly, he'd had time alone with Jane this morning.

He wanted more. He wanted Jane. He wanted to win the competition and finally have what he had always desired—Jane's heart.

Nicholas pushed back from the hearth, intending to join the others. If winning the competitions would get him what he wanted, he had to win them all from here on out.

Jane slipped from the keep as soon as she was able to reassure her suitors that she was unharmed. When they had finally retreated to their chambers to change and freshen themselves, she had headed for the stables. She had to make certain her horse was not lame because of today's accident.

She opened the side door to the stables and entered. Instantly, the scent of fresh, sweet hay pervaded her senses.

"Who's there?" Egan called out a moment before he appeared from around the stalls. "Oh, 'tis you, milady." He clutched a small wooden bowl in his hands as he came toward her. "How can I help ye?"

Jane smiled. "I came to see my horse, Diana. Where is she?"

"Her usual stall," he replied as a look of remorse crossed his youthful face. "She's bruised and battered. I was about tae treat her wounds." His gaze dipped to the bowl in his hands.

"I can see to her, Egan." Jane reached for the bowl of ointment.

"If you insist, milady. I'll be right here if ye need me."

"Thank you, Egan." Silently, Jane moved to the stall where her horse lay upon the ground. She dropped to her knees beside her.

"My dear sweet Diana, what have I done to you?" she asked, leaning down and pressing her cheek against the horse's neck. She set the ointment aside and ran her hands over the faithful animal's coat, assessing for a fever.

With a soft whicker, Diana nuzzled Jane. Continuing to stroke her neck, Jane ran her hand over Diana's withers, shoulder, forearm, until finally she reached her lower leg. Diana allowed her master to carefully inspect each leg, from knee to hoof, for damage. Only slight bruising appeared on both fetlocks. The front legs must have taken the brunt of the assault.

Jane reached for the bowl of herbal liniment oil she had invented herself. She was pleased Egan found the lard mixed with lavender oil and crushed mint as useful as she had. Her own horse enjoyed a rubdown with it after a long ride.

"Come on, girl. I need you on your side."

The animal shifted onto her side as if sensing what Jane intended to do. It was not the first time Jane had rubbed down her horse, but never for such abuse. "That is a good girl," Jane cooed as she soothed the oil into Diana's sore and battered legs. "I am so sorry you had to suffer for me." She massaged the final leg, then continued to stroke the animal's back for a time.

Today's attack had been unexpected. She truly thought she would be safe amongst her suitors out in the open, but apparently she had been mistaken.

Who was out to harm her? The girl they had met at the cottage? A servant? It made no sense.

Jane sat back on her knees. But could that person be someone in her household? Whoever it was had access to her routine, even to a change in her daily activities.

Forcing the thought away, Jane gave Diana a final stroke on the neck, then stood. "I will be back to check on you later," she said as she closed the stall door. She turned and startled as she came face-to-face with Bryce.

"Ministering to the animals now, are you?" he asked, his voice heavy with sarcasm.

Jane straightened, refusing to allow her cousin to see how unsettled she was by his presence. Where was Egan? "What do you want, Bryce?"

"You know what I want." He stepped closer to her in an act she knew was meant to intimidate her.

"Well, you cannot have Bellhaven."

"It should be mine. And I would accept you along with the estate as a welcome prize." He lifted his hand to stroke her cheek.

The feather-light touch sent chills through her. She edged away, stepping to the side, out of his reach. He carried no weapon, but he needed no blade to harm her if that was his intention. His strength could overpower her, though she was far more agile. And without all that anger to weigh her down, she could outmaneuver him, she prayed, if it came to that.

"Why this ridiculous competition?" he asked with a penetrating stare.

He let her step farther away. "I need a husband."

"Then why not spare the others and accept me? That way we can keep Bellhaven between us. It can be as much yours as it is mine."

The castle was never his, and if she had anything to say about it, it never would be. Her gaze connected with his. "I might have been presented with evidence earlier to prove my father is—" She broke off as her throat tightened.

"He is dead. You have had proof of that."

"Perhaps, but not of Jacob."

He sighed. "When are you going to see what is before you, you naive fool?"

"I remain hopeful. That is all."

"Hope never did anything for anyone." He shook his head.

Jane sighed as she studied him. He was handsome, intelligent, and from their youth together she knew him to be resourceful. She knew he had taken the death of his mother hard. But was that enough to fill a person with hate? "What happened to you, Bryce, to make you so angry?"

He startled. "Why do you care?"

"You are my cousin."

He turned away, hiding his gaze from her. "Do not look at me like that."

"How am I looking at you?"

"As though you care."

"But I do."

"Why waste your precious time on me?"

"I have done nothing over the years to make me the target of your hate. Who are you really angry with, Bryce?" Jane swore she could almost hear her cousin's heart beating faster. His breath hitched.

Her body relaxed. She had touched on whatever it was that made him so uncontrolled and angry. Someone had hurt him, and deeply.

"If you ever need to talk, I will listen. Perhaps talking about it will help you find peace," she said softly.

"And you think that will change me?" He spun to face her once more, his shield of anger firmly intact. "You seriously overestimate your abilities, cousin."

Jane was no longer afraid. Something inside her said Bryce would not harm her. His bluff and bluster was merely an act to cover his wounds, whatever they might be. "When you are ready to talk, I will be here."

For a heartbeat, his gaze softened, then the hardness returned. "I do not want your sympathy. I want this castle." He pushed past her, heading for the door. "I will have it, too. One way or another, Bellhaven will be mine."

"We shall see," Jane whispered to the emptiness that remained. No one would take Bellhaven from her without a fight, especially her own cousin.

Nicholas climbed the stair, heading for Jane's bedchamber in his search for Lady Margaret. He could not find her below stairs, and a maid in the hall said she had seen Lady Margaret carrying something up the stairs.

He paused at the open doorway and looked inside just as Lady Margaret placed Lord Lennox's standard across the back of a chair, then leaned his sword against the seat back. Her fingers lingered on the flat of the blade for a moment before she pulled them back.

"If it is true that Lord Lennox is dead, there is no more honorable way to die," Nicholas said softly, entering the chamber.

Lady Margaret spun around, startled. Hurriedly she brushed at the corners of her eyes with her fingers. "I am being a sentimental fool."

"He was your brother. You have every right to be saddened by his loss." Nicholas realized in that moment he had missed seeing Lady Margaret during his two-year absence from Bellhaven as well. Jane's aunt had always been a calming influence in both Jane and Jacob's lives.

Lady Margaret forced a wobbly smile. "I am trying to be strong for Jane's sake."

"You and Jane are so alike. You do not have to be so strong all the time. Let others help you." Nicholas stepped fully into the room and held out his arms.

The older woman waited all of a heartbeat before she tucked herself into his embrace. He allowed his warmth and strength to flow into her. "It will be better soon. It has been . . . a difficult day."

"For us all." He tightened his arms around her.

Lady Margaret pulled back to stare into his face. "Do you truly believe someone in this very castle is trying to harm Jane?"

"Yes." Nicholas offered the woman a smile as he set her from him. "Now then, are you better?"

She drew a deep breath, then nodded. "Much."

"I came to find you to ask your help."

"With what?" Lady Margaret asked.

"I need to find a particular servant girl who works somewhere here in the castle," Nicholas said grimly. "She is young, perhaps around eighteen, blond hair. She said her name was Clara, or Clarisa."

Lady Margaret frowned. "We have a Clara who is blond and about that age. She works in the kitchen. We also have a Clarisa. But she is a dark-haired maid. She is a score and five and the mother of twins."

"This girl said she was the sister of the woodcutter."

Lady Margaret's face paled. "Peter was an orphan."

"Was?"

She nodded. "He rode off with Lord Lennox and Master Jacob to battle and has not been seen since."

A chill moved through Nicholas at her words. "Can you send both girls to me in the hall? I will speak to both."

"The girl," Lady Margaret asked, "why do you want her?"

"I believe she is either involved in Lady Jane's accidents or knows who is."

"Merciful heavens." Lady Margaret straightened and a look of purpose came back into her eyes. Her brother's death was not forgotten, but for now she had a way to move beyond it—with action.

"I will meet you in the hall shortly with both girls," she said, and hastened from the chamber.

Alone, Nicholas looked back at the chair, bearing the Lennox standard and Lord Lennox's sword, one last time. *God's blood.* He had told Lady Margaret the truth. There was no more honorable way to die than in battle. He knew the truth of that. But why did Lord Lennox and Jacob both have to die in such a painful, violent way?

In the silence, bitter memories of another type of violence tugged at Nicholas. Even now he could smell the tallow candles of his father's hall, feel the stone floor beneath his knees, sense the eyes watching from a distance and not a one of them moving forward to stop his father's lash.

The lash came down hard, but with such talent as to neither break skin nor muscle. Only bruises would remain this time. Nicholas gritted his teeth, trying to summon the anger that had seen him through these endless nights of torment.

The anger would not come, only exhaustion. If only his father would cease for a moment, let him catch his breath, explain what had happened.

Nicholas shuddered as the lash came down again, two, three, four times. He fell to his hands, but not to the ground. Never would he collapse fully. His own pride would never allow that. He hitched a breath. "Father," he rasped, praying the word would jolt some rational part of the man's mind. "Please listen . . . to me."

The lash came down harder. Nicholas bit back a cry of pain, fighting the black terror that threatened to choke him. His father never listened to him. Why would he start now? All he cared about was his drink. And when he drank, he got angry. Nicholas was the target simply because he refused to allow anyone else to be. But tonight, his father was completely past reason.

A Laird for Christmas

Something had to change. Perhaps it was time to flee his home, seek refuge somewhere else, anywhere else. Protect himself for once from the cruelties of a madman. Even as the thought formed, Nicholas knew he could never leave. If he did, someone else would take his place and he could never live with that.

The lash came down, again and again, draining him of life, of hope. He would have wept, but his tears had left him years ago, only humiliation lingered, and that rocked him to the depths of his soul until it smothered everything there. Would there ever be an end to the nightly torture? He had done nothing wrong except be born a Kincaid.

The memory tore through him, streaked across his back, and lanced his heart so deep that for a moment he could not breathe. That was the past. Nicholas straightened. This was not the time for memories. It was a time to be on guard and alert. If he did not, someone might get hurt.

Jane.

It was Jane who had rescued him from that hell with her smile. Near her, a part of himself that had been dead for an eternity came back to life. She had given him something to live for, hope for, dream about.

No one would ever hurt her the way he had been hurt. He would protect her, and even if she chose another to be her husband, he would see she came to no harm, now or anytime in the future.

The thought of Jane with another man was like a hundred pricks of a sharp blade. He forced the sensation away. He would concentrate on Jane's safety. Her future and his could wait another day.

Nicholas left the chamber, closed the door, and went up to the battlements for a breath of fresh air. When he felt more in control of himself and his emotions, he went down to the hall to await Lady Margaret and the girls.

When he reached the great hall, the three women were already there.

"This is Clara and Clarisa," Lady Margaret said, introducing them both.

His gaze immediately moved to the flaxen-haired girl and disappointment filled him. She was not the same girl from the woods. He had been hopeful he had misheard her name.

Lady Margaret gazed at him expectantly.

He shook his head.

Her face fell.

"Do either of you know another young woman named Clara or Clarisa? She may or may not work in this castle," Nicholas asked.

"Nay, milord," Clarisa said with a quick curtsey. She stared at his shoes. "I know no one else by that name."

Clara met his gaze, steady and strong. "No."

She was not the girl, but he could sense she knew more than she was saying. "Does your mother work here in the castle?"

"Nay. I'm the only one from my family."

"And your surname is?"

She paled slightly. "MacGuire."

The MacGuires again? "How did you come to work here?" Nicholas asked, noting that the girl started rubbing her hands together as he continued his interrogation.

"My family sent me here two years ago when Lord Lennox inquired about a young kitchen maid who might someday take over for Miss Marthe."

"Is this true?" he asked Lady Margaret.

"My brother did hire a few new servants about that time. Jane could tell you more about it as she has always been more involved in the day-to-day activities of the estate than I have been."

"Is there some other post besides the kitchen you can shift Clara MacGuire to until I can speak with Lady Jane?" Nicholas asked Lady Margaret.

"Don't send me away," the girl cried out.

"You are not being sent away, merely given different duties until Jane can be consulted." It would not do to have the girl in the kitchens where she would have easy access to Jane's food. Poison had yet to be used against Jane, but they had to consider everything from this moment on.

The first rule of war was a surprise attack. With the maid out of the kitchen, there would be one less potential for surprise.

With only lanterns to guide them, Jane and David headed through the outer bailey toward the one hill inside the castle gates. They were alone, and yet they were not. The other men had insisted if Jane were going out of the keep that they follow as guards in case whoever was after her attacked once more.

Jane looked over her shoulder to see five dark shapes and five lanterns following behind her. They kept their distance, giving her and David privacy, but they were there. She was not certain if the fact thrilled or annoyed her.

With supreme effort, Jane shifted her attention to where it belonged—on David. He had won the last competition. Despite the danger she had faced that morning, and the news she had received about her father, she owed him the courtesy of her exclusive attention during this time. After all, it was why they were all here. No matter what else might happen to her or around her, she had to marry by Christmas Eve. "Where are you taking me?" she asked, forcing a levity she did not yet feel into her voice.

David offered her a rare smile that lit up his usually somber eyes. His mood was carefree and playful this evening. Not two words she usually equated with the serious boy from her youth. "We are almost there." David carried a long slim object wrapped in linen under one arm and a bulging basket in the other. The smell of freshly baked bread wafted from the basket, indicating he had brought dinner along with him. No doubt Marthe had supplied him with all Jane's favorites. The entire staff had warmed to the idea of her finding a husband, and as quickly as possible.

Jane and David stopped at the crest of the hill. He set down his lantern, then spread a thick pelt over a patch of ground that had been cleared of the snow. No doubt David had come out here earlier, preparing for this event.

Once the large pelt was in place, he sat down, then stretched his tall, muscular frame out upon the fur. Moonlight glistened on his neatly trimmed brown hair. He worn a soft linen shirt and breeches covered by a thick fur cloak. "Come join me," he said in an inviting tone. Lying there with his hand outstretched, he looked sinful, elegant, and far too good for her nerves. Raw sexual energy shimmered off him in thick waves.

She startled at the thought. David was always so safe. She did feel safe with him tonight, yet she also felt a new awareness growing between them, something that had never been there in her youth. She set her lantern on the edge of the blanket opposite his before she accepted his hand and sat down on the blanket beside him. She arranged her own cloak to cover her legs.

The night was clear and cold. Jane inhaled slowly then let the air slide from her lungs, creating a wreath of mist to hang about her momentarily before vanishing. Above them the stars sparkled like a million jewels in the sky. "Why did we come out here for our time alone?"

He cast an ironic glance over his shoulder. "To be alone." He shifted the cloth covering the basket and withdrew a chunky loaf of bread, a wedge of golden cheese, a small wooden platter bearing sliced, roasted pheasant, and two dried apples. "Your other suitors are always too much at hand."

Jane smiled. "A moonlight meal?" she asked, once again returning her attention to her suitor.

"I wanted to give you an experience you would remember," he said, offering her a pewter plate and a two-pronged fork, before withdrawing a flask from his basket, then pouring her a cup of mead. She could smell the sweet honeyed scent as he passed her the flagon. "Have you ever had a supper for two under the stars?"

She took a sip of the wine. "Never."

"Good." He poured himself a glass of mead, then started serving their meal. "This meal is just the beginning."

"It is good to have you here, David. It seems like years since you have been to Bellhaven." It had been many years. David and his father used to come to the castle often. Then several years ago, they just stopped coming. No explanation was given. Her own father never mentioned the Buchanans again. It was as if they had ceased to exist.

"It has been a long time," David said.

Jane picked at the wedge of cheese David had offered her. "Was there something that happened to keep you and your father away?" Jane asked, suddenly curious as to why he had vanished from her life so suddenly.

He frowned, thinking. "I am not certain, and looking back now, I cannot imagine why I ever allowed that to happen." He popped a piece of meat into his mouth, chewed thoughtfully, then continued. "I only remember that last night vaguely. My father was upset about something your father did or said. It was not long after that that my father turned ill. I got involved in his care and in taking over the estate."

David's words faded and Jane knew his thoughts had turned to his own father's death. "Death is a part of our life. It is inevitable for us all."

"Yes, but a violent death is not natural," he said softly. "Would you like to talk about your father?"

"Nothing I say will bring him or Jacob back. I have proof now of Father's death. Jacob is still a mystery." She stared down at her plate, her hunger no longer present. "I miss them. I want them back. But wishing it so will not make it happen." She drew a deep breath then released a rush of mist to coil with the chill night air. She brought her hands to her chest, covering her heart. "I would know if they were dead. I would feel it here. And I do not, but with the proof of my father's death . . ." She straightened. "I have to accept what has happened, and what I must do now."

"Marry one of us?"

"Yes."

"As much as I hate to admit this, there is not a man here who would not make you a fine husband, Jane. I have studied my competition. They all appear to be fond of you, and all are steady enough to provide you the support you will need as mistress of Bellhaven."

"Even Bryce?" she asked with a chuckle.

"Even Bryce," David said with amusement in his tone. "Bryce's venom is merely his way of showing his disappointment not to be next in the line of succession." David's face grew serious once more. "I want the man you choose to be me, but I want you to make a decision that will make you happy for the rest of your days."

"Thank you, David. It means a lot to hear you say that."

His smile returned. "By the heavens," he groaned. "When will I ever learn? Now I will have to work twice as hard to win your hand from my competitors. Perhaps I should get started. This night, I want to take you somewhere you have never been before."

"Where?" Jane asked, suddenly curious about what he had planned for her.

"To the heavens." He turned toward the linen-wrapped package he had carried with him. Spreading the fabric apart, he revealed a long cut of leather and two clear, spherical objects. He placed the large glass piece at the far end of the leather, smaller glass closest to him, then rolled both into a cone with the leather. Placing the narrow end up to his eye, he turned his gaze toward the sky. "It is a perfect night for stargazing, clear and bright. Have you ever seen the stars up close before?"

David turned and offered the strange contraption to her. "Place this—it is called a telescope—against your eye. Close the other one and focus your gaze on the stars."

As he extinguished the lanterns, she did as instructed. With only the light of the moon to cast a silvery light over the night, Jane looked up and gasped. The stars appeared so close, as if she could reach out and touch them. "Is this magic?"

David laughed. "It is a new kind of magic."

She turned back to David. His face was alive. His eyes sparkled like the stars she had just seen up close. Never had she seen him so animated. Whatever this new magic was, it certainly agreed with him. "How does it work?"

"Basically, a telescope is a long tube with magnifying lenses at both ends. The end you put to your eye has two lenses that curve outward. These lenses magnify the image. At the far end of the telescope are inwardly curved lenses which draw in the light. The distance between these two sets of lenses can be changed to focus the image and make it clear."

His smile shifted to a more pensive look. "There is one flaw, however. As this light passes through the tube and hits the lens nearest your eye, the image is magnified and appears close, but it also appears upside down. This is because the light entering the telescope bends the image. I have not figured out how to correct that just yet. But I will."

"I am certain you will." Jane put the telescope back to her eye and looked once again at the night sky. The usual pinpoints of light became more jagged, with light spiking out from several points. Even if the stars were upside down, they were magnificent. "The stars are so beautiful."

Before she could register his presence, David slipped behind her. His chest pressed against her back and his legs bracketed hers. His hands moved to cover her own. "Let me guide you," he said softly against her ear. He shifted her hands to the west. "Over on the western horizon at this time of year, you can see the planet Venus."

Jane felt the warmth of David's strong hands against her cool flesh. She breathed in his spicy scent, trying to focus on Venus while her thoughts shifted to the purpose for this time alone. David was handsome, reliable, a good protector, and curious about the world around him. He would make anyone a fine husband. This evening she had seen him smile more than she had ever remembered. He seemed happy, content in the thought of sharing a life with her. But was he the *one*?

She cared for David, but could she grow to love him? Would he help her forget her first kiss, her first love, and his ultimate betrayal? Jane frowned, forcing the thought away.

David. Tonight was about David.

The planet before her eyes was bigger than anything she had seen in the night sky before. The edges of the planet seemed so sharp and almost unreal. "It seems so odd that these stars and planets are here every night and that anyone who looks up can see them, yet they appear so unique and special and intimate through the lenses of your telescope."

"Tonight, the heavens are for you." He shifted her hands once again to the north.

A million stars appeared, all clustered together. Again her breath escaped her in a rush. "My father told me about the Milky Way."

"You recognize it. Wonderful. It was in 1610, through the use of one of the first telescopes, that Galileo Galilei discovered the first proof that the Milky Way was made up of countless stars."

David moved her hands again toward the eastern horizon. A large globe appeared. It seemed close enough for Jane to reach up and touch.

"Is that the moon that appears so big?"

"Yes, the moon is the brightest object in the night sky but gives off no light of its own. Instead, it reflects light from the sun."

"What are the shadows I see?" Jane asked, fascinated with this new look at the moon.

"Those are not shadows, but craters. Researchers think they were volcanic," he replied patiently.

"It is spectacular to the naked eye, but magnified—" Jane could not find the words to describe what she saw. Warmth filled her chest as she continued to study the heavenly bodies. She was happy, truly happy, when only a few hours ago she had wondered if she would ever know that emotion again.

Impulsively, she turned and stretched behind her to plant a kiss on David's cheek. "I will remember this evening every time I look at the stars."

He moved in front of her, his eyes searching hers. He lifted his hand and ran his finger down her jaw. The gentleness of his touch sent a chill through her. Would he kiss her? Did she want him to? She was not certain as he stared at her with those dark, hungry eyes.

Then he ran the pad of his thumb over her lips and she shivered at the sensation. The air between them was rife with tension. The force of it took her breath and made her both weak and strong at the same moment.

Just when she was sure he would kiss her, he lifted the telescope from her fingers and leaned back. The heat in his gaze shifted to pain. "I want to kiss you, Jane. But I will not. If you choose me as your husband, I will bare my soul to you. Not before."

Her heart pounded as he stood and started packing the dishes and his telescope away. Their time alone was over and David had appeared to enjoy himself tonight, until the very end. In the last moments it had become obvious that he wanted her, yet she held all the power in this adventure.

She had the power to unleash each of her suitors' passions or to deny them. It was more power than she had ever had in her life. Her father and brother had ruled over her. She had been allowed to care for the castle, but not really make the decisions. Not like she would now.

In that moment, she suddenly realized it was important for her to choose a mate who would allow her to keep that power—make her choices, live by her decisions, and to do what was right for her people.

"David." She turned to him, her hands clasped before her. She had to be bold and ask the question she needed answered. "If I were to marry you, would I be allowed to discuss decisions made about the castle and its people with you?"

His brows drew together as he studied her. "A man's role is to be the leader and protector of his family. A woman's place is to oversee the household and the children. Are we to take on different roles than those?"

Jane tensed at his response. She had hoped to have more of the freedoms she experienced now, but she realized David, or any of her other suitors, would not want to be minimized in his role as laird of Bellhaven. "Can I ask you another question?"

"Always."

"Does it bother you to be one of six men vying for my hand?"

David clung to the picnic basket, his tension and his response obvious without words. "To be honest, yes. But every one of us knew what we were getting ourselves into when we accepted your aunt's invitation. For one of us, the hardship will be worthwhile. For the others," he shrugged, "we will find our way eventually."

"But—"

"Trust yourself and what your aunt has put before you, Jane. In one of us you will find what you need."

It was her turn to smile. "Thank you, David, for that reassurance, and for this wonderful night." She slipped her arm through his. "Shall we join the others?"

"Only because we must," he said with a chuckle. He gathered the supplies and the unlit lantern. With only the light of the night sky to guide them, they joined the others to head back into the safety of the castle walls.

Bellhaven Castle. Just looking at the tall, imposing towers and the pinkish-gray stone brought a feeling of love and contentment to fill her chest. She would do anything for Bellhaven.

Even marry one of these men, she finally realized. Jane proceeded through the inner bailey to the keep—the core of her home. In order to keep the castle, she only needed *one* husband.

One.

Later that night, unable to sleep, David wandered the hallways of the keep. He cursed himself with every step he took. He should have kissed Jane. Never had he felt the burning of desire as strongly as he had tonight.

He hated feeling vulnerable. Hated that he wanted her.

David shook his head. No, he had done the right thing, avoiding that kiss. He could not have taken her lips then forgotten about her later. Once he took a wife, it would be forever.

David clenched his jaw when he realized where his feet had taken him—just outside Jane's chamber door. He pressed his hand against the wood and splayed his fingers. Closing his eyes he could imagine Jane sitting atop her bed, could once again see that turmoil in her eyes.

She hated this game as much as he did. She had a kind and gentle soul, and playing one man against the other was not for her. She was far too level-headed for that.

Fire pounded through his blood as he continued to imagine Jane on the opposite side of the door. He could almost feel her pain, her indecision. She was usually strong, so capable. He had never met a woman to match her.

"I choose you," he had imagined her saying to him tonight.

He would give anything to hear those words, to have her look at him with desire in her eyes, to want him more than any of the others. He held back a groan as his body tightened. His cheek burned where she had kissed him.

He clenched his hands at his sides. Right now all he wanted to do was kick open her door and kiss her until she melted in his arms. To have her touch him, hold him, welcome him. But it was not going to happen that way. He sensed Jane holding herself back tonight. She was uncertain where her heart lay.

No matter. He was not giving up. Not yet. There had been a connection between them once. He could not ask for more than that right now. With a heavy heart, he forced himself to leave her door.

Looking at the stars had been a good start at turning Jane his way. She was not there yet. He had to think of another way to engage her heart, not just her mind.

10

Seven days remained until Jane had to choose a husband and marry him. It seemed an eternity, yet she knew it was not. However, today was not a day for another competition as other things required her attention. Today she needed to tend to the castle.

She had arranged for the men to spend the morning practicing their sword play. On the walk back to the castle last night, she could feel their restlessness. Perhaps a day of battling each other without her as the prize would help calm their nerves.

Jane gathered her cloak around her shoulders as she walked through the chill morning air. Her routine each morning was to check on the welfare of her castle. Today, however, she wondered how the serfs were fairing in the winter season. Without them, the castle would have no income. She would deliver gifts of food and coin to each family on St. Stephen's Day, but she had best start her preparations for that event soon.

She walked from the keep, across the inner bailey, to the kitchen and bake house, through the inner gate and into the outer bailey. As she walked, she considered what difficulties having sixty extra men in the guard, brought by her six suitors, had fallen to Angus and his men. More residents would no doubt affect Angus's responsibilities, add expenses to the castle's finances, create extra workload on the kitchens, and stretch the housing abilities of the servants' quarters. She had wanted an army, and she'd been granted that wish. Now Jane hoped Angus and the others could manage the extra load.

Making her way toward Angus to ask him about the burden on the castle, Jane lifted the hem of her gown to keep it from getting soiled. Her low boots crunched in the layer of snow that still lingered despite the past two days of sunshine.

Jane greeted her people and listened to their needs as she progressed through the castle. She took in the sights that never ceased to fill her with pride—the pinkish-gray stone buildings, the well-kept mews and stable, the well-equipped forge, the outer buildings for the servants as well as the fine stained glass windows of the chapel. She had spent the last two years supervising and often working alongside the servants to wash every corner of the castle and rid it of the foul smells that had once been ever present. Now only the fresh breeze from the forest beyond filled every corner of Bellhaven.

Jane tipped her face up to the morning sun. The weak rays barely warmed the land, but even so, if she closed her eyes she could immediately see the castle as it would be in the summertime, with its lush gardens and loaded fruit trees. It was under her care and direction that the castle had become both desirable and profitable.

At the thought, she opened her eyes and her footsteps slowed. The gatehouse stood before her, closed to their enemies. But more threatening at the moment than her enemies were the men who had learned Jane was without protection. The Lord Fairfields of the world were eager to take what they could from an unprotected female. Adding to the danger was Jane's newly acquired reputation as a woman easily seduced.

Jane drew in a sharp breath. On unsteady legs, she pushed herself to continue forward on her original mission. She could not undo what Nicholas's hurtful words had done to her reputation, but marrying one of her suitors would at least help her protect what she valued more than her virginity—her people and her castle.

Feeling stronger and more in control with every step, Jane proceeded toward where she knew she would find one of her most loyal servants.

Angus, who served as both steward and bailiff, saw her approach. The overly large man shuffled out to greet her. "Milady. How are ye this fine mornin'?"

"Can you tell me no one approaches to attack us?"

He bowed. "I can."

"Then I am well and hopeful our situation will only improve," she replied with a genuine smile.

"It already has improved." Angus's gaze shifted to the open field, where her suitors and their men took up arms against each other in a mock battle. The sound of steel striking steel rang throughout the outer bailey.

"Yes, but the question still remains, are they enough to keep Bellhaven safe?"

Angus folded his arms over his chest and nodded. "We're better off than we were a few days' past with sixty more men to defend this castle."

That much was true. The warriors each of her suitors had brought with them increased their ability to fend off an attack. But it was not the fear of attack that filled her thoughts at the moment. Instead, her thoughts and her gaze shifted to her suitors.

After a brief conversation about how Angus fared with the extra men in the castle, Jane bid him a good morning. Her gaze still drawn by the men, she hurried to the bastion closest to the open field and entered the stone structure. She made her way up the stairs. At the top of the tower, she moved to the edge, peering through the crenellations.

Below, the men battled, unaware of her presence. Her suitors sparred, but not with the usual blunted swords. Nay, they used weapons with sharp blades and pointed tips. Jane tensed. What possessed them to take such chances with their lives?

David and Nicholas were paired against each other, giving and receiving forceful blows with their swords. They were equally matched, she thought, as she watched them move their lithe bodies up and down the field, neither tiring.

Lord Galloway and Colin fought each other with less fervor. Both had obvious talent. However, neither man seemed to have his heart in the battle.

Her gaze moved to the two remaining men. For a moment, Jane felt her knees go unsteady beneath her as Bryce came at Jules with a lethal strike.

Jules managed to block the blow just in time to avoid losing his head. He looked tired, unsteady, and pale.

Bryce growled and came at Jules again.

Jules met his sword, held it, but Jane could see the muscles of his arms quiver beneath the strain.

She held her breath as Bryce forced Jules's sword down. Her cousin punched Jules in the stomach with his free arm, sending him to the ground. Bryce kicked his side.

Jules rolled, but he did not avoid Bryce's booted foot as it connected with his head.

Jane clutched her hands together and prayed that Jules would find his feet. The man was still too weak from his incarceration to battle the others. She had not considered Jules's strength when she had sent them off this morning.

Jane tried to cry out a warning as Bryce raised his sword. Her voice failed her. Her chest tightened. The sword came down, arcing toward Jules's chest. He did not move, did not react.

Then Bryce went flying as Nicholas slammed into him. The two men landed in the snow. Bryce's sword tumbled from his hand.

Lord Galloway scooped up the weapon, keeping it away from Bryce's grasp.

Bryce cried out in rage as he scrambled to his feet.

Nicholas was up a heartbeat later, just in time to duck a fist aimed at his face.

Before Bryce got in another punch, David and Colin grabbed her cousin by the arms, pulling him back.

"Enough," David shouted.

Nicholas hurried to kneel at Jules's side. Jane held her breath until she saw Jules open his eyes. "I am not dead yet," he croaked.

A rush of relief filled her. She clung to the stone for support. Then as though sensing her presence, Nicholas's gaze lifted, connecting with hers.

He gave her a curt nod, then returned his attention to Jules, helping him to his feet.

"This is not over," Bryce called as Nicholas led Jules away.

"It is over." Colin jabbed Bryce in the ribs.

The man doubled over, then tried to shake himself free of the arms that held him. "Let me go."

"Only if you promise to cool that hot head of yours," Lord Galloway said impatiently.

Bryce shook himself free. "He started it."

David strode to stand before Bryce, leaving only a handbreadth between them, his presence intimidating, his body vibrating with authority. "I am ending it. Now leave us."

Bryce stepped back and turned away, heading for the inner bailey.

Jane straightened despite the fact she was suddenly weary. Bryce had always been a melancholic child, but he had never been violent. What had happened to him in the years since she had seen him? Something had to have happened. There had to be an explanation for his anger. Perhaps she should speak with him again and either force him to tell her what disturbed him so, or warn him to check his emotions or leave.

Right now, however, it was Jules who needed her attention. She never imagined the day would turn to disaster merely because she needed to attend to the castle's business. Jane retraced her steps back to the keep, stopping near the hearth in the great hall to gather a basin of hot water and several strips of linen in case Jules had wounds that needed tending.

At the doorway to Jules's chamber, Jane stood and looked at the man who lay in the bed. He was still as death. She entered the room and approached the bed. His eyes remained closed.

A small candle burned on the small table near the bed. The light was sufficient to illuminate Jules's face. His lip was bleeding and one eye was rapidly swelling into a purple mass. He was still dressed in his jerkin and breeches, and the others who had helped him were nowhere in sight.

Jane set the water and linens on the table. She dunked in one strip of linen, wrung out the water, then applied the wet cloth to Jules's bleeding lip. At the contact he groaned. "Jules?" she whispered as she wiped the blood away.

"Jane?" he rasped, and opened his eyes.

"How badly are you hurt?" She lowered herself to the bed, her gaze moving to his torso, his ribs, where Bryce had kicked him. A blossom of red stood out against the silver padded jerkin he wore. She pressed her fingers to his side and her fingers drew back bloody.

"It is not from Bryce," Jules bit out.

Jane stiffened.

"'Tis a previous wound from gaol that Bryce reopened," Nicholas said from the doorway. He entered the chamber holding large strips of linen and a dagger. Ollie followed behind him and busied himself at the fireplace, adding more logs and coaxing the flames to burn higher.

Nicholas sat on the bed across from Jane. It took him less than a breath to rip Jules's jerkin down the front and pull it off his friend.

At the sight of Jules's bare chest, Jane's cheeks warmed until she saw what Nicholas had known all along. The exposed wound started at the base of his ribs and continued around to his back. Nicholas rolled Jules onto his side to reveal his entire back, laced with wounds.

Jane gasped. "A lashing?"

At her words, Nicholas tensed. His hands stilled for a heartbeat before he recovered. No doubt seeing his friend in such a state disturbed him. "This wound that starts on his side and goes around his back is the deepest." He took the wet cloth from Jane's hand and wiped away the blood. It was immediately replaced by fresh blood.

"As I suspected." Nicholas brought his gaze to hers. "He is bleeding too fast to sew him together." His voice was grim.

"The knife then?" Jules asked weakly.

Jane winced. Nicholas intended to seal the wound with a hot knife. She reached for fresh linen and pressed it against Jules's wound. Perhaps if she just slowed the blood flow.

"I'm sorry, milady," Ollie said as he thrust the knife into the fire. "At this point, only a knife will do. He's been sufferin' for too long."

Jane nodded.

"Jules," Nicholas coaxed softly. "There is no other way. After all you have been through, we cannot lose you now to a wound. The hot blade will hurt like the devil, but then you will be fine."

Jules nodded and closed his eyes.

"Jane, your task will be to hold his shoulders. Do not let him roll onto his back."

She pulled the cloth in her hands away and set it aside before placing her hands on Jules's shoulders, holding them firmly.

Ollie handed Nicholas the thickly wrapped hilt. Even from a distance, Jane could feel the heat of the fiery orange blade.

Ollie positioned himself over Jules's body and pushed the edges of the wound together.

Not hesitating, Nicholas pressed the hot knife to Jules's flesh. Jules became, if possible, even paler than before, but he did not cry out.

The stench of burning flesh brought bile to Jane's throat. She drew a sharp breath, hoping to steady her reaction. She could not be so weak, not when Jules was so brave.

With a steady hand, Nicholas sealed each section of the wound until it was closed.

"'Tis finished," Ollie said, taking the knife from Nicholas's hands. He returned a moment later with salve.

Nicholas gently raised Jules into a sitting position and applied the soothing salve, then spread more across the other lash marks on Jules's back before wrapping a bandage around his ribs. When he was done, he settled Jules back against the pillows.

Jules closed his eyes with a sigh. "Thank you," he rasped before he lapsed into an exhausted sleep.

"Ollie, stay with him," Nicholas instructed. He held out his hand to Jane, helping her to her feet. "Come with me. You need fresh air."

She curled her fingers around his. She needed something to wash the scent of Jules's burning flesh from her senses, but nothing would ever take away the memory of him bravely enduring such horrific pain. "I am to blame," she said when they were out in the hallway, heading toward the stairs to the upper level of the keep and, hopefully, the tower.

"You did not put the lash to his back."

"No, but I should have worked harder to free him from gaol." Outside, a blissful breeze wafted across the tower, cold and refreshing. Jane drew her hand from Nicholas's and moved to the crenellations, gazing out over her land. This tower was where she always came to think. Staring out over the castle walls and the hills beyond usually gave her a much-needed perspective when the weight of her burdens seemed too heavy. Standing here now brought her no such relief.

Silence surrounded them. She could feel Nicholas's presence behind her. "Perhaps this game of suitors was a poor idea."

"Without your 'game' Jules would still be in gaol. No amount of bodily damage or pain will make him less grateful to be here."

"He should be safe within these walls," she whispered.

"And so should you." His hands moved to her shoulders and turned her to face him. "We are all glad to be here, no matter what happens. We all want you to keep your castle and to find happiness."

Happiness?

Jane felt her throat tighten. She had been happier in the days since they had arrived than she could remember for a very long time.

"You have been so alone."

She nodded.

"It must have been very hard."

It had been hard. "I would do anything for Bellhaven." For the third time in less than a week, she felt tears begin, tears of fear and sorrow. She had kept her grief locked inside for so long now.

The next thing she knew, she was gathered against Nicholas's solid chest and wrapped in his arms. She tried to hold the tears back, and she was successful until he skimmed a hand over her hair. Reason fled and she allowed the tears to come. She clung to him and wept. She wept for her father, who had tried so hard to be everything his son needed after the loss of their mother, even if he had often failed. She cried for her brother who, despite being two years younger, tried to protect her from all harm—real or imagined—and who teased her and loved her with equal devotion. She cried for her mother who died giving her brother life.

And for a heartbeat, she wept for herself and the situation she now found herself in. She had to marry in such a short time. At least she would have her choice of men she liked instead of being forced to tolerate someone like Lord Fairfield, who only wanted to conquer her and take all she had.

She pulled away and batted at her tears with the back of her hand. She turned away. "Forgive me," she said in a tight voice. "It has been a tiring morning."

She felt his hands on her shoulders again. Nicholas turned her around, and despite herself, she looked up into his eyes. "Stop trying to be so damn strong. We are all here to help you. Please let us help you."

"I have shouldered the burden for six months," she said softly.

"You have been carrying the burden of Bellhaven since I first came here as a young man. Your brother and father offered you protection, but you have been overseeing the castle for years." He brushed away her remaining tears with his thumbs.

His words were only the truth.

He drew her back against his chest. "Will you let me help you?"

"What can you do?"

"I would be the husband you need. The protector you crave. Your friend for a lifetime."

She relaxed into him, let his strength flow through her. In his arms, she felt fragile. Protectable. Safe. To feel as if she could lay aside her burdens for the moment was an unusual sensation. But then reality returned, and a familiar hurt settled inside her. It was Nicholas who held her. Nicholas. The man who had only added to her burdens. She drew back, putting some necessary space between them. When he was further from her, she could think more clearly. "How am I to trust that you will never hurt me again?"

His features darkened. "Tell me what I did, Jane. How did I hurt you?"

"You left me behind, for one thing."

"Is that the wedge you have forced between us? My leaving at your brother's command?"

"There is so much more to it than that. You know there is. You hurt me in unimaginable ways."

"How, Jane? Please talk to me. Tell me what I did. If I do not know, how will I ever make amends?"

She tried to talk, but her throat tightened as fresh tears threatened. Jane dropped her gaze to her feet, hiding her weakness. By the heavens, what was wrong with her? She never cried, yet now she could not seem to stop.

She forced the tears back and said what she had longed to say since that first day in her hall. She met Nicholas's gaze once more. "Why did you start rumors about me?"

He frowned. "Rumors about what?"

"My sensual nature." She forced the words out.

"What are you speaking of?" His expression turned troubled. "The passion we shared two years ago was precious and sacred. I would never betray you in that way."

And yet he had. Tears forced their way forward once more.

He reached for her.

She took another step back, out of his grasp. She could not continue the discussion. Not now. Not until she could regain a sense of control over her emotions. "It matters not. The 'game' is what is before us. Only the winner of the competitions will gain my hand and all that goes with it."

"I only care about Bellhaven because it is important to you, Jane. You are the prize I seek, only you." Nicholas's voice filled with determination. "I must know more about these rumors, but if you wish to discuss them later, so be it."

He straightened. "If you fear me leaving you again, those days are gone." He paused. "If it is the competition that matters, then prepare yourself, because I intend to use every tool in my arsenal to convince you of my devotion."

The intensity of his gaze shook her down to her toes.

Nicholas acted as though he wanted to put the past behind them. Could she do it? Was she ready to let go of her anger and her hurt and start fresh with this man who had occupied her dreams and her nightmares for the past two years?

Given the urgency of her situation and the fact she would marry in less than a week, did her damaged reputation truly matter? Or was it her pride he had damaged beyond repair?

"What would you do if I gave you a second chance?" she asked, challenging him.

"Give me that second chance and I will prove to you that I am the only one who could ever make you happy."

A shimmering coil of hope brought gooseflesh to her neck and arms. She did not want to believe him, but she did. "I am still angry with you." It was a half-hearted attempt to hurt him.

"I can accept that."

"You will get no special treatment."

The beginnings of a smile pulled up the corners of his mouth. "I would not expect any." He held out his hand.

She accepted it, and he laced his fingers with hers. Silently, they walked back into the keep.

Perhaps it was time not just to forgive Nicholas, but also to let go of those things that weighed her down. She was allowing her sadness to poison all her hours and days with worry and fear. Six gorgeous men awaited her in the keep, men who were eager to marry her, but also eager to find and stop whoever meant to harm her.

A chance like this would never come to her twice. It was time to embrace this competition and the men who had answered her call. Tomorrow, she would begin anew.

The next morning, with the help of her maid, Jane dressed quickly in a simple gray gown. She pulled her hair away from her face with a ribbon, allowing it to hang long and free down her back. Finished with her morning ablutions, she headed through the door of her chamber. At the top of the stairs that led to the great hall she paused. From the sound of male voices, she knew her suitors and their men had gathered for their morning meal.

Slowly, Jane descended into the great hall and looked about the room. Instead of the cold stone walls, she saw warmth in the pink-gray stone, heard the sound of the men's laughter, and smiled. Laughter was not something she had heard at Bellhaven in many years. She liked the sound. Perhaps this truly was a new beginning for her, for Bellhaven.

If it were not for the fact that someone was trying to harm both her and Margaret, or that when she had woken this morning her father's sword and standard were gone, this new life of hers might actually be perfect.

Jane took the final step that brought her into the chamber. As she did, the voices diminished and all eyes turned to watch as she made her way to the dais. She took her seat beside Lady Margaret.

"Did you sleep well, my dear?" Margaret asked.

"I did, but I have a question for you. Did you come into my chamber last night and collect my father's sword and standard?"

"Nay. Why?" Margaret asked, puzzled.

The warmth in the room paled. "They are gone."

"Gone?"

"They were on the chair where you left them when I went to sleep and when I awoke, they were not. I was so hopeful that you took them away. . . ." As Jane's words faded, so too did the voices in the hall, leaving only silence.

"Why would someone steal the tokens of your father?" Lord Galloway asked, abandoning his half-eaten slice of cheese.

"Perhaps one of the servants moved them," David offered.

Jane shook her head as her smile faded along with the color of the walls. Not pink, but only gray stone stared back at her. The realities of her situation were as stark as ever, despite her best efforts. She shook her head at David's assumption. "I asked my maid. She knew nothing of their removal from my chamber."

Nicholas's features darkened. "The danger to Lady Jane continues."

"We should rotate a guard outside Lady Jane's chamber from now on," Colin offered, as all the levity in his features shifted to worry.

"As well as one of us remaining with her at all times," Bryce suggested. At the statement, everyone turned to look at him with varying looks of disbelief. "What is it? You all look as though I have grown two heads. I have made no secret that I want to inherit the castle, but that does not mean I wish any harm to come to my cousin."

"Enough of this dire talk," Jules interrupted. "Jane was so happy a moment ago when she walked into this chamber. All our talk of danger and intrigue has robbed her of that." He winced as he pushed back from his seat at the table, then stood. "I cannot tolerate that sad expression on your face a moment longer."

"Do not concern yourself with me." She motioned for him to return to his seat.

He ignored her, instead coming around the table to stand beside her. "You have had enough sadness and hardship of late. I want to see you smile again."

Lord Galloway raised his goblet. "Hear, hear. We could all use a bit of levity."

"What do you suggest?" Lady Margaret asked, casting a hesitant smile at the nobleman beside her.

"There are only six more days 'til Christmastide, and yet you would hardly know it by the look and mood of Bellhaven. I say it is time to put Lady Jane into the Christmas spirit, right here. Right now."

A low rumble of voices filled the hall as not only her suitors, but their men, discussed the virtue of the idea.

Margaret stood and clapped her hands, bringing silence to the hall once more. "What a lovely idea. We will prepare for a banquet tonight with food and musicians and dancing."

"Who will join me for an expedition into the woods?" Jules asked the others.

"Jules, you are in no condition to travel on a horse or by foot," Jane argued.

"It is unwise for Jules or Jane to leave," David replied with a scowl. "Both of you will remain here with two of us and half our men, while the rest of us gather greens and bring them back to decorate the hall."

Lord Galloway nodded. "Splendid idea." He stood, and after bidding Margaret a good day, moved to stand beside Jules. "Count me in to gather greens."

"I will go as well," Colin said, "There has been too much heartbreak around here of late. It is time to change all that."

With mixed emotions, Jane watched Colin, Lord Galloway, and David gather several of their warriors before they left the hall. It had been two years since the Lennoxes had done anything more at Christmastide than burn a Yule log in the hearth and sip mulled wine with the castle residents. This year they needed the holiday to be so much more.

Jules was right. Christmastide was a time to be grateful for the blessings she had received. Decorating the hall was just a start to what Jane hoped would be a happier time for all of them. Bellhaven, and all the residents who lived there, deserved to hear laughter once more.

Later that evening Jane entered the great hall with a renewed sense of excitement. She had taken time before the meal to dress with care. She wore a pale pink gown with a tight satin bodice that had paned sleeves lined with a darker pink and a matching underdress. With her maid's help, she had styled her hair in a mass of tight curls. Her mother's pearl eardrops and necklace completed her attire.

At the base of the stairs, she surveyed the chamber that had been so sparse and unadorned this morning. Everywhere she looked, she could see evergreen boughs and holly. Decoration graced the long tables and the hearth—even the iron chandeliers were covered with greens. The scent of pine filled the great hall, transforming it into a magical woodland.

These days, many other noble families had given up the old ways, having large meals with the castle residents, preferring instead more intimate gatherings with their families. For Jane, her people were her family. She liked the family sense that dining together created.

Jane could not help but smile at the full chamber tonight. It had been months since they'd had so many residents under the roof of Bellhaven. Happier than she had been in a long time, she took her place at the head table. "Thank you, all. The decorations are superb. I could not have imagined what a splendor you would create."

"The night has just begun." Lord Galloway stood and made her an elegant bow before he approached. He had dressed in the style of his countrymen, in the colors of his clan, green and black and yellow and orange. His plaid emphasized his broad shoulders and muscular physique. Her heart sped up at the sight of all that lean power and strength. "Would you care to dance?"

"Supper has yet to be served," Jane replied with a lighthearted laugh.

His gaze shifted between her and where Margaret sat at the table on the dais. "I wish to be the first to dance with you," Lord Galloway said, but his gaze did not return to Jane. Instead, he focused hungrily on her aunt.

Jane raised a brow at Lord Galloway's unexpected interest. "There are no musicians," she offered.

"Who needs music?" Colin asked, stepping in between the two of them. He took Jane's hand, encouraging her from her chair. "Follow my lead."

Colin drew her to the only open space near the hearth. The tables would be drawn back after the meal to make room for dancing. Colin did not seem to mind the small space.

He drew her close and she could smell his warm, clean skin. They began the dance with a promenade, then faced each other and took three vigorous steps forward then clapped. Seven steps to the left, then turn around twice. The steps of the dance faded as Colin leaned in close, "I hope you do not mind the intrusion on Lord Galloway's time with you. The man left an opening, and I took it."

Jane smiled. "I suppose that is what you all must do. Look for opportunities to make your claim."

Colin gave her a devastating smile. "I am making a claim." Jane shivered with anticipation or fear. No one was ever as honest with her as Colin. With him, she knew exactly where she stood.

She forced her thoughts back to the dance as she went up on her toes, then turned and resumed a promenade. Dancing with only the beat of her heart to guide her was far more difficult than she expected. Or was it dancing with Colin that was the challenge?

Before she could consider the idea further, Bryce was before her. He slipped his hand in hers, leaving Colin standing alone. Bryce offered her a smile. "You look enchanting tonight. Aphrodite's equal wrapped in pink." No menace hung in his words.

Colin backed away from their dance with a frown as Bryce twirled her farther down the room.

"If you all must dance with me before the meal, I am afraid I will be too exhausted when the musicians truly begin."

"You have far more stamina than that, Jane," Bryce said, his smile increasing.

Relief filled her at the sight of his smile, the second one in as many moments. Perhaps he had figured out that his usual sourness would not advance his position with her in this competition. He pointed his toe and led her forward with faultless grace.

"Bryce," she asked, hesitating for a step. "Will you promise me something?"

He frowned. "That depends on what you ask."

"Promise you will never attack Jules the way you did today."

His hand flexed in hers. "He is not well. I wanted him to stop pretending that he is."

"As his bruises can attest, you made your point."

An amused gleam softened his features, and she caught a glimpse of that boyish charm she remembered. "I give you my word. I will not attack him again."

"Thank you, Bryce," she said with a touch of relief. Jules would hate that she had made Bryce make such a promise. But never again would she witness her friend being abused like that while she did nothing to stop it.

Bryce led them across the floor again. She followed his well-practiced lead and returned her thoughts to the evening ahead. Tonight she wanted to be happy and pretend she had nothing to worry about other than dancing and laughing. The realities of her daily life would return soon enough. In the meanwhile she had handsome men to promenade with about her hall.

When the servants came into the hall with a roast boar garnished with apples and holly, a dozen pheasant decorated with their own feathers, and a tower of pastries piled into a likeness of Bellhaven Castle, her guests met the display with applause and cheers. While the kitchen staff took the meat to the carving table to strip the dishes of their culinary magnificence and carve them to be served, Bryce led her back to her seat at the long table on the dais.

"It pains me to seat you here," he said as he glanced at his rivals, "but I will not protest, as I am sure you all expect," Bryce said, releasing her hand and taking a seat at the far end of the table.

Slightly bewildered by Bryce's sudden change in behavior, Jane took her place. Nicholas sat on one side of her. David on the other. Jane's heart hammered as she greeted them both. She had a true affection for both of these men. Jane groaned inside. Who was she kidding? Affection was putting it mildly. David had been sweet and gentle with her last night. His touch had made her heart race and her body quiver, while one look from Nicholas made her melt.

She cast a glance about her table. Colin and Jules greeted her with a nod. Bryce met her glance with a bland smile for a heartbeat before he looked away. A part of her sighed. His transformation was not as thorough as she had hoped. Aunt Margaret and Lord Galloway were engaged in an animated conversation. Her aunt's cheeks glowed.

Jane smiled. Even her aunt was not immune to her suitor's charm. She drew a steadying breath. *Put it out of your mind. For tonight just enjoy and be grateful.*

The tension of the moment was broken when Egan approached each guest with a basin of rosewater. A second servant followed with a fresh white linen towel.

Jules stood somewhat awkwardly from his place at the table, no doubt from the pain of his wound. He raised his cup. "*Slàinte mhath*," he said, toasting the others. The Gaelic words for good health were greeted with the customary response of "*slàinte mhor.*" Great health.

Nicholas and David said nothing as they narrowed their gazes, sizing each other up. The tension between them thickened to the point of being unbearable until Marthe, the cook who worked as a footman tonight because of the banquet, set plates of meat, vegetables, fruit, and bread before Jane and her guests.

"You look like a vision of your mother tonight," David said, smiling softly.

Jane returned his compliment with a smile. "I cannot always recall what she looked like," she said honestly. That fact used to bother her. How could she forget her own mother? But over the years Jane had accepted the reality. She remembered all the important things about her mother, if not her face.

David brought his hand to rest gently on Jane's arm. "You are her twin with your hair curled that way."

"Thank you, David, for saying so."

He leaned closer. "After supper may I walk with you in the moonlight?"

Nicholas frowned. "May I dance with you when the musicians start up?"

David and Nicholas locked gazes, their faces devoid of all humor. Jane felt her cheeks flame as she answered neither. Her own gaze moved down the table to where Margaret sat. Her aunt offered Jane a knowing smile. Margaret had assigned the seats for tonight, no doubt in an attempt to pit David and Nicholas against one another.

A long moment later, both men shifted their attention from her to their meal. With the intensity of their gazes off her, Jane finally felt her blush begin to fade until David spoke once more.

"You must visit Hathaway Hall sometime soon," he said, chewing contentedly on a braised turnip.

"If touring our estates is part of your 'selection plan,' then Westfield Abbey is at your disposal." Nicholas frowned and swallowed.

David dragged a hand through his hair. "I never meant to suggest that my estate might aid in your decision of me as your husband."

"Did you not?" Nicholas reached for his wine and gulped it down.

Jane ignored them both and sliced her meat into tiny pieces, tasting none. She stared down at her plate to see a disorderly pile of shredded meat as her earlier happiness faded. Despite the fact they were not engaged in a competition at present, the men were still competing.

When David finished his meal, he excused himself from the table, saying he wished to join his men and prepare for another round of training in the morning.

"Are you not hungry?" Nicholas asked Jane when they were alone.

She sat back in her chair. "I find I have no appetite this evening."

"Perhaps you do not know yet what you hunger for?" He smiled at her.

The innuendo in his words brought warmth back to her cheeks.

He reached for a spiced, dried fig and pressed it to her lips. "You must keep up your strength for dancing and other pleasures, Jane."

Cinnamon-flavored sweetness flooded her mouth and the heat between them thickened in intensity. She looked away from his compelling gaze as the word "pleasures" resonated in her thoughts. He had no idea the pleasure he brought her with a simple touch or a glance.

She shifted in her chair, suddenly uneasy with the intimacy of their seating. She looked down at the table and realized her mistake. His large and capable hands held another fig, and memories suddenly assaulted her of those broad, powerful fingers splaying against her back, holding her close earlier today.

"Your cheeks are flushed," Nicholas said softly. "Are you too warm?"

Not warm. Melting. At his closeness, she felt as though her blood was running molten just beneath the surface of her flesh. She quickly picked up her goblet and drank deeply.

"Another fig?" he asked.

She set her goblet down. "No, thank you." Her goblet was immediately refilled. "Is it not time for the dancing to start?"

His hand released the fig onto his plate and dropped casually to her knee. "There is plenty here to amuse us," he said, reaching beneath the table and sliding his hand up her leg.

She went rigid, her gaze flying to his face. He was looking straight ahead, but a whisper of a grin tugged at his lips. He knew what he was doing to her. "Nicholas."

He turned to her. A flush mantled his cheeks. "You still respond to my touch," he whispered.

The warmth of his palm burned through the layers of her dress and undergarments, and her limbs began to tremble. Her hand was unsteady as she reached for her goblet again.

His hand moved higher, tightened with warmth, hunger, demand.

A demand she must not answer. She made the mistake of closing her eyes and sensation flooded her. She snapped her eyes open and staggered to her feet. "It is time to dance."

Her announcement was met with cheers and laughter from the men at her table as well as their armsmen.

"Who will we all dance with? There are only two ladies here," Colin asked.

Jane's gaze connected with Marthe's as she cleared the head table. Marthe nodded to her unspoken question. In response, she signaled her staff to set down their loads. Clearing the meal could wait. "There are twenty maids available as partners. Since there are no other options, perhaps this once we could break societal rules and allow the armsmen to dance with the servants."

Jane motioned to the musicians who had set up in the gallery. Immediately, the lilting strains of music filled the hall. The tables were moved back and all the females came forward, accepting her guests as partners.

Lord Galloway made a bow to her aunt Margaret, then pulled the woman to her feet and into the dance. On a trill of laughter, Margaret swirled away, her color high, her eyes sparkling.

Jane could not help but smile. Her aunt looked happy, truly happy in Lord Galloway's arms, as the hall resounded with the merry sounds of music and laughter.

"Shall we join them?" Nicholas slipped his hand in hers and guided her to the dancers. Caught up in the music, Jane soon found herself laughing out loud, pulled into the excitement. All the dancers joined hands and circled faster and faster about the hall before they broke and whirled away. Laughter bubbled up in her throat and she felt almost too breathless to release it. They changed partners and Jane stepped back, needing a moment of rest. The dancers beside her were only streaks of crimson, blue, green, and gold.

"Jane," a voice called, breaking into her reverie. She stilled. A hand reached out and pulled her from the whirling throng and behind a pillar.

She gazed up to see Nicholas's face before her. His raw penetrating gaze sent her blood pounding through her veins. The fabric of her gown that had once been so soft suddenly became heavy and abrasive against her skin.

"We must join the others." The candles in the hall blurred into blue-orange flames and the beat of the music echoed deep in her body.

"No one will even notice we are gone."

Before she knew what he was doing, he cupped her head with one hand, brushed her bottom lip with his thumb, and bent his head to capture her lips.

Jane could not move, could not think as his warm lips parted hers. The scent of cinnamon and bay leaves invaded her senses. Never in her life had she felt anything like his mouth on hers. This kiss pulled her back into all she remembered, yet it was different as well. This kiss was fierce and hot and startling.

Every nerve in her body fired. She moaned low in her throat, though the sound was claimed by the music that pulsed around them. She had forgotten how devastating his kisses were. The warmth and strength of him pressed against her, numbed her to all else. She clutched at his shoulders, wanting desperately to taste more.

He pinned her to the pillar. His chest pressed against hers, making her even more aware of his lean, hard muscles. She wrapped her arms around his neck, pulling him closer as her head swam. Her knees weakened and she sank deeper into him.

"By the heavens," he breathed, his voice a caress.

The music ended. Jane pulled back, suddenly aware of her surroundings.

"Not yet," he growled, holding her close.

A minute ticked by. She dropped her hands from his neck and took a step sideways. Her cheeks burned. What had she done? One look from him and she became everything his rumors had claimed her to be—*a passionate seductress.*

"Jane, do not retreat from me. Not again."

She took another step away from him, bringing her fingers to her still-throbbing lips. She gave him a wistful look. "I should never have allowed that to happen."

"Do not fight what is between us."

She tensed, fighting the warmth that flared at his words. "There can be nothing between us, Nicholas, but this competition. A competition between you and five other men."

"There does not have to be." He took a step toward her.

"Nicholas, please?" She held up her hand, praying he would stop. If he touched her again she would shatter. The pain of longing mixed with the reality of the past. "I have forgiven you, but the wounds are still too raw."

Nicholas dragged in a breath. He ran his hands through his hair. His chest tightened as he looked into her face and saw the truth of her words, all those she held back, and those she had held in for so long. He saw for the first time what he had sensed since his return to her life. She had built a wall between them.

He did not know how to breech it.

He only knew he had to.

She lowered her gaze and drew in a breath. She took another step back, drawing away literally and emotionally, reinforcing that wall. "Please let me go."

He held her gaze, forced himself to. "I understand your fear."

"How could you when I do not even understand it myself?" Her face paled. "With you I am in danger." She shivered. "A danger I do not even understand."

But he did understand. She was afraid to go back there with him again, back to the void where only sensation and passion existed, where they both lost themselves in an attempt to be whole. "I can say a million times that I will never leave you, or do anything to harm you, but my actions will eventually speak louder than words."

She drew a careful breath, turned away, but did not leave.

He took the few steps that separated them, halted behind her.

She said nothing, but also did not move away.

Gently, he reached out and wrapped his arms around her, pulling her against his chest. He pressed his head against her hair and waited until she relaxed. "I am here when you are ready."

She leaned back against him. He tightened his hold and swore on his heart that never again would he let her go, no matter what stood in their way. He pressed a kiss to her head. He knew enough about her not to coax her into more. She had to come back to him willingly and in her own time.

He could wait, at least until Christmas Eve. He had to make her remember all they had shared. He had until Christmas Eve to make things right, to give her some reason to believe in him again.

The next morning Jane rose early, before the first light of dawn appeared. She had not slept well, and her mind was even more restless than her body, still filled with foreboding about the competition today. Nicholas's kisses still lingered on her lips.

She found herself pacing her chamber, trying to remember all the reasons she should never allow herself to fall for the charming laird again. When she was with him, it was as if those years did not matter. Every moment and every touch took them back to the place they had been before. No, that was not true—their encounters were even more intense than they had been before.

Too restless to stay in her chamber, Jane grabbed a cloak and headed down the long hall toward the stair that led to the wall walk. Outside, fingers of pink-orange light forced back the night. Dawn would soon be upon them.

Jane drew a deep breath of the chill morning air as she strolled the long walkway, heading toward her favorite spot near the field where the men practiced. By the time she reached her usual nook in the crenellated stone, she realized two things.

Nicholas could take her back to the moment before he had left if she would only let him. But did she want him to?

Secondly, she was not the only one up at this hour. Peering over the edge of the castle wall, she studied the dark figure alone in the lists. The glow of a torch illuminated a small area where the man stood as still as a statue. His head was bowed, but she knew without seeing his face that it was Jules. He held a sword in his right hand.

He was dressed only in a lightweight shirt, breeches, and boots despite the chill of the morning air. The warmth of his breath coiled with the silence of the morn. Slowly he straightened, then bowed as though to an imaginary adversary. His movements were slow and methodical at first. He kept his body loose, relaxed. His stance was balanced, his back straight, his chest and torso forward. He slid his feet across the ground, reducing the chance of losing his balance. To win a fight meant staying in control. And it looked as if Jules was in control of both his mind and body this morning.

Jules maintained his weapon from the middle of his body to the top of his head as he met and blocked blows from his imaginary opponent, before proceeding with several strikes of his own. With his elbows bent and his sword close to his body he moved up and down the open space. His agile body was poised and confident as he flowed through the steps of the battle again and again until sweat soaked his linen shirt and curled the ends of his blond hair. His steps were light, his stroke sure, honing muscle he had lost during his incarceration. Only a slight hitch in his step gave away the fact that he was still recovering from his wound.

Jane watched in fascinated wonder as Jules's steps grew stronger, more certain. She knew without a doubt, it was Bryce's abuse that had prompted this early-morning practice. Jules would never show his physical weakness again.

She watched him in silence until dawn gave way to early morning. When he had finally tortured himself enough, he headed inside, leaving her alone with her thoughts. She leaned her head against the cold stone of Bellhaven and closed her eyes.

Jules deserved a chance to win a better life for himself than the one he had been given. Was that life with her or someone else? Around Jules she did not feel her body raging with fever or her mind swirling with dizziness as she did when Nicholas drew near. But perhaps that was better. Remaining in control of herself and her thoughts might be exactly what she needed in a husband, not the fiery longing Nicholas unleashed.

Jane drew a slow shaky breath. A quiet moment ticked past. Trusting Nicholas with her heart could be self-destructive, hurtful, even devastating. He had not loved her, not in the way she had loved him. It would be foolish beyond measure to walk that path again, would it not?

She opened her eyes and stared out across the bailey just now coming to life as servants began their daily routine. Could she deny the passion she and Nicholas shared and instead take up with someone and something else far more bland but safe? No closer to an answer, Jane turned around just as the door to the keep opened.

"There you are, dearest," Aunt Margaret said. "When I could not find you in your room, I suspected I would find you here." She took Jane's cool hands in her own. "How long have you been out here?"

Jane shrugged. It seemed only minutes had passed, but it was probably much longer than that.

"What is troubling you?" Margaret asked with a frown.

"Why do you ask that?"

Margaret gave her a level look. "You always come up here when something is wrong."

Jane smiled. Her aunt knew her well. "I could not sleep."

"Too excited about the next competition?" Margaret asked with a twinkle in her eyes. "And which of those gorgeous men you will spend time alone with next?"

"Not exactly," Jane replied hesitantly.

Margaret's smile faltered. "Jane, you are thinking about this far too much. You are supposed to let whatever happens happen."

"I tried being more whimsical about it all, truly, but that is not who I am."

"I realize that, dearest." Margaret released Jane's hands and her smile returned. "You must be yourself, just as your suitors must show their true colors as well. That is what your time alone is supposed to provide—insight into their hearts."

Jane sighed. "It is far more complicated than you make it sound."

"Matters of the heart have been complicated since Adam first met Eve in the Garden of Eden." Margaret reached up and cupped Jane's cheek. "Your heart is no exception. Steel is forged with fire. Jewels are created under pressure. And love only comes to those who risk it all."

"Love batters you and rakes you raw."

Margaret's lips quirked at the next competition the men were to face. "Something other than your suitors' hearts will be raw after the next competition. I am glad you liked my idea of having them sew for you. It is this sort of challenge that will lay them bare to you. Just wait. You will see."

Jane's lips pulled up at the corners despite her attempt to remain serious. "Their bloody fingers?"

That infuriating twinkle was back in Margaret's eyes. "Oh, there will be blood, and a whole lot more. Come." She reached for Jane's hand. "We do not want to miss a moment of this."

Lady Margaret was right. Later that morning, Jane had never seen David, or Nicholas, or even Jules look so out of place in a solar. Colin and Lord Galloway and Bryce all wore frowns upon their faces. None of them were happy to be here. The thought made Jane smile.

Each man folded his big body into one of the chairs set in a semicircle around the chamber. The announcement that they were to have a sewing competition was met with a mixture of trepidation and horror. Bryce growled an obscenity. Jules's brow furrowed. Colin simply stared at her, his shock obvious. David's expression darkened. Nicholas released a heavy sigh. Lord Galloway smiled.

Angus and Ollie set two baskets in the middle of the men. One basket was filled with cloth, shears, and needles, the other with a multitude of colored spindles of thread.

"This competition is a test of your skills in a more intimate way," Lady Margaret announced.

"I would rather we had a sword fight," Colin groaned as he picked up a needle and tested the point against his thumb. He drew his finger back as the needle pricked his skin, then frowned fiercely at the blood that welled upon his skin.

"Your challenge is to create something with a Yuletide theme for Lady Jane from the items here. You will be given until the chapel bell tolls twelve."

David lifted a length of cloth with the edge of his fingers as though it might bite him if he grasped it fully. "We can make anything?"

"Your goal here is to please Lady Jane," her aunt reiterated. "Think about her as you make your plan."

Jane saw a flash of temper in Bryce's gaze. His mouth pressed into a thin line as he battled against himself. He paused, took a breath, then turned to Margaret. "Who will be the judge?"

"Lady Jane, of course." Margaret glanced about the room. "Are you prepared?"

Jules frowned. "As ready as we will ever be."

Nicholas nodded and reached for a square of green brocade. She could see the tension thrumming through him as he turned over ideas in his mind.

Not one of her suitors looked pleased with this latest challenge. Jane's lips quirked. With her suitors off balance for a time, she might be able to regain a little of her own.

"Good luck," Lady Margaret said, taking Jane's hand and leading her toward the door. "We will return in two hours."

Two hours.

Nicholas stared at the green cloth in his hands. He had to create something grand for Jane this morning if he were to win more time alone with her. What in the heavens could he create in two hours that would win him Jane?

He groaned as he selected a needle and a spindle of gold thread, then looked about the solar. The goal for this challenge was not to be the best, but simply not to be as terrible as everyone else.

"The only stitches I have ever laid were in a comrade's shoulder," Colin said as he selected a length of gold cloth.

"You are not alone there." Jules plucked one piece of fabric after another from the basket, searching for inspiration among the remnants.

Only Lord Galloway looked pleased with the situation into which they had been thrust. He had grabbed a length of brown fabric and had already completed sewing the ends together into a casing of sorts. He then stuffed other pieces of fabric inside, before closing the ends. He tied a knot in the string and snipped the excess with his shears, looking very at ease with the process.

"Are you making a small pillow?" David asked, as he also noticed Lord Galloway's comfort with a needle.

"No," the confident laird answered as he set several pins across the length of the pillow. He took a handful of empty spindles and wound gold string around each one.

A chill of foreboding shot down Nicholas's spine as he watched Lord Galloway continue his work in silence. The man appeared to know what he was doing.

Nicholas noted he was not the only one staring at Lord Galloway.

"We are all in trouble if he actually creates something with all that string." Bryce frowned down at the mass of fabric in his hands. The white fabric had been stitched into what might have resembled a body if the observer had indulged in his cups.

Nicholas narrowed his gaze and truly tried to see what it was Bryce was creating. The body appeared to have the pox, if the telltale dots of blood were to be regarded as part of his design. "What is it?" he finally asked.

Bryce pressed his lips together, studying his own creation. "Jane was so pleased with the doll Jules gave her during our first competition, that I thought perhaps she would like another."

"What does that have to do with the Yule season?" Jules laughed.

Bryce became rigid as he cast Jules a frosty glare. "It is an angel. She named her puppy by that name. It must mean she likes angels, even just a little."

Jules laughed, delighting in Bryce's discomfort. "You might want to add some wings."

"The thought had occurred to me," he replied in a curt tone.

David ignored the lot of them as he sewed quietly in the corner. His fingers worked not with thread, but with folding the length of yellow cloth in his lap.

"This is not meant as a complaint," Bryce said. "I really do hate this challenge."

Colin frowned. "Where did you learn how to do that, Lord Galloway?"

Lord Galloway looked up from his many spindles. "I had five sisters. There was no one to fight with, so if I wanted company, I had to learn my way around the solar."

"I feel very emasculated," Jules complained.

"I feel out of my league," Colin countered.

Nicholas glanced about the chamber as the men complained about their attempts to sew. He doubted women ever complained about sewing. More like they complained about the men in their lives while they sewed. The thought made him smile.

David growled and threw his folded cloth on the floor. "What is Jane trying to do to us with this test?"

"This was not her idea," Lord Galloway offered.

David stood and strode about the chamber like a wild, caged beast. "Then whose idea was it?"

"I might have mentioned it to Lady Margaret," he said with a smile.

David's fists tightened, and he shot across the chamber until his hands were about Lord Galloway's throat. "You pompous ass."

Nicholas threw down his fabric and pulled David away. "Leave him be, David. We all have our strengths. Yours was definitely hunting."

Lord Galloway massaged his abused throat. Several acknowledgments were echoed around the room.

When the fight left David, Nicholas released him. "Time is slipping by with such nonsense. It would be better spent finishing your creation than killing off the competition."

David returned to his seat and started folding his cloth once more, grumbling beneath his breath the whole time.

He needed to take his own advice, Nicholas realized with a glance about the solar. The other men were much further along with their creations. His gaze settled on Lord Galloway, who worked on silently. He had tied the thread of several lengths of string to the pins and expertly moved the spindles back and forth, creating a lacy pattern with the string. Nicholas released a silent groan. How could any of them compete with a man who knew how to make lace?

Jane waited until the toll of the bell died before she reached for the door latch. Two hours had passed. The competition was at an end. A part of her was curious to see what they had created. Another part of her was less eager to have to choose a winner.

"Are you ready to see how they fared?" Margaret asked from beside her.

"They are awfully quiet." Silence was all that greeted them from the opposite side of the door. "Perhaps they have killed each other with the pins?"

"Do not be dramatic, dearest. They are most likely as nervous as you are."

She was nervous, but determined to get the selection of her next champion over with. Steeling herself, she opened the door and went in.

The first surprise was that they were all alive and watching her every move as she stepped into the chamber. The second surprise was that the room was clean. The fabric had been neatly gathered and placed back into the basket. The shears, needles, and thread were collected and returned to their proper places.

The third surprise was that each of the men waited not in his chair, but on their feet, their movements arrested as though only a heartbeat before they had been pacing like caged animals about the chamber.

"Goodness," Lady Margaret exclaimed, giving voice to the thoughts running through Jane's head. "You all completed your task. That is excellent. Simply marvelous." Her aunt moved to stand near Lord Galloway. She offered him a coy smile and color flooded her cheeks.

Jane watched the exchange between her aunt and Lord Galloway with interest. Her aunt never blushed. And the look she gave him before leaning against the wall at his back was almost as though she were under some kind of spell.

The tension in the chamber was thick as Jane moved into the room slowly, allowing herself time to digest her aunt's fascination with Lord Galloway. David stood off to her left. One glance at his dark expression revealed his trapped desperation. His eyes sparked with undisguised temper.

A quick glance at the others revealed the same caged energy. None of them were happy about the competition Lady Margaret had foisted on them.

Returning her gaze to David she asked, "What have you created for me, Sir David?"

David slowly unfolded his hands to reveal a bright yellow folded star.

She offered him a smile of appreciation. "How very clever of you to fold the cloth into angles, then secure it with thread."

"It was all I could think of," he admitted, his gaze dropping to the star. "Leave me in the wilderness for days on end with no food or water and I can survive. But sewing, it is the worst sort of torture and not something I ever wish to do again." Tension coiled in his wiry frame.

"Tell me why you chose a star."

"It is supposed to be the Christmas star, the one the wise men followed to lead them to the Christ child."

"Very well done, David."

At her words he met her gaze once more. Some of the tension in him vanished. "Good enough to declare me the winner?"

"We will see," she said, moving to her next suitor. Nicholas leaned casually against the wall by the hearth. He met her gaze boldly, confident as he held out his offering of a light green handkerchief with what appeared to be a stitched holly leaf and berries in the center if she squinted her eyes enough to make the mass of green and red into a form. He had tried his hand at needlepoint. That fact itself warmed her heart. He knew from their earlier days together how much she detested needlepoint. Although she could say without a doubt that her skills, even as poor as they were, outstripped Nicholas's talent with a needle.

That he had tried to make a connection with her over thread and needle warmed her to her toes. She turned the handkerchief over and inspected the sewn edges. The linen was folded neatly, but the hemming stiches were uneven, and after every three or four stitches, the thread bunched into a knot. Again, she hid a smile. She could see he had tried his best. "What a useful as well as pretty creation, Nicholas." She set his creation on a small table nearby. "Every time I am taken by the chills or fever, I will think of you."

He frowned. "That is not a good thing, is it?"

"'Tis part of life, and you did well," Jane said.

Nicholas leaned back, his frown increasing as she moved on to Bryce.

Her cousin proudly displayed a mass of white fabric that might have been in the shape of a body, though it was oddly deformed and dotted with red spots.

"It is an angel," he said when she remained silent, studying the object.

"Of course it is," she breathed, pleased that he had informed her of such. She never would have guessed correctly otherwise. She took the angel from his fingers and held her up to the light. Large, bold stitches ran up and down the fabric, forming her body and what must have been her wings. Bryce did not have a dainty hand, but regardless the blood-spattered object she held showed he had indeed tried and sacrificed much of himself in the process. She dropped her gaze to his abused hands. "How are your fingers? Should I have one of the maids bring you a tisane to soak them?"

He moved his hands behind his back. "They are the wounds of my efforts, and just like battle wounds, they will heal eventually."

Jane blinked, then searched his face, his eyes, seeking that unruly temper that usually simmered beneath the surface. What had happened to change

Bryce so completely since his abuse of Jules in the lists? Was his newfound patience and humility an act, or had he truly changed?

She liked this new side of Bryce. She narrowed her gaze. A part of her was still suspicious, expecting the temperamental boy she had known to appear at some unsuspecting moment. "Why an angel, Bryce?"

He straightened. "It is supposed to be a likeness of you," he said in a low-toned voice.

After a pregnant pause during which she assessed and considered his true motive, she replied, "I am honored by your gift." But was his effort enough to make her declare him the winner and give him the time he so obviously wanted to perhaps explain his change of heart?

Jane stepped toward Jules, hoping as she did that one of the creations would be far superior to all else so that her decision would be an easy one. Before her skirts had settled, Jules offered her his creation.

"If you thought Nicholas's gift was useful, then mine is also that and necessary." He handed her a pair of soft leather gloves.

Though the cut of the thin leather was uneven, she exclaimed, "Well done, Jules." From her own experience she knew how difficult leather was to sew. She slid a hand into first one glove then the other and flexed her hands. The seams were loose enough to allow air to brush across her hands, which might be an admirable quality in the summer, but certainly not in the snow.

Jane flexed her fingers, admiring his work. As she did, several of the stiches came loose and two fingers popped out.

"I can fix that," Jules assured her.

She studied her leather-covered palms, avoiding his eyes. She knew what she would see there—eagerness and a plea for her to choose him as the winner. She had seen it in all their eyes so far. "These gloves are very thoughtful, Jules. With a little repair, I imagine they will be quite delightful during this winter season."

She met his gaze.

He beamed with pride.

Her chest tightened. It had been such a long time since she had seen any sort of pleasure on Jules's gaunt face. A part of her wanted to see that pleasure continue, and it would if she declared him her champion. Putting the thought out of her mind, she drew in a tight breath, removed the gloves, and set them near the other gifts before moving on to Colin.

"Milady," he greeted her with a bow of his head.

She allowed her gaze to travel to his hands. In them, he held a mass of pink—it was the very same fabric from the gown she had worn yesterday eve at the banquet.

"I know the challenge was to make something that might represent Christmastide, but I could not come up with an idea." Colin held up his offering. "This is what came to mind. Because there were no flowers in the garden when we went there, I decided to create one for you today."

It was a flower. Jane accepted the unruly tangle of fabric and thread. After a long moment of study, she said, "You have captured the chaos of a rosebud before it is about to bloom into a beautiful flower."

His brows drew together for a heartbeat before he smiled. "Ah, yes, that was my intent."

She brought the bud to her nose and closed her eyes. "I can imagine the first scent of spring upon the petals."

She opened her eyes at the touch of his fingers upon hers. "You are nothing if not kind, Lady Jane," he said, offering her that gorgeous smile of his.

She placed Colin's creation on the table with the others and moved to her final suitor.

Lord Galloway's pose was casual as he leaned one shoulder against the wall, his gaze fixed on both the woman beside him and the woman who approached at the same time. Something was different about Lord Galloway this morning. He still offered Jane his usual seductive grin and he had arranged his body so that it was difficult to ignore all his male perfection—perfection that no one with functioning eyes would rate as less than phenomenal. His manliness was guaranteed to distract any living, breathing woman.

Jane shifted her gaze to her aunt. And distract her aunt he did. He took Jane's hand and pressed a light kiss to the back. Margaret's gaze fixed on each movement, followed his every breath. Jane blinked. Never had she seen her aunt so enthralled.

Lady Margaret was smitten with the man.

Jane pulled her hand away and stepped back, suddenly uneasy with the thought of this man vying for both her and her aunt's attention. Her nerves tightened. "Lord Galloway, what do you have to show for your efforts with needle and thread?" Jane asked, praying the article would be something much worse than Colin's attempt at a flower.

"For you," he said as he slowly unfurled the golden mass in his hand. The fabric rippled with the movement, then settled to reveal a triangle of gold fabric trimmed in a narrow band of delicate lace.

Groans of disgust sounded behind her as she stared in awe at his creation. "You made this? In two hours?"

He picked up the edges and settled the garment about her shoulders.

The light, airy shawl molded to her. Jane brought her fingers up to feel the smooth edges of the lace. "How in heaven's name did you create lace?"

He gave her a devilish smile. "I was raised in a house of women. I know a great many things that are more of the feminine persuasion."

Jane fixed her gaze on her aunt's face. Margaret greeted her with a sad half smile. "The winner of this competition could not be more obvious."

The weight of the shawl suddenly became oppressive. Jane slipped it from her shoulders. How could she possibly declare any of the other men the winner after such a display of craft? She found it difficult to comprehend what had transpired with her aunt in the matter of a few days with regard to Lord Galloway. Did the man notice the way her aunt looked at him? Could he get out of the way of his own magnificence to even see her at all?

"Lord Galloway, I agree with my aunt. You are the obvious winner here." He beamed.

Lady Margaret turned away.

Jane's heart fell, but some small part of her mind persisted in churning through ideas. There had to be a way . . .

"I have already determined how we will spend our time alone," he said in a low, raspy tone. He placed the shawl he had created over her arm. "You can wear this tonight for our intimate supper . . . alone," he said, looking over her shoulder with a satisfied grin. The look was no doubt aimed at his competition. "We will not be leaving the castle, so there is no need for chaperones. Give me a few hours to arrange things, then I will send someone for you."

She nodded absently as Lord Galloway took both her hands and kissed them. "Until later, my dear."

Dinner alone.

At his words, an idea formed that had nothing to do with the two of them being alone. Deep in thought, she leaned against the wall and sighed.

"He has that effect on me as well," Margaret said, turning back to watch Lord Galloway leave the chamber.

Jane pushed away from the wall. Eagerness filled her. The man might have a dinner to prepare for, but she had a few plans of her own.

"Margaret," she said, grasping her aunt by the hand and hauling her past the men who remained in the chamber. "Come with me. There are things to be done."

"I am pleased that you are finally getting into the spirit of this competition, but my dear, I have no heart to help you prepare for this occasion."

Jane smiled and cast a look back at her aunt's puzzled expression. "You will. Trust me. By the end of the night, I hope your heart, along with other parts of you, are truly engaged."

13

Jane's heart began to pound in expectation as she followed Egan up the staircase to the west tower. He hesitated at the doorway before opening it to the outside.

"His lordship asked that you put this on before joining him," Egan said, handing her an oiled fur cloak.

"Do you remember your instructions?" Jane asked.

The young servant nodded. "As soon as I deliver you, I am to go find Lady Margaret and tell her you are unwell and that you need her assistance," he repeated for the third time in the past hour.

She smiled at his indulgence. "Thank you, Egan."

A stain of pink came to his cheeks as he threw the door open and announced her presence.

She steeled herself for the night she had planned. Her aunt had no notion of what she intended. Margaret had simply moved through the steps of Jane's preparations for her time alone with Lord Galloway with a sad look in her soft blue eyes. When Jane had set her aunt in the chair before the dressing table, she had asked what Jane's intentions for such a thing were. Jane merely stated she was trying a new style on her aunt in preparation for the wedding.

Margaret had gone along with the scenario when Jane had demanded she try on her best gown, and then proceeded to lace the dress a bit tighter than was her norm, molding the gown to her aunt's trim form. Then she had had to endure one last heartbreaking glance from her aunt when Egan had come to collect her. Margaret had wished Jane well and turned quickly around, no doubt in an effort to hide her pain.

The memory faded as the chill evening air registered against Jane's cheeks. She looked about the tower as a funny little ache centered in her chest. Lord Galloway had converted the tower from its militaristic purpose to a romantic alcove.

He had gone to a lot of trouble on her behalf. On her left, illuminated by ten torches all around the circular tower, were a small table and two chairs. He had covered the table in a cream linen cloth, then set two places with pewter plates. In the center of the table a candle was lit and a bottle of wine stood ready to pour. Beside the wine rested a tureen of what smelled like roasted meat stew.

Lord Galloway stood on her right, unaware of her presence. His dark head was slightly bent as he gazed at a cheery little fire he had set atop a stone slab. He stood with one booted foot propped up on the slab. One hand rested on his knee, the other at his side. He wore no cloak, only a soft black jacket, a soft linen shirt, and dark breeches. Despite what she had planned, Jane could not help but notice the sheer male beauty of his wide, masculine shoulders, his broad back and narrow hips.

There was something in the sober way he was staring into the fire that touched her heart. Then, as if sensing her presence, he suddenly straightened and turned to her. A smile came to his lips that did not quite reach his eyes. Could it be that his thoughts were on someone other than her?

"Come over by the fire," he said, holding out his hand.

Jane accepted it and allowed him to pull her toward the flames. A cocoon of warmth encompassed them. Despite the heat, she shivered. It was time to put on the performance of her life.

Jane swayed on her feet and groaned.

Lord Galloway's grip on her hand tightened. His brows came together. "Are you well?"

"I am dizzy."

He led her away from the fire to the chairs and set her into one. "How long has it been since you have eaten? Perhaps you need food?"

Jane wrapped her arms about her middle, doubled over, and moaned. "Merciful heavens, I think I am going to be sick."

The door to the tower opened and Margaret raced toward her. "What has happened now?" her aunt asked, her ashen face wreathed with concern. She kneeled at Jane's side.

At the pained expression on her aunt's face, Jane truly felt gore rising in her throat. When she had devised the plan to get her aunt to trade places with her for the night, she had not considered Margaret's worry.

"It is merely a momentary thing," she assured her aunt, trying to straighten, then doubled over again. "I suddenly feel a little ill. I can attempt to go through with tonight's events. Surely the nausea will pass."

Jane stood. "Perhaps I need a little air." She staggered over to the crenellated wall and forced herself to draw an overly dramatic breath.

Lady Margaret stood, then stiffened as though suddenly realizing Lord Galloway's presence. "Lord Galloway," she breathed, her gaze pinned to his.

From her vantage point, Jane watched as Lord Galloway stood perfectly still. His gaze lit on Margaret's face a moment before shifting to her aunt's long curls, which Jane had artfully coiled with a strand of pearls. He skimmed over the long line of Margaret's neck, across the square neckline that exposed the tops of her full breasts. He swallowed thickly as he continued down her thin waist, over the curves of her hips and down to her feet, then back up again.

His look was personal, and possessive.

Jane hid a smile as she doubled over again, issuing another heartfelt groan. The sooner she was out of the way, the sooner her aunt and Lord Galloway could continue with the evening.

Margaret twisted toward Jane. "My dear, let me take you inside."

"No, I cannot leave Lord Galloway alone after all the trouble he went to on my behalf."

"You cannot stay. Not in your condition," Margaret said. "You need a warm fire and a cold compress to the forehead."

Jane shifted her gaze to Egan, who waited at the door. "I could see to those things, milady." He came forward and took Jane's arm as she had instructed him, helping her forward.

"But what about Lord Galloway?" Jane screwed her face into a look of heartbreak solely for her aunt's benefit.

"I suppose I could stay with him, if he would welcome my company in place of yours?" Her gaze filled with a mixture of disbelief and hope.

The somber expression that had been in Lord Galloway's eyes since Jane first arrived suddenly vanished. A look of utter contentment came over him as he took Lady Margaret's hands in his own and led her to the table. "I would be honored to have you as my guest."

Jane leaned on Egan to complete the deception as they headed out the doorway and down the stairs. Out of sight, she straightened, thanked Egan once again for his role, and headed for her bedchamber feeling better than she had in a very long time.

Margaret's breath stuttered in her chest when she realized the sensual look in Lord Galloway's dark brown eyes was all for her. "I am scared to death to be here with you."

"Most women are terrified to be alone with me," he teased with a lazy, devastating smile. He watched her as if he never wanted to stop.

"Not because of your reputation," Margaret said.

"So you know of my many exploits."

She felt a small thrill of satisfaction. "Of course I do. I know everything about you. I had to before I allowed you access to my niece."

She watched in wary alarm as he leaned toward her, his face closer to hers than it had ever been. She hurriedly took a sip of her wine, then another, trying to settle her nerves. When she ran out of excuses not to look at him, she returned her gaze to his probing stare.

"I have done some investigating of you as well, my love," he said. "And I am not displeased with your past." The husky sincerity of his voice snatched her breath away again.

"My past?"

"Your husband. His demise."

Her cheeks flushed. "He died in my arms."

"I can think of no better way to die." He lifted his hand and grazed her cheek, then took the wine from her hands and set it on the table. His gaze turned warm and sensual.

"You must be mad," she said, her voice quavering. Sensation rippled up and down her spine. The heat of his touch scorched her.

"Mad about you." He drew her closer, taking her chin between his thumb and forefinger and lifting her gaze to his. "And the challenge you pose. How exciting to be the one who survives your passion."

"You are meant to be Jane's suitor." Margaret's voice squeaked.

"There are five other men who would welcome my withdrawal from this competition."

Margaret's entire body started to tremble at his intimate touch. That alarming heat was doing strange things to her head. Her vision blurred.

He brought his lips to hers and savored her slowly before leaving her lips to kiss the line of her jaw. Her heart raced. Sounds muted. The world stopped.

Delicious sensation danced over her flesh as his lips brushed back and forth across her ear, then his tongue touched the lobe and began delicately tracing each curve, slowly probing. She shivered as waves of tension shot through her.

Her vision doubled, then cleared. At her trembling response he tightened his arms around her, supporting her. His lips traced scorching kisses down her neck. His warm breath stirred her hair and warmed the pearls that hung there against her neck. "How did I not see your loveliness the moment I entered Bellhaven Castle?" he whispered, his voice achingly gentle as his mouth retraced the path it had come.

Margaret clung to him as her head suddenly throbbed. Her vision blurred again. She shook her head. A grave mistake, she realized, as her stomach roiled in agony. She gasped and pulled back, gazing with desperation into his face.

"Margaret?" he asked with a frown.

Her mouth went dry. "Awwa abbaww." She struggled to swallow. Her tongue thickened. Her chest constricted.

"My love, what is it?" Lord Galloway gazed at her with concern.

An acid taste lingered on her tongue. Her stomach twisted. Her lungs burned. On a groan, she pitched forward, collapsing into his arms.

"Margaret!"

Poison. Lord Galloway's face was grim as he sat at the edge of Margaret's bed. "Someone poisoned the wine with hemlock," he told Jane with barely contained anger.

That wine had been meant for her. Blood roared in Jane's ears. She could not breathe. She balled her hands into fists and felt her nails biting into her flesh as she fought for composure. She welcomed the pain—it gave her something to focus on rather than her guilt.

The doctor had been to see Margaret. He had given her something that had forced her to heave up the contents of her stomach. Doing so had saved her life.

Jane felt tears deep inside her, building, gathering force until they nearly choked her. Yet she refused to let them fall. The only thing that mattered at present was her aunt.

"Should I have the healer look at you while he is here?" Lord Galloway asked, concern deepening his voice. "Your stomach?"

Her lies threaded through her pain and weighed her down. "I am recovered." Tears scalded her eyes.

Lord Galloway studied her. "Do not blame yourself for any of this."

Jane swallowed roughly. She could not lose another person she loved. There had been so much loss already. "If only I had stayed. . . . "

"Then I never would have confronted my feelings about your aunt." He offered her a calm, serene smile. "If not for you, my heart might not feel so full it might burst."

At his words, the grief she had been holding at bay welled inside her, spilling onto her cheeks in hot, wet tears. "Why would someone do this?" she asked in a broken voice.

"Someone wants you out of the way. Obviously they are going to great lengths to see that happens."

"That they were able to poison the wine means they are in this castle."

"We will find them," he assured, "before they succeed."

Jane brushed the hair from her face with a shaking hand. "I will not give them a chance to harm Margaret again." She met Lord Galloway's gaze. "Will you take her away from here? Away from me? On her own, she will be safe."

"Not . . . going," Margaret rasped. Her eyes fluttered open and she drew a labored breath.

"Margaret." Lord Galloway's eyes glittered brightly.

Margaret's gaze found his, as she noticed he was in the room. "You stayed . . . with me?"

"Always." The passionate force of his voice almost convinced Jane he could hold back death if he chose to. He stroked Margaret's cheek softly.

"Jane." He turned to her. "There is something I need to tell you." He lifted Margaret's hand and placed a kiss upon the back of it with tender care. "I am withdrawing from the competition." He set Margaret's hand down and reached up to brush a lock of her hair off her forehead. "My heart is here, with your aunt."

Only an hour before she had thought herself incapable of feeling ever again, but to her surprise stirrings of hope blossomed. "I could not be happier for you both," Jane said with a smile.

Margaret blushed at her newfound love. "Let us hope . . . your heart . . . survives our first night . . . together."

Lord Galloway laughed and pressed a kiss to Margaret's lips. "Then you had better hurry and get better so we can find out."

Jane rose from the bed and headed for the door. Three was suddenly a crowd in the small bedchamber. She needed to leave them alone. Her aunt would be safe in Lord Galloway's care.

News of the attempt on Lady Margaret's life moved through the castle like a flame on dry kindling. Upon hearing the news, David raced into the field where Nicholas and Jules were sparring. "Lady Margaret has been poisoned."

"Is someone with her?" Nicholas asked, stopping his sword midstrike.

David nodded as he tried to catch his breath. "The doctor is here."

"Does Lady Jane know?" Jules sheathed his weapon and wiped the sweat from his brow with the back of his hand.

David nodded. "Lady Jane and Lord Galloway are with the doctor and Lady Margaret."

"How did this happen?" Nicholas's face darkened.

"Someone poisoned the wine intended for Lady Jane with hemlock," David said with a frown. "Lady Margaret drank it by mistake when she took Lady Jane's place during her time alone with Lord Galloway."

"Lady Jane switched places with her aunt?" Nicholas asked in a puzzled tone.

Jules's lips lifted in a half smile. "That is good news for the rest of us."

"Perhaps," David replied.

"Where is Bryce?" Nicholas's gaze narrowed. "Where was he when all this happened?"

Jules shook his head. "Bryce has changed or at least I pray he has."

"Has he?" Nicholas asked. "Or does he want us to believe he has?" He raked a hand through his hair. "God's teeth, when will this end?"

"When Lady Jane marries." David verbalized what he knew the others were thinking.

"Then we had best see that happens soon," Jules exclaimed.

David nodded. "Our worst fears have been confirmed. Whoever wants to harm Lady Jane lives within the castle."

Jules trapped David's gaze, his own unflinching. "Then why are we standing around here? Let us split up and go find Bryce, or the villain, or both. We must do something."

"Agreed," Nicholas said. "I will go to the keep and gather the servants. I want to find the girl from yesterday, Clara, and see if she has someone who can vouch for her whereabouts this afternoon."

"I will go through the kitchen, searching for any sign of hemlock or other poisons." Jules set his jaw. "That is the last time someone will get at her in that manner, if I have anything to do with it."

"I will take the grounds," David stated. "Be suspicious of anyone and everyone."

"Even ourselves?" Jules asked with a frown. "I would hate to think one of Lady Jane's suitors would harm her."

"Bryce still has the most to lose," Nicholas stated.

Jules nodded. "Let us not convict him until he has a chance to explain his whereabouts."

Below stairs, Jane entered the great hall to find Nicholas pacing like a caged animal before her staff. Not a flicker of emotion disturbed his austere features, yet Jane could clearly hear his mental cursing. He had been questioning them for the past hour while she had been with her aunt.

"Any closer to an answer?" she asked, even though she already knew his response.

"No," he said, keeping his gaze upon Clara.

Her eyes were rimmed in red as was her nose, and she clutched a plain white handkerchief in her hands. She sniffled and dropped her gaze to her feet. By the look of things, Nicholas had not spared her feelings in his interview.

Jane frowned at the girl. It did seem rather odd that a lethal concoction be found in a bottle of wine intended for her consumption only a day after Nicholas mentioned that someone might use poison to harm her. "Tell me what you know."

"Most of the servants saw nothing unusual. Clara might have something to tell us if she can ever move past the dramatics." Nicholas frowned, his steady, impossible-to-escape gaze on the girl who used to work in the kitchen.

Clara sniffed again and looked up to find both Nicholas and Jane staring at her. "I swear on my life, I had nothing tae do with that poison."

Nicholas stood before her. "Unless you would like to be relieved of your duties permanently, it is time to tell us everything you know."

Clara paled, then nodded.

"Start with your afternoon. Lady Jane and I both saw you at the midday meal. What did you do after that?"

Clara looked down at her fingers. "I cleaned up after the meal and helped with the dishes."

"You were asked not to go back into the kitchen."

"I did what ye asked. I stood at the doorway and passed things through tae Marthe," she said, adding a sniffle for emphasis.

"Clara has not been back in the kitchen since ye banned her, milord," Marthe confirmed.

"Go on," Nicholas encouraged.

"I spent most of the afternoon in the great hall, cleaning the floor and preparing the tables for the evening meal. 'Twas there that Ollie asked if I'd help clean the ashes from the fireplaces above stairs."

Nicholas looked at Ollie, who nodded his confirmation.

"I paid attention to that task and that task alone as I was—still am—terrified to lose my position altogether." Her gaze flicked up to Nicholas. "I'd finished three rooms, and just set to enter Lord Galloway's chamber, when I saw something very odd." She paled further and met Nicholas's gaze. "I've heard tales of Her Ladyship's ghost, but I've never seen her myself."

"You saw my mother?" Jane interrupted. She had heard the servants talk of an image of her mother haunting the north tower and hallway. Jane had gone there many times over the past several years, hoping, praying to see the specter herself. Despite her longing, her mother had never appeared.

"I was in the north hallway." The girl shivered. "I've heard the other servants talk about seeing an image of yer mother." She wrapped her arms about her waist. "'Twas her, the ghost had to be her."

Jane reached out, feeling suddenly unsteady, and caught Nicholas's arm. She wanted to believe in the miracle that her mother had somehow appeared. Yet she had known long ago that her mother would never smile at her again, never again call her "my angel." At the thought, old grief welled up and threatened to spill over. Jane tightened her grip on Nicholas's arm and fought for control.

Nicholas pulled her close against his side as he continued. "Describe what you saw," he demanded.

"I only saw her from the back. Long blond hair. A blue skirt. A shawl about her shoulders. I'd swear 'twas the Lennox tartan."

"You never saw her face?" Nicholas asked.

Clara's shoulders slumped. "Nay."

"So you might not have seen the ghost of Lady Lennox after all?" Nicholas's frown was back.

Clara's eyes widened. "It had tae be her. Who else could it be? All those tales. . . ."

"Which way did she go?" Nicholas asked. Irritation simmered in his deep voice.

Clara grimaced. "I followed her down the hallway and around the corner, but once I turned the corner, she was gone. Vanished."

"Have you ever seen Lady Lennox before today?" Nicholas asked.

Clara's face turned ghostly white. "Nay, I've only heard the stories."

"So you have no reference by which to judge if this were truly Lady Lennox or not?"

The girl blinked. "Nay."

"What time was all this happening?" Nicholas asked.

She paused as though caught up in thought. "Around dusk. I hurried tae get all the fireplaces cleaned before the men finished their supper."

"Did you hear anything odd during this exchange?" Nicholas pursued.

Clara frowned, hesitated, then said, "Aye." The word stretched, became stronger. "After Lady Lennox disappeared around the corner, I heard a soft creak and felt a whoosh of air, but by the time I made it into the hall both the sound and the air were gone."

Nicholas narrowed his gaze on the girl. "Was there anything unearthly about the woman you saw?"

Clara drew a shallow breath and shook her head. "From the stories, I had expected her to be floating above the ground or something."

Nicholas turned to Jane. He gave her a gentle smile. "Would you like to see the place where Clara claims she saw your mother, or would you rather wait here?"

"I would like to come with you." Jane straightened, once again feeling her legs under her. She stepped away from Nicholas. She ignored the sensation of loss that came from his absence. "Where are the other men?" Jane saw a vague shadow of disappointment in Nicholas's sherry-colored eyes.

"Jules is turning the kitchen over, looking for signs of poison. David is searching the grounds. Bryce and Colin are missing at the moment," Nicholas informed her. "If there is anything more amiss, we will find it. In the meanwhile, let us have Clara show us where she saw this apparition of your mother."

Jane dismissed the rest of the staff, then turned to follow Nicholas and Clara up the servant's staircase. She tried not to think about Nicholas. There were plenty of other things she could think about. She drew a sharp breath as she battled the memories with all the powers she possessed. She searched deep within herself for some time in the castle that did not lead her back to Nicholas.

The problem was she had lived within these stone walls all her life. Yet it was the times she had spent here with Nicholas that had turned her rather dull and ordinary existence into something of a dream. With him at Bellhaven, the walls never seemed so cold, or the space between them so empty. The memory of her time with Nicholas was set apart in her mind in a brief, shining moment.

She remembered what it felt like to have hope, however transitory. When she had looked into Nicholas's eyes she had felt comfort, and for the first time in her life she had experienced her own strength when his hand wrapped around hers. In him she had found a sliver of contentment in a world that largely ignored her. She had felt important, like someone thought she was precious and worth fighting for.

But he had not fought for her in the end. And what was once magical ended as quickly as it had begun, leaving her to face the true emptiness that was her life, especially after his betrayal. For better or worse, she was the keeper of Bellhaven—its ancient walls, its legacy, and its people.

Jane reached out and touched the cool stone as they passed from the stairs to the hallway outside the north tower. She had transferred all her hopes and dreams from one particular man to the castle that would remain long after both of them were gone from this earth. She had honestly thought that keeping the estate running smoothly would do it, would fill her with the same sense of satisfaction she had experienced in Nicholas's arms.

Looking at him now, at his dark brown hair and chiseled face, his powerful body, his confidence, she knew she had been wrong. Her steps faltered as she took in the whole of the man who had been thrust back into her life. For a heartbeat she could not think about who might be trying to kill her or what was at stake if she did not marry soon. All she could think about was the past and how much she had loved this man.

He turned to smile at her.

Her heart lurched.

She said she had forgiven him for hurting her with his rumors, and she had. But would she ever trust him as blindly as she had before? Fear stood in her way when it came to Nicholas. He had not thrown stones or daggers at her head, or tried to poison her food, but he had killed a part of her two years ago—a part of her that he had created, nurtured, and claimed to love.

"Is this where you saw the figure?" Nicholas asked Clara.

The girl nodded. "Then she disappeared around that corner over there."

Nicholas held out his hand to Jane as he had so many times in the past. "Are you ready?"

Did he know the true weight of his words at that moment? Was she ready to move forward into a new relationship with him?

His gaze connected with, held, and challenged hers. And something inside Jane softened. It could not be easy for Nicholas to be here at Bellhaven and forced to share her with five—four—other men.

Was she ready?

Jane reached out. Her fingers trembled. She touched the warmth of Nicholas's flesh, smelled the scent that was his own, and her pride melted. As though no time had ever passed, his fingers curled around hers.

"I am ready if you are," she said, then realized the double entendre of her words. A blush crept up her throat. "I mean, yes. Let us discover the truth."

He gave her a direct look, his gaze probing, his smile edged with dangerous intent. His gaze dropped to her lips.

Jane shivered and tried to pull out of his grasp.

He did not let go. "Do not run from me, Jane. Not this time," he asked, his voice a raw whisper.

She looked into his eyes and realized in that moment just how much she cared about him, how much she wanted him to care about her. Her heart fluttered. For the first time, she could not summon a single reason to tell him no. "Lead on."

Nicholas held her gaze and nodded. "The first task ahead of us is to discover the 'secret' of the ghost of Lady Lennox."

Clara paused around the corner. "This is where she vanished." She shivered. "May I leave you now? I have no wish to see that ghost twice in one day."

"You may leave."

The girl nodded and hurried back the way they had come, leaving Nicholas and Jane alone.

"Do you believe in the supernatural?" he asked.

She pressed her lips together before replying, "If you mean, do I believe my mother is here as a ghost? No. She has been dead for so long . . ." Jane swallowed roughly, and this time when she tried to pull away, he let her go.

Emotion surged as a memory of the past filled her mind. She saw her mother and herself almost fifteen years ago, walking hand-in-hand along this hallway to the tower where they could look out over the land and watch for her father to return. Jane closed her eyes, trying to will the memory away. The image in her mind only sharpened.

Jane opened her eyes. She missed her mother so much in that moment it hurt deep inside herself. Margaret had been a wonderful substitute, but nothing could ever replace her mother's love. Jane took a deep breath and tilted her chin up. "I am sorry, Nicholas. You will have to explore the hallway on your own."

He startled. "Where are you going?"

She did not answer as her feet hurried away, heading to the one place in the castle that could help clear her thoughts.

Colin Taylor might have no knowledge of who he was by birth, but he was not ignorant of human nature. And in his experience, men did not let go of their anger as easily as Bryce had let go of his.

Under the cover of darkness, Colin followed Bryce out of the castle, staying out of sight. Bryce had taken no horse, so he must not intend to go far. But why leave the castle, when everything he wanted was within its walls?

The wind blew softly across the moors; Colin was grateful, for it brushed away the footsteps he was not able to conceal. Bryce moved with assurance, as though he knew the lay of the land, and even in the darkness could find what it was he sought.

After walking for a time, they approached an outcropping of rocks. Bryce stopped in front of them as another man came out of the shadows to stand beneath a circle of silver-white moonlight. "Do you have information?" Bryce asked.

Colin shielded himself behind a nearby rock that was big enough to conceal his body, yet close enough to see and hear what the other two had to say.

"I have a copy of Lord Lennox's will, along with a few other tidbits that I could gather about the others," the stranger replied in a gravelly voice. The cool light illuminated only half of the man's face, giving him a vaguely sinister appearance. He seemed, from what Colin could see, to be about the same age as Bryce, in his late twenties.

But where Bryce was neatly garbed with golden, unblemished skin and a raw handsomeness that at times made him seem unreal, the stranger was blemished and rough, despite the elegance of his fashionable jacket, frothy white shirt, dark breeches, and black boots.

"What kind of tidbit?" Bryce asked. His voice held a note of anticipation as he accepted rolled sheaves of paper from the other man.

"Lord Galloway's money is invested heavily in an Englishman, Thomas Savery, an inventor who a few years back patented a device called the steam pump. From the looks of things, the earl is poised to receive a fortune for his investment."

"God's teeth," Bryce erupted. "News like that will not help me annihilate my competition."

The man shrugged. "You paid me to find out about them. I never promised it would be bad news."

"Go on," Bryce said on a sigh.

"Jules MacIntyre's release from prison did not come at his father's hand, but through an unknown source that I traced back to Edinburgh."

"Do you have any leads on who it was yet?"

"Nay," the man said. "I have several inquiries out. Someone will talk soon. We must be patient."

"Patience is not one of my virtues. What about the others?"

"Colin Taylor is the most interesting of the lot. He has no past. I could only trace him to a foundling home in Glasgow which he left at a young age to squire for Lord Pickering. It is quite remarkable he was able to do something so distinguished. Such privileges are reserved for titled sons."

Bryce nodded.

"Sir David Buchanan has been known to wager a fair bit in the last several years. But he is still quite flush despite his losses."

"And Nicholas Kincaid?" Bryce asked. "There must be something there. What about the reports of a dalliance he once had with my cousin? Did you find anything to substantiate those rumors?"

The stranger shook his head. "No one knows where those rumors started. And about the man himself, I talked to several of his retired staff. They were all very close-lipped when it came to talking about his past—almost as if it pained *them* to talk about it."

Bryce frowned. "And you did not pursue it further? That is what I am paying you for," he ground out. "I need more. Go back and fulfill your task."

The stranger recoiled. "I have done my duty, just as you demanded. Do not blame me if there is nothing further to be dragged out of the people who know these men."

"And the will?" Bryce nodded to the papers in his hands. "Is there any news there?"

The stranger frowned. "His Lordship sealed up his daughter's inheritance right and tight if, after he is declared dead, she marries before Christmas Day. But if she doesn't marry by the stroke of midnight on Christmas Eve, for any reason, the title and the estate pass to you."

Even at a distance, Colin could tell Bryce's expression was one of pleasure. "All right, Barker, you did well with the will. However, I'll not be paying you a farthing more until you dig up something useful on these men. I need to know exactly who they are and how they can be blackmailed into ceasing their pursuit of Lady Jane."

Colin kept silent as the minutes ticked by while Bryce and his investigator arranged their next meeting two nights hence then said their good-byes. Deep in thought, Bryce stalked back to the castle.

Colin waited only until Bryce had passed before heading after the investigator. He intended not only to foil Bryce's plans to dig up dirt on his competitors, but also to know more of what the man had found out about his own life. If the investigator had discovered even the smallest of clues, it would be more than Colin had ever had.

And if he was determined not to talk, a few nights of isolation in Bellhaven's dungeon might loosen the man's tongue.

Jane lit the last of many candles and stood back to observe the labyrinth in the chapel. It took up the entire surface of the floor at over forty feet in width and length. There were no sides to this maze. The pre-Christian design had been adopted by her ancestors, no doubt in imitation of the Chartres cruciform labyrinth. Just like the meditation maze in France, this one was open, and one or more persons could walk the path at the same time.

She had no idea which of her ancestors had carved the meditative path into the stone floor during his lifetime, but the creation dated somewhere in the twelfth century, around the time when Richard Lennox had ruled over Bellhaven. She had always assumed it had been his creation. Why he had built the concentric circles on the floor of the chapel, she knew not either. But she had always been grateful for the time she and her mother had spent here in contemplation and prayer.

Jane removed her shoes, then stepped up to the path that would take her inside the labyrinth. She took her first chilly step onto the path and tried to clear her mind. A tiny gulping sound of grief escaped her and a single tear rolled down her cheek as she allowed the memories of her mother to wash over her.

No matter how much she wanted the stories of her mother's ghost to be true, she knew they were not. If her mother were still in this world, she would know. It would be the same sensation she felt now, the same conviction that told her her father and brother were not yet gone from this life. She still felt them deep within her soul.

The cool stone chilled the bottom of her feet through her stockings as Jane took slow, even steps through the winding path. She allowed her progress to calm her as the yellow-gold light of the candles illuminated her way. She quieted her mind, only aware of her breath as it filled her body then forced its way out.

Silence surrounded her. The muscles in her neck and shoulders began to relax, and her thoughts shifted from her mother to Nicholas. They had both driven her here tonight, but it was Nicholas who remained with her. Was she ready to confront what she and Nicholas had been? What they still could be if only she let him back into her heart?

Was it the competition that had him pursuing her—the threat of someone else vying for her affections? Would he make her want him again, body and soul, only to deny her in the end?

Or was it something more—something she dared hope for?

"Jane?" A soft voice broke through her thoughts.

Nicholas. Had she conjured him with her thoughts?

"Jane." The voice came again.

Jane stopped walking and turned slowly toward the chapel door. Nicholas stood there, his features softened, and for a heartbeat she saw not only sadness, but fear, before the look vanished.

"Why did you follow me?" she asked, forcing back a twinge of annoyance at his invasion of her sacred space.

"You should not be alone. You should never be alone until we find who is after you."

"I am not alone. I am with God."

"God cannot stop a flying dagger," he growled beneath his breath. He strode toward her, onto the labyrinth.

"Stop."

He halted. His brows drew together.

"If you want to talk to me here, you have to walk the path. But first you must remove your boots."

He frowned down at the floor, then took several steps back toward the opening in the concentric circles. "Surely you jest?"

"No. I am quite serious." She saw the uncertainty in his gaze, felt his hesitation. "The labyrinth can be very inspiring if you give it a chance."

Silence settled heavy between them.

With a sigh, he bent down and removed his boots, set them aside and took a step. He hurried along the path.

"Slow down," she said in a calm, serene tone. "Use the path for reflection or inspiration."

He was silent for another long moment before he said, "Can we talk as we both walk?"

"No." She gave him a quick, teasing smile. "Not one word until we both reach the center."

"The center?" he groaned.

"Let the path give you whatever it is you need." The conversation flowed between them as it used to with no tension or reserve.

"I need you to listen to me," he said.

"Only after you have quieted your mind and listened to your soul." She drew a steadying breath and started back on her journey toward the center, weaving back and forth along the circuitous path.

"Another challenge for me alone?"

She stopped and gave him a measured look. "We could bring the others here if you would prefer."

"No," he replied quickly, and started walking, more slowly this time. "I want you all to myself."

Jane hid a smile. She and Nicholas walked in silence. As they traveled toward the center, they passed each other once, twice, three times. Their hands brushed. Their gazes met. Her heart fluttered, and she could feel the tension thrumming between them. The sound of her own heartbeat echoed in her ears, matching her steps. She increased her pace.

Nicholas's stride lengthened and his gaze shifted from warm to molten gold as she reached the center and waited for him there. Each step he took seemed to take a lifetime, until finally he entered the center and stood across from her.

He drew her to him, lifted her hand, and brought it to his lips. His eyes locked with hers. He kissed her fingertips, then turned her hand and pressed his lips to her palm. He let them linger just long enough for her to remember what his kisses had been like, to feel his heat.

He had called her a passionate seductress. When those words had first come back to her, they had hurt her to the core. But with him here, standing before her, when it was only the two of them, the term did not seem as harsh as it once had. With Nicholas, passion came easy. Seduction was a natural extension of two people who cared about each other.

The question was, did she still care about him like that? Did she want to play the seductress to his passion once again? Could she survive it if she did?

"What did you want to talk to me about?" she asked, her voice a whisper as she tried to deny the sensations racing across her hand, her flesh.

"I want you to see that I am here, standing before you." With a hold on her hand, he tugged her gently, drew her a step closer. Still holding her captive with his gaze, he bent his head and pressed his lips to her wrist.

"I see you." Her pulse leapt as he spoke.

He brushed his lips back and forth across her tender flesh. "No, Jane, you do not. But you will. Eventually you will see that I am here. I am not leaving. Never again."

A long moment passed while she looked into his eyes. Jane tried to keep her mental distance, to hold tight to the calming effect of the labyrinth on her soul, but she could not, not with his sherry-colored eyes calling to her. She was drawn in by the warmth in his gaze, by the touch of his lips on her sensitive skin.

"I have not decided who is to be my husband." She said the one thing that could put some distance between them.

Nicholas paid her no heed, as though he sensed what she was trying to do. She was never very good at hiding her emotions. With his arm at her waist, Nicholas drew her gently against him. "Husband or not, you own a piece of me, right here." He placed her hand over his heart. "You always have."

She smoothed her hand against the soft fabric of his shirt as though searching for proof that he did possess a heart. Her fingers trembled, but there was no fear in her eyes. "If I were in your heart as you say, how could you leave me so easily and say the things you did?"

"I would never do anything to hurt you, Jane. Not intentionally." He looked into her eyes. "Your brother demanded I leave. And I did. It was the worst decision of my life. If I had to do it all again, I would lay down my life rather than leave you."

In the flickering light of the candles, she studied him. "I knew Jacob was not happy, but it was Father's approval you needed."

He raised both hands, framed her face, tipped it up to his. "Jacob never gave me the chance to speak to your father or to you." Nicholas took a slow, steady breath as he held her.

"Why are you telling me this now, after all this time?"

He kept his gaze locked with hers as she searched his eyes, his expression, most likely considering what she saw. "I want you to know I did not leave you because I grew tired or bored. I left because I was given no options and I think you knew that even then."

The moment stretched and her gaze remained unwavering. He could sense her hesitation to open herself up to hurt once more. "I was told nothing, other than that you were gone. The knowledge of why you left does not change anything. It is my heart, not my mind that needs persuasion."

She wanted proof.

Her heart had been his once. Could it be his again? He brought his lips to hers and kissed her tenderly, giving her a chance to back away.

But she did not resist. Instead, she melted into his embrace. Need flowed between them, hotter than he remembered. He graciously accepted the gift, and with his tongue stoked the embers into a fire. He would use their attraction, fan it into a bonfire, while she made up her mind about who to marry. He would reassure her of his devotion. He could make her believe in him again, that he would always be there, be there to love her every night and every day. Because he was not sure what he would do if she decided to remain apart from him.

His hands left her face to move over her shoulders and back. He gathered her closer, allowing the familiar heat and the fire to follow as it always had between them, consuming her reservations and the ability to think. He let the demanding heat devour him as one thought settled in his heart. He was back in her life and back in her arms. He was not going to let her go no matter how many suitors stood in the way.

Jane groaned and broke their kiss, pulling back slightly. "We cannot do this," she breathed against his lips.

"For once, follow your heart, Jane. Not what your head is telling you." His entire body throbbed and ached at the loss of her touch. He closed his eyes and breathed in her sweet feminine scent. She would step back too soon and the moment would be gone.

As though reading his thoughts, she pulled away, putting distance between them.

"I trusted my instincts once, only to be made a fool. I cannot do that again and survive."

"Jane—" He reached for her.

She stepped further away. "No, Nicholas. I cannot lose myself in your passion again, no matter how much I might want to. I do need to use my head to decide which of my suitors will be the best choice for me and for my people. Passion can have nothing to do with that choice."

Nicholas stood in complete silence as her words washed over him. Passion had everything to do with this choice. Did she not see that together they made sense, they were happy, and the world seemed right?

Apart, nothing worked, felt right, or prospered. But only when she stopped denying what was between them did he stand a chance of winning her back.

I choose you. He would give anything to hear her say those words. But he would have to wait.

"Very well, Jane. I only want what is best for you." His heart heavy, he offered her his arm. "Allow me to escort you back to the keep."

She shook her head. "I can find my own way back."

Nicholas nodded and headed for the door. He had work to do if he were to convince her that the "way back" was with him.

After Jane fell asleep that evening, her dreams drifted for a time like mist over the moors, coalescing without shape or form. The sweet, lingering sensations of Nicholas's kiss remained on her lips.

Nicholas.

Her thoughts wandered back through the mist, over the land bordering Bellhaven. Men and women from neighboring clans twirled and tumbled in her mind until the images cleared and she saw a single woman with her golden hair streaming in the wind, running over the mossy ground in her bare feet. The hem of her dress was shredded and caked with dirt. A sash in the colors of the MacGuires blurred then became the familiar colors of the Lennox red-and-green tartan.

The dream twisted and turned. Her heart raced. Her pulse quickened as the sounds of laughter came to her ears. She felt a strange mixture of sadness and joy as the woman stopped running and turned instead toward Jane's bed. The flaxen-haired woman stood over the bed, staring down at Jane with a menacing glare.

Jane thrashed in her bed, tried to wake up. To no avail.

"How dare you," the woman said, lifting a dagger and thrusting it downward, through Jane's heart.

Jane's chest constricted. She cried out and came awake with a start. She sat up and grabbed her chest. No dagger rested there. Her heart thumped beneath her hands. She drew a shuddering breath as her senses reoriented to her chamber and the darkness.

She drew a shallow breath. The dream had seemed so real, frighteningly so. Jane could still feel the presence of another even though her eyes told her she was alone. She paused, listening in the darkness. The sound of her own breathing was all she heard.

Driven by a sudden irrational fear of being alone in her chamber, Jane grabbed her dressing gown and left her room to find Margaret. She made her excuses to the guards at her door as she ran past them, down the corridor, to her aunt's chambers. Without hesitating, she opened the door. A single candle burned next to the curtained bed, casting shadows against the wall.

Her heart hammering, she slipped under the covers of the bed next to her aunt, as she used to do when she was a child.

Margaret opened her eyes. "Jane?"

"Is it all right if I disturb you?"

"You never disturb me," Margaret replied, shifting on the bed to allow Jane more room.

"How are you feeling?" Jane asked as she settled on the bed, grateful that her aunt was improving.

"I am happy to be alive." Margaret smiled, and Jane could see that her aunt's blue eyes were no longer hazy and unfocused as they had been earlier. Instead, a brightness of spirit entered her gaze as she gathered Jane next to her side. "I am better than I have ever been."

"Truly?" Jane rested her head on her aunt's shoulder.

"Truly," Margaret replied. "Tonight Lord Galloway asked me to marry him."

Jane pulled back. "He did?"

Margaret nodded. "You could have blown me over with a feather."

The remnants of Jane's dream faded as joy filled her heart. She laughed, the merry sound filling the room. "That is marvelous."

Her aunt bit down on her lip. "I am not certain it is."

Jane scooted back, no longer needing reassurance. "Are you not convinced of his feelings for you?"

"Oh no," Margaret replied. "He is devoted, of that I am certain. You should have seen him today while I was in the grips of the poison. He kept begging me to stay with him, not to leave this earth before we had a chance to act on our feelings." Margaret's cheeks flamed. She brought her hands up to cover them. "Imagine, at my age, blushing about a man."

"You are not old."

"I will admit, around Lord Galloway, I do feel young."

"Then what is it?" Jane asked. "I know he cares about you. I have seen the way he looks at you, as though he wants to devour you."

Margaret gave a nervous laugh. "That is the problem, but in reverse. I am afraid 'tis I who will devour him."

Jane shook her head and gave another laugh. "What is it about the Lennox women? We are so strong when it comes to defending our land and our people, and yet when it comes to our personal relationships, we fall victim to irrational fears?"

"You do understand." Margaret sighed. "I know what happened with Thomas will never happen again." She crossed herself. "At least I pray it will not. But that does not stop the fear."

Jane patted Margaret's hand affectionately. "Let me ask you something that you asked me not many days ago—do you love him?"

Her aunt smiled a smile that lit up her face and seemed to brighten the room. "With all my heart."

"Then let that love guide you."

Margaret laughed. "I should be the one giving you advice, since we started this whole competition to secure you a husband."

Jane smiled at her aunt, feeling an overwhelming sense of joy. "I am pleased you have found someone to share your life."

Margaret opened her arms and Jane moved into her embrace. Relief flashed across her face. "Thank you, Jane, for being happy for me."

Jane pulled back. "It looks like both of our lives will be very different come Christmas Eve."

Margaret's smile faded. "I told Lord Galloway I would not marry him until you were settled and I could leave you with someone I trusted."

Jane forced a smile to hide the sudden stirring of her nerves. "Six more days. Five suitors. Three more competitions."

Margaret's mouth quirked. "When you say it that way, it does not sound very romantic."

Closing her eyes, Jane let the word tumble around in her brain. *Romance.* She was not certain how much more romance she could take.

The next morning, upon waking, Nicholas stretched and put aside his memories of last night with Jane. He had to concentrate on winning the prize for good, regardless of any competitions or other foolishness. Today her suitors were to compete by running an obstacle course that Angus, Egan, and Ollie had constructed at the far end of the open field.

Nicholas quickly folded his great kilt, then dressed and hurried downstairs to breakfast. The stakes of this next competition were higher than they had ever been before.

He and David met in the great hall. Over breakfast they reviewed all the information they had separately gathered last night. "The girl, Clara, claims the ghost of Jane's mother is somehow responsible for placing poison in the wine."

David frowned over a bit of salted pork. "Why would a mother do that to her child in this realm or any other?"

Nicholas's hand halted as he set down his ale. At times he had longed for his father to do something so sinister—to do anything to end the torment he had put Nicholas through on a daily basis. Poison would have been kind. . . . He shook off the thought. "The servants revealed nothing. Were you or the other men able to find any sort of evidence at all?"

"I made a rather startling discovery," Colin said, sliding into a chair across from them. "He is currently occupying space in the dungeon."

Nicholas and David shared a startled glance. "You found the villain?"

"I do not think so," Colin admitted. "But the man has been working for Bryce, gathering information on all of us in an attempt to rule us out as marriage partners for Lady Jane."

Nicholas snorted. "So the 'I have changed act' is just that, an act?"

Colin shrugged. "It appears so."

David's frown deepened. "When did you apprehend this man?"

"Last night after we broke from supper, I followed Bryce out of the castle where he met with Barker. That is what the man calls himself."

Nicholas held David's gaze for some moments before saying, "Then Bryce could not have been the one to poison the wine."

David shifted in his seat. "If not Bryce, or any of the rest of us, or the servants, then who? Because I am not inclined to believe a ghost did it, or carried out any of the other attacks on Lady Jane or Lady Margaret."

Nicholas caught and held David's, then Colin's, gaze. "Perhaps it is time to do a little ghost hunting after the competition today?"

David nodded. "We could set a trap. But this time we would be prepared for whatever folly the villain has planned."

"An excellent idea. It is time to turn the tide in our favor." Colin finished the last of his breakfast and pushed away from the table. All three men stood.

"But first we have an appointment with destiny," Nicholas said with a grimace. He was strong, and his life with his father showed he could endure pain when needed. But agility was not his strong suit. Though today, for an eternity with Jane, he would find whatever skills he needed to be declared the victor.

Most of the castle's staff lined the outside of the open field, waiting for the contenders for Jane's hand to appear. Excited chatter filled the morning air as Jane took her seat in the stands. Only a short moment later, the voices around her grew louder, the chatter almost deafening as the challengers approached.

Jane tightened her grip on the arms of her chair as the five remaining suitors entered the lists for their fourth challenge. She had known they would dress for the part they would have to play today, but nothing could prepare her for the sight of them rounding the corner, all dressed in plated armor.

They were the army she had so desperately tried to gather, but they were so much more. They were her hope for the future. She knew she should be thinking of their safety during this feat of skill and torturous trial, but the sight of them, in all their glory, took her breath away. She had never thought she would be intrigued by power, but today, and with these men, she was.

"Goodness," Margaret said, the word as breathy as Jane herself felt. "They are quite a sight, are they not?" Her aunt was seated beside her, with Lord Galloway hovering close on her opposite side.

With an effort, Jane pulled her gaze from the men to look at her aunt. The color had returned to her cheeks, and apart from the weakness in her limbs that still lingered, she appeared unharmed despite her trial. "Are you well enough for this?" Jane asked.

"Of course." She reached for Jane's hand and patted it reassuringly. "I would not miss this challenge for anything. Besides, Lord Galloway has seen me through the worst of my illness." Margaret sent a breathtaking smile to the man beside her, a smile that illuminated her face and made her aunt appear years younger.

Lord Galloway captured her hand and brought it to his lips. "Our journey has just begun."

Jane shifted her gaze back to her remaining suitors and to the contraption Angus, Egan, and Ollie had created. This test, more than any of the others, would prove to her who she could trust to head up her army. She forced all thoughts of Nicholas away. For the moment, she had to focus on her military needs more than physical ones.

The men approached Angus, who stood with five pieces of straw of varying lengths hidden in his fist. The men would draw straws to determine the order in which they would attempt the obstacle course.

Jules drew first and pulled the shortest straw.

Jane inwardly groaned. Of all the men, he was least likely to succeed in this challenge due to weakness and injury. He could have benefitted from watching the other men progress through the trial before he had to take his turn. However, such a benefit was not to be his this day.

The other straws were drawn. The order determined—Jules, Colin, Bryce, Nicholas, and David. The first man to complete the course was the winner, regardless of who had yet to take their turn.

Jane tensed as Jules approached the first challenge of climbing one vertical wall, then another. He scrambled up the first wall with enthusiasm, but the second wall was taller and proved to be more of a challenge for his injured body. He clung to the top with only one arm as he struggled to pull himself up. Several long moments ticked by before he fell to the ground, defeated.

Angus rushed to Jules's side and helped him to his feet, escorting him off the field and out of view. Jane shifted in her chair, debating if she should remain or go to Jules's aid, when Colin took the field. He bolted over the walls as if they were no challenge at all, then dropped to his knees to crawl through a mud pit covered with a low net of barbed spikes.

Jane held her breath as he gained his feet and jumped through a ring of fire before entering the section of the course that held five swinging logs. They moved back and forth at uneven intervals. Being hit by one of them would send him to the ground in defeat. Colin made it past the first, then the second. He hesitated at the third, moved to take a step forward, and the second log hit him in the back, sending him sprawling.

Ollie rushed forward this time to drag Colin off to the side of the course and signaled for Bryce to step up and take his turn.

"What happens if none of them make it?" Margaret asked, her hands clutched together.

"Then perhaps we will choose the man who made it the farthest?" Jane offered. Three more competitors. Surely one of them would finish.

Bryce climbed the walls without hesitation, but then he ran alongside the mud pit. The crowded roared their disapproval as he moved to the swinging wood. He captured one of the smaller logs with his hand, forcing it to stop swinging, then reached up with a dagger he pulled from his boot and sliced through the rope suspending it from the wooden frame above.

Jane sat forward in her chair. "What is he doing?"

"Cheating," Lord Galloway growled, standing. "I will take care of this."

Margaret caught his hand, pulling him back toward her. "There is no need for you to take on Bryce. We established no rules." She shrugged. "We did not say there would be a penalty for skipped obstacles."

Bryce tucked the two foot log under his arm and ran past the spider walk on a horizontal rope ladder with swinging clubs, past the balance beam. Two of David's warriors rushed him, but Bryce knocked them to the ground with the log in his arms. He ran unchallenged past the final ring of fire to the finish.

Bryce tossed the log on the ground and pumped his arms in the air. "I won."

"He cheated!" The crowd hissed and growled their displeasure, the sound increasing with every heartbeat.

Angus picked up a horn and with a blare of sound cut through the noise. Silence followed. "Only Lady Jane can determine the outcome," Angus proclaimed.

All eyes turned to Jane. She in turn looked at David and Nicholas. Both men's expressions were dark. Jane drew a slow, even breath. They both wanted a chance to compete, and part of her wanted to give them that opportunity. Yet a heartbeat later, it was that very irritation on Nicholas's face that steeled her answer. He wanted to win. He wanted the opportunity to spend time alone with her again.

Her body warmed at the thought, but her mind rebelled. He had hurt her when he had started rumors about her passionate nature. He had forced her to suffer both other men's repugnance and rude offers. She had an opportunity to make him suffer some small measure of what she had endured. The beginnings of a smile tugged at her lips. It might not be fair to the others, and she would be the one to pay for this folly by spending time alone with her cousin, but all that paled in comparison to what she would gain with this one act of rebellion. "I will accept Bryce as my champion," she announced.

Beside her Margaret gasped and the crowd roared, the noise heightening to a fever pitch.

"Are you certain?" Margaret asked.

Jane watched Nicholas's features turn icy before he headed off the field with David at his heels. "I can tolerate one night alone with Bryce." She returned her gaze to her aunt's. "Bryce and I used to spend time together as children. He was different back then. Perhaps this time with him will help me understand what has changed. Despite his change of heart, he still seems so angry."

Margaret frowned. "And perhaps dangerous. I am not certain this is a good idea at all."

Jane stood. "I will make certain he has no opportunity to harm me. Besides," Jane reached down and patted the dagger she kept concealed on her calf. "If he tries anything, I am not defenseless."

At her own words, Jane's mood darkened. Nay, the only time she seemed defenseless was when she was in Nicholas's arms. With a sigh, she left the stands, heading back to the castle. She had a prisoner to deal with before her time alone with Bryce.

Jane stood in the stable near the prisoner's horse with her puppy, Angel, pouncing in the hay near her feet, searching for something to play with. She had saddled the man's horse herself while she waited for Angus to bring the informant to her. Footsteps sounded outside. Jane's hand hovered above her hidden dagger until she saw the familiar silhouette of Angus appear in the doorway of the stable.

"I've brought the man to ye," Angus said, and he propelled the man forward.

"I demand to be released," the man said, trying desperately to twist out of Angus's iron grasp on the back of his jacket. At the sight of Jane, he stopped moving and simply allowed the big man to escort him forward.

Jane frowned at the odor that clung to the man. His shirt was covered in dust. His boots were scuffed and his face marred with a streak of mud across his right cheek. Still, he might be dirty, but other than that, he had escaped the dungeon of Bellhaven relatively unscathed. "You are free to go, Master Biddleton, as long as you promise never to return again."

Barker Biddleton narrowed his gaze on her. "Bryce MacCallister hired me. I was only following his orders."

Jane straightened to her full height. "Your orders come from me now since you are on my land and I am the law here."

He swallowed. "I meant no harm."

"You have delivered all the information that you retrieved on my suitors?"

He nodded. "I know how to write. I put it all on paper and handed it over last night."

Now all she had to do was get the papers from Bryce and she could correct whatever mischief Barker had stirred up. She did not care what he had discovered on any of her suitors. She of all people knew what happened when falsehoods were spread, and worse, believed, by others. "Very well. Your services are no longer required. You may leave."

He stood there a moment. It was a moment too long as far as Angus was concerned because the servant jerked Barker up by the collar and the back of his pants and nudged him closer to his horse.

Taking the hint, Barker mounted. He offered Jane a nod, then rode his horse out of the stable.

"I will make certain he leaves," Angus said, ambling after the horse.

Jane watched them go. She did not like the idea that Bryce had spied on his competition in the hopes of tarnishing their reputations. Had her cousin been wise, he would have taken more care with his actions. Instead of endearing him to her, his actions had the opposite effect.

She had no choice but to spend time alone with Bryce this evening. That was his earned reward. But nothing said she had to stay with him for long. A few minutes with him, a brief conversation about how disappointed she was by his behavior, and she would be in her bed and asleep before long.

She bent down and lifted Angel in her arms, hugging the playful puppy to her chest. "What do you think about an early bedtime tonight?"

The puppy wagged her tail.

"I could not agree with you more." Jane laughed as she headed back to the keep.

Bryce knew he had taken a big risk, cheating as he had during the obstacle course challenge. But what other choice had he had? If he had played fair, David or Nicholas would have won the challenge, and neither man needed more time alone with Jane. She was too attached to both of them for Bryce's own comfort.

He might have had to cheat to accomplish his goal, but he would use this opportunity to persuade Jane to see his side of things. After tonight, she might very well agree that marrying him was the only solution to her problem.

And he had the perfect evening planned. Bryce looked around at the scene he had set. He knew his cousin better than any of the other fools here. He remembered what had made her heart take flight when she was young. Such things did not vanish with age. He smiled to himself as his gaze moved over the lanterns he had set along the edge of the frozen pond. Then his gaze shifted to the huge bonfire that roared on the east side of the pond. He had cleared the area of snow and had built a small wooden bench so that they could sit together and watch the flames. The heat from the fire would keep them warm while they remained outside and away from the others.

The ice, the fire, the solitude. All these things would work to his advantage tonight as he wooed Jane. Satisfaction brought a true smile to his face. Nothing would end this night too soon.

Moving to the edge of the pond, he waited for Jane to appear. She came only a few moments later, escorted by Lord Galloway. The other men walked behind them. At the sight, Bryce allowed himself a moment of irritation. The other men would stand nearby all night in order to protect Jane.

Bryce straightened as his cousin approached. He was determined to ignore the others. He took Jane's hand in his and instead of pressing a kiss to it as he wanted to, he simply placed her fingers on his arm. "Milady, welcome to the past. This night, we will spend time together as we used to when we were younger."

"Let us get this over with," she said with a touch of irritation before signaling the others to retreat. They all left, except Nicholas, who hesitated a moment before he turned and walked back toward the edge of the walled garden gate where the others waited. They were out of earshot, but close enough to lend aid should Jane need it.

Bryce put the others from his mind and turned back to Jane. Her greeting was in no way encouraging, but he smiled at her nevertheless. The smile of a man who knew her well enough to bring her around.

"What do you have planned?" she asked, raising a hand to brush back a loosened lock from her temple. When she noted his eyes following her fingers, she dropped her hand to her side.

"Come," he said, gently guiding her to a bench near the bonfire. "Let us sit for a while and talk."

Jane nodded and took a seat on the bench. She had left enough space for him to join her, but he did not sit down. Instead, he moved back a little, giving her space to get used to the idea of them being together.

She turned away from the fire and met his gaze. "I want to talk to you about Bar—"

"Your army," he interrupted. "Not the army your suitors brought to you."

Jane's eyes widened. "Without them, I do not have an army."

"Not yet. But you could have one tomorrow with my help." He reached into his sporran and pulled out one of the papers Barker had delivered to him last night. He unfolded the coarse linen paper and handed it to Jane. On the sheet were the names of forty men.

Her brows drew together. "What is this?"

"This ledger bears the names of all the men who have agreed to fight for you, for us, should you choose me as your bridegroom."

For a heartbeat, excitement flared in her eyes before they clouded with worry. "Bryce, why did you hire an investigator to uncover information about my other suitors?"

His pulse thudded in his ears. "How could you know that?"

"Barker was captured." She frowned at the paper in her hands. "He brought you this, and other things—information about the other men."

Bryce shifted uncomfortably. "He did."

Jane frowned. "Why did you do that?"

He shrugged. "I have never had an advantage in my life. I wanted something that might turn you away from the others. It was an unfair advantage, but one I felt I needed."

"Cheating will not take you far in life," she replied.

He quirked his brow. "It achieved me time alone with you tonight."

Jane sighed. "Did you find anything?"

He shook his head. "The only information that was even slightly interesting was about Colin."

Jane's expression hardened. It was not at all the look he wanted to see on her face. "You will hand over the report about Colin." She rustled the paper in her hands. "Barker brought you these names as well?"

"Aye."

She set the list on the bench beside her. "I will think on this offer." Then she brought her gaze back to his, and her eyes narrowed. "Bryce, I know there is a good person inside you. I used to know that boy."

He closed his eyes. He could envision the boy he used to be. What had happened to change him?

"Can I give you some advice?" Jane's voice brought him back to the moment.

He opened his eyes and nodded.

"Stop trying so hard. Be yourself. Be the man I know you are."

He could not resist sitting next to her. As he did, he prayed for a spark of attraction to flare between them. Something, anything. He shifted closer, waiting.

Her face remained unchanged.

Disappointment rocked him, but he forced the emotion away. Pity. She was not attracted to him. But many couples started marriage with far less. He straightened, changing tactics. "Cousin," he said, the word punctuating the crackle and hiss of the flames. "Do you remember when we first met?"

She nodded. "It was shortly after my mother . . . died."

"My mother and I came here to offer our condolences and to help where we could," Bryce continued. "You were three. I was six years old."

"I remember."

"You were grieving over the loss of your mother. Your father had no time for you. Lady Margaret was taking care of your baby brother. You needed a friend, someone to listen to you, to care about what you felt and thought. That was me."

Bryce rubbed his temples as the memories flooded back. "We took walks around this pond, and when the ice froze over, we skated over the ice. We laughed." He paused. "And sometimes we cried."

"We were both different then," she said with a sigh. "We were both so young. It was before life had a chance to leave its mark on us." She started to say something more, then stopped. Instead, she put her hand in his and squeezed.

He felt the warmth of her touch, smelled the soft scent of roses. His heartbeat thudded in his ears and a layer of the ice surrounding his heart started to melt. Bryce squeezed his eyes shut, battling memories with everything inside him. This night was supposed to expose her vulnerabilities and leave her raw, not the other way around.

"We did have fun together back then, did we not?" she asked softly.

He nodded, not trusting his voice. There had only been that one time in his life when he had allowed himself to feel something other than hatred for everyone in his family, and that was his time with Jane. Though he and his mother had only stayed a fortnight, it had been long enough to show Bryce all he had been missing.

After that, he had been forced to return home to the man who constantly reminded him of what a soulless failure he was. The emotional abuse had continued for years. And although he had returned to Bellhaven on many occasions after that, he and Jane had never again been that close.

His hope was that tonight would change all that.

The bonfire before them kept the chill air at bay and cast a red-gold light across the frozen pond. Bryce gripped Jane's hand more securely in his own and got to his feet, taking her with him. "Would you like to see what I have planned?"

She nodded as he drew her to the pond's edge, then knelt in the snow before her, slipping pattens onto her feet. "We are going skating just like we did so many years ago." When he had finished with her pattens he slipped a larger pair over his own boots. He held out his hand and waited for her to accept him. His goal had changed. He would not push or prod or manipulate Jane tonight. What she did, she did of her own volition. He wanted her to see he could be that boy he had been so long ago—a friend and a companion.

"Do you like the idea?" he asked, tucking a flyaway strand of hair behind her ear.

Jane smiled. She could feel the night wrap around her, pulling her back into the past, until she was a young girl, standing on the edge of the pond with him. "Yes, Bryce. I like it very much. It has been so long since I have taken the time to simply have some sport."

"Tonight, sport is all I want for you."

She hesitated a moment. "Is the ice thick enough?"

"I tested it earlier. I would never endanger your life unnecessarily, Jane, you have to know that."

Despite all the mad events that had happened in the past month that made the others suspect Bryce of foul play, she did believe he would never harm her. What reason would he have for doing so? If she died, he would inherit. If she failed to marry, he would inherit. If she married him, he would inherit. Even if she married someone else, Bellhaven would be his unless she had children of her own. There were so many reasons for him not to harm her. Why would he risk everything by committing a crime that could take it all away?

She looked over the pond, with the shimmering lights around the edge, and smiled. Bryce would never harm her. He had far too much to lose if he did.

Without hesitation, she put her hand in his and together they stepped out onto the ice. Laughing, she allowed him to pull her across the slippery surface of the pond. Cool air shivered across her cheeks and tangled in her hair.

Bryce looked happier than she had seen him in many years as he twirled her around, his laughter joining hers. Backlit by the huge blanket of a starry night, his eyes were no longer filled with pain.

At the center of the pond, they stopped moving, "Thank you for this night, Bryce," she whispered. She brought her fingers up to settle over his heart. "No matter what happens with the rest of your days at Bellhaven and with the competition, will you promise me to keep a bit of the boy you were in here?"

"I did not think I could. Too much has happened to strip me of my goodness," he said, his voice tight with emotion. "But perhaps, in time . . ."

The night was full of sounds as they continued skating. The bonfire crackled and popped. A soft breeze rustled the branches of the apple trees near the pond. A hiss, a pop, and a keening whine grew ever closer.

Jane stopped skating. She looked around her.

"What is it?" Bryce asked with a frown.

"That sound."

He released her hands and turned toward the fire. "Perhaps one of the logs—"

A thunderous crash sounded.

Jane gasped at the sight of a cannonball, cleaving through the thick ice.

Time slowed. The sound of cracking filled the air. Fissures spread from the hole across the surface of the ice. The pond rocked. The ice cracked, opened, and Jane pitched forward. Her scream dwindled as she fell, ending abruptly with a loud splash.

18

Jane could hear her own breathing, sharp and gasping. Only a hand-breadth from her, Bryce reached out, trying to grab her as he, too, was swallowed up by the frigid water. Down they went, into the cold, dark depth.

Jane fought against the weight of her skirts and her cloak tugging her down. She released her cloak. Slowly, torturously, she dragged herself up with her hands, fighting for each inch, fighting to keep the darkness at bay. She needed to grab something solid. She reached out. She could not think. The black fog in her brain was paralyzing. Then air hit her face and she gulped in a breath, urging herself forward. She was lifted clear out of the water and nestled in a strong embrace.

"Praise the saints." Nicholas's voice cracked as he picked her up in his arms and pulled her against his body, his warmth. A cloak went around her shoulders, then another.

"B-Bryce?" she asked, her teeth chattering. "I-Is he a-alive?"

"David went in after him," Nicholas's voice reassured.

Her heart pounded frantically against her ribs and she heard her own panicked breathing, fast and shallow, as she waited for someone to report on Bryce's condition.

Her mind was still sluggish, still grappling with what had happened. She strained to hear over the shouts and splashing water.

"A cannonball annihilated the ice."

"God's teeth. When are we going to catch this villain?"

"From the trajectory, it looks like the weapon was fired from the south tower."

"I will go take a look."

"I see David."

"Throw me a rope."

"We got him!"

"Pull him up."

The voices all blended together as Jane shook her head, desperate to clear the fog of confusion. "I a-am b-better now," she stated, forcing a calmness she did not feel into her voice.

Nicholas set her down and tightened the cloaks about her body. "David pulled Bryce up from the bottom."

And as if they did not have enough to contend with at the moment, it started to snow. Light flakes at first, then heavier. Through a veil of white, Jane took in the scene. Bryce lay on the ground, pale and lifeless. His thoroughly soaked cloak tangled about him like a frigid cocoon. David plucked the cloak away while Colin turned him onto his side. Both men's clothes were clinging to them with wetness as they kneeled beside Bryce on the frozen ground. David pounded on Bryce's back with violent force. "Cough it up, you fool," he pleaded.

Bryce jerked, then retched, the water leaving his body. His chest moved up, then down, and a slight curl of mist coiled toward the sky.

"He is breathing," David announced, his gaze connecting with Jane's a moment before he and Colin lifted Bryce by the arms and settled his arms about their shoulders. "We must get him back to the keep."

Nicholas slipped his arm around Jane and pulled her against his side. Feeling suddenly unsteady, whether it was from the accident or his nearness she was not certain. No matter the cause, she was grateful for his support and leaned against him as they made their way back inside.

Over a murmur of voices, David, Bryce, and Colin climbed the stairs inside the great hall to the bedchambers above. Nicholas helped Jane up the stairs and they arrived at Bryce's bedchamber just as the men set him on the down-turned bedding. David piled two blankets atop Bryce's body. "Has someone sent for the doctor?" Jane asked.

"I have," Lady Margaret said as she swept into the chamber. She delivered a steaming washbasin to the bedside table. Egan followed in her wake. He sat at the edge of the bed and began to wipe away the grime from Bryce's colorless cheeks with a hot towel.

Lady Margaret's gaze shifted to Jane. "Dearest, are you unharmed?" she asked solemnly. "When I heard the news, I was so frightened."

"I am well," Jane reassured her aunt. "Bryce suffered far more injury than me."

Jules left the crowed bedside to add several fresh logs to the fire, trying to heat up the chamber and bring Bryce's temperature back to normal.

"Jane?" Bryce groaned. He reached out toward her.

Jane left Nicholas's side. She sat on the bed opposite of Egan and took her cousin's cold hand in her own shaking one. "I am here, Bryce." She smiled down at him.

He met her gaze and tried to smile. "Our evening . . . did not go . . . as planned."

She reached up and brushed a soggy lock of hair from his cheek. He was deathly pale. It filled her with a cold, expanding dread. "You are still with us. For that, I am grateful."

She caught David's gaze. "Thank you."

He nodded.

"Bryce is not the only one who needs some attention. Go, all of you, to your chambers," Lady Margaret said with a concerned frown. "Get out of your wet clothes. I have arranged for the kitchen staff to bring hot water. I say a few baths are in order tonight."

Lady Margaret caught Jane's arm and turned her toward the door. "Standing about in wet clothes will not help any of you. Egan will bathe Bryce, make him comfortable, and change him into clean clothing while we wait for the doctor to arrive."

With Lady Margaret's help, Jane continued to her chamber. She hurried to the fire that burned there and nearly stood in the grate until her chills had settled. When her hands had stopped shaking from cold, she doffed her wet clothes, washed herself in a basin of hot water, then dressed before heading down the stairs to the great hall. She paused on the bottom step, listening to her suitors, who had gathered there after their own ministrations.

"The bastard has to slip up sometime," David growled from his place at the long table. His hair was still wet, but other than that, he bore no sign that anything out of the ordinary had transpired.

"Will it be before or after someone dies?" Jules prowled the dais in agitation.

"The cannon on the south tower was still warm when I got there," Colin said, looking tidy and as handsome as ever. "But there were no clues as to who fired the weapon. None."

"As much as I hate to admit this, it is as if we are dealing with a ghost," Nicholas said, raking a hand through his hair.

"Nay!" Lord Galloway thumped his fist on the table, his brown eyes narrowing. "The villain is real. And now we know that person is not Bryce."

"Or any of the rest of us, as we were all together at the time of the attack." Colin frowned.

"Unless one of us has an agent doing their bidding," Jules retorted.

Jane shivered at the accusation. They had to find the attacker—and fast, before the men started fighting one another. She did not know why, but she was confident none of her suitors were responsible for all the attacks on her, Margaret, and now Bryce.

"Perhaps it was that man Barker, whom Bryce hired to do his bidding?" Colin suggested.

"It was not he." Jane stepped down into the chamber and approached the others. "I questioned him this afternoon, then released him. I would hazard to guess that since Bryce is now among those of us who were attacked, the attacker wants to make certain the succession of Bellhaven does not go through the Lennox-MacCallister bloodlines."

"At least we have a motive if nothing else to go on," Lord Galloway replied.

Nicholas stood and offered Jane his chair. "What do you know of the estate's holdings?"

Jane accepted the seat. "Very little other than the wealth of our estate is in the land surrounding Bellhaven. Properly farmed, it could produce far more revenue than it does now."

"Your father and brother had not seen to that with the tenants?" Jules asked with a frown.

Jane shook her head, trying to recall all her father and brother had discussed. "For some reason, Father seemed hesitant to change anything about the land. I overheard him talking with Jacob once that his men had found silver and gold particles in the ore dug from Ben Haven on the eastern border of our land."

David frowned. "They never mined the shaft?"

"Not to my knowledge," Jane replied. "Again, he seemed hesitant to do anything to alter the estate from its present way of life."

Nicholas's gaze narrowed. "Is the estate failing in any way?"

Jane paused at the question. "Nay. It produces adequately. We want for nothing, except an army to protect us."

Jules stopped his pacing. "What other motive could there be besides the inheritance of the estate?"

"Revenge," David said quietly. "My apologies, Jane, but your father was not known for his amiability."

"No offense taken," she said, catching David's eyes. "I am aware of his faults." She shuddered, closing her eyes for a brief moment, clinging to a fraying thread of hope that he and Jacob were still alive. Despite the emotional rift that had come between them after her mother's death, he was still her father and she loved him.

Jane opened her eyes. "My father was human. He made mistakes like anyone else. I am unaware of him treating anyone unfairly in his dealings with the estate."

Except her.

Jane tucked the thought away, deep inside. None of that mattered now. She straightened. The only thing that mattered, besides staying alive, was getting married in less than a week.

Five more days to be precise.

"Lady Jane," Lord Galloway said, breaking into her thoughts. "I knew your father, but not well. Did he have any other close friends who might have known more about his activities than perhaps his own family?"

"The only two friends in the peerage who visited here often were Lord Fairfield and Lord Wigan. Both sent messengers expressing their condolences shortly after my father failed to return from that last battle. When it later became known that Jacob might have been lost as well, Lord Fairfield came himself." She drew in a short, sharp breath at the memory of her father's friend's arrival; at his daring proposal to make her his mistress and take over her land without so much as a fight.

Nicholas caught her expression, his frown deepening. "What did he want?"

For a heartbeat she was tempted to remind him of his soiling of her name and opening her up to indecent proposals like the one Lord Fairfield had offered. Then she drew another breath and changed her mind. They had been down that road before. Nicholas claimed he had not hurt her. She knew otherwise.

When she did not reply, Nicholas stood. "Let us bring Lord Fairfield here and ask him ourselves."

"Nay," Jane said, scraping the chair against the floor in her haste to stand. "I will not have that man in this castle. Never again." Jane locked her cold hands together, suddenly jittery and afraid. Lord Fairfield only reminded her of the things she could not control in her life. Her anxiety heightened a notch as she backed away from the table. "You will obey my wishes on this, Sir Nicholas, or you will be dismissed from this competition."

Nicholas watched as Jane's expression closed, shuttered.

Her lips thinned. "Do you hear me?" She straightened and looked haughtily at him.

The look in her eyes dared him to challenge her. He would do nothing to jeopardize his place in the competition for her hand. "I will not bring him to the castle." His voice came out as a resigned growl.

"Good." With a crisp nod she turned and left the room.

All eyes turned to him. They were all silent a moment before Jules asked, "What was that about?"

Nicholas frowned. While he did not understand what had just happened, he intended to find out. And while he had given her a promise not to bring the man inside the castle, he had said nothing of going to the man himself.

Jane did not want him to talk to Lord Fairfield, which only increased his desire to seek the man out.

"I suddenly feel unwell. I will see you all on the morrow," he said to the others before heading for the stairs.

He had no intention of going anywhere near his chamber. As soon as he walked up the front stairs, he headed down the back ones, out of the keep, and to the stables, where he readied his horse and mounted.

As stealthily as possible, he rode from the stables and quickly crossed to the iron portcullis. He commanded Angus to raise the gate, then slipped over the drawbridge and into the night. The horse's hoofbeats were muffled by the ankle-deep snow as he set his steed to flight. Of a common hue with the night, the pair were quickly swallowed by the darkness.

It was under that core of darkness that Nicholas hurried toward his goal.

For some reason, he and Jane had taken a step backward tonight. She was irritated with him about something that had to do with Lord Fairfield.

Filled with grim determination, Nicholas guided his horse over the snow-covered land. He would see Lord Fairfield and have his answers before the night was through.

Jane slipped into Bryce's chamber later that evening, eager to see how her cousin fared after his accident. As she approached the bed, Bryce turned toward her, his blue eyes glittering in the candlelight. "You will be well soon," she said, taking a seat next to the bedside. "You and I are both lucky to have escaped unharmed."

"I am sorry I took you out there."

Jane frowned. "You had no idea someone would fire a cannon at the pond."

He nodded, slowly. "I should have thought of your safety. This bastard seems to have no reservations about attacking you whenever and wherever he can."

She was silent for a moment before asking, "How do you feel?"

He smiled faintly. "Like my head is going to explode."

She shivered. "If that cannonball had landed a few more paces to the left—"

"I would have been killed."

Jane shuddered at the stark brutality of the words. "Yes, but I am glad you were not." She reached out and took his hand in hers. "Is there anything I can do for you?"

He shook his head. "But there is something I can give to you." He reached for the rolled papers on the bedside and handed them to Jane. "This is all the information I gathered on each of your suitors. Use it however you will."

Jane smiled down at him, allowing her pleasure to flow into that smile. "You are a good person, Bryce. I always knew you were."

"Thank you for believing in me." He squeezed her fingers.

"There has to be something I can do for you, Bryce. Name it."

"Marry me," he said with a teasing, half-hearted smile.

Jane sighed. "Something other than that."

"Stay with me for a while." His voice faded and his eyes drifted closed. In another moment he was sleeping soundly.

Jane leaned back in her chair and studied his face. There were so many things she did not know about her cousin. Such as why he struck out at the world before it had a chance to strike him, or why he covered his emotions with a devil-may-care attitude.

Deep in her heart, she knew he was not the one responsible for her accidents. But they had better figure out who was, and quickly, before anyone else was caught in a murderer's web.

"I will take it from here, Hemsley." Closing the door on the servant who had escorted him in, Nicholas strode into Lord Fairfield's dining room and interrupted his supper.

Lord Fairfield looked up at the intrusion. "Who are you and what are you doing here?"

Pulling out a chair on the opposite side of the table, Nicholas dropped into it. "I am Sir Nicholas Kincaid, and I am looking for you."

The middle-aged man with a balding head set down his fork with a thump. "Why?"

"Because I need answers."

The older gentleman narrowed his gaze on Nicholas. "And you think whatever you seek 'tis important enough to disturb a man's dinner," he said with a deep sigh.

At Nicholas's nod, the man picked up his fork and knife and started attacking the piece of meat disguised by a thick brown gravy in the center of his plate. "Answers about what?"

"Lord Lennox and his daughter Lady Jane. Do you know them?"

"You know I do or you would not be here disturbing me." Lord Fairfield did not look up from his plate as he continued to cut his meat into bite-sized pieces.

"Why would someone want to harm the heir to Bellhaven Castle?" Nicholas inquired.

Lord Fairfield looked up and frowned. "By heir, do you mean Lady Jane Lennox?"

"Aye."

Lord Fairfield's face reddened. "Then nay, I have nothing to say on the matter."

Nicholas yanked the plate away at the same moment he plucked the knife from Lord Fairfield's hand, pointedly studying the blade. "I would start talking if I were you."

The man sat back, his expression a mixture of anger and fear. "What do you want to know?"

"Let us start with Lord Lennox. Who were his enemies?"

Lord Fairfield swallowed roughly as his gaze settled on the sharp knife. "Lennox was a very secretive man. Even though I have known him for half my life, I barely scratched the surface of the true nature of the man."

Nicholas set the knife down, but still within his reach, and returned the plate to Lord Fairfield. "Can you give me some specifics?"

Lord Fairfield continued eating. "He had a lifelong feud with the MacGuire clan."

"About what?"

He shrugged as he chewed. "I little know, or care."

A moment ticked past. Nicholas picked up the knife.

Lord Fairfield sighed. "Lennox and Seamus MacGuire had no love for each other. Something to do with the clan leader's daughter."

Nicholas leaned forward, confronting him directly. "Anyone else?"

Lord Fairfield shook his head and continued to eat.

"Then tell me, what is *your* relationship with Lady Jane Lennox?"

Lord Fairfield's head came up and he frowned. "The vixen deserves her fate."

Nicholas rolled the blade in his hand, keeping his growing irritation at bay.

After a second Lord Fairfield added, "I went to see her after I heard of her brother's death."

Nicholas sharpened his gaze. "See her or challenge her for her father's lands?"

He returned Nicholas's gaze, his expression tightly checked. "Very well, if you must know the truth, I challenged her. I offered her my protection in return for Bellhaven. I figured a girl of her nature would need someone to warm her bed before too long."

Nicholas clenched his fist around the knife. "You offered her marriage?"

"Take a woman of her reputation to wife?" Lord Fairfield smiled without humor. "Nay, I offered to take her as my mistress."

Anger flared in Nicholas's gut at Lord Fairfield. "Her reputation?"

Lord Fairfield flicked him a look that was part irritation, part assessment. He picked up his last morsel, chewed, swallowed, then set his fork aside. "I am an old man. I could use a little passion and seduction in my life before I die. But that harpy refused my protection. She deserves whatever disaster soon comes her way."

Passion and seduction. Those words twisted inside him. Momentarily, he forced the emotions away. "What kind of disaster?" Nicholas asked through gritted teeth.

"The clans all know what kind of woman she is. Fast and loose. And with no male to protect her, she will be attacked, and by an army much greater than mine in time."

"Whose army?"

"The MacGuires, the MacLeans, even the crown once they learn she is holding the castle and lands on her own. 'Tis anyone's guess."

Nicholas stood and brought the knife down right next to Lord Fairfield's hand. "Lady Jane Lennox has an army. And as for her reputation, the woman has been wronged. You spread *those* words to the clans." The words fell from Nicholas's lips, but inside his brain a connection finally clicked. Jane's anger at him upon his arrival. Her accusation that he had hurt her, harmed her reputation with their innocent dalliance. Her words of forgiveness for a wrong he had no notion of committing.

Jane had been wronged. Not by him, but because of him. Someone had spread rumors, rumors that were believed and acted upon by men like the one before him.

Nicholas pushed back from the table. "Never set foot on Bellhaven land again, or it is my blade you will have to face. Do you understand?"

His pallor a sudden ghostly white, Lord Fairfield nodded. "I understand."

An urgent need built inside Nicholas. He could hardly speak, could not think. The emotions churning inside him were so deep, so powerful, he was not certain he could step toward the door. Without knowing it, he had harmed Jane. Two years ago he had made no secret of his affection for her in front of her servants. Had one of them spread the vicious lies about her?

But he was also at fault. In fact, he was entirely to blame for leaving her behind to face the ridicule alone. On legs that felt wooden, he pushed himself forward, out the door, and to his horse. He sucked in a huge breath of the cool night air, grateful that it revived his senses.

He had to see Jane.

Tonight.

Dear God in heaven, what had he done to her by leaving her two years ago?

Jane heard footsteps in the hall that stopped in front of her door.

She sat up in her bed. At the pause in footfalls, her heartbeat stumbled and she reached for the dagger beneath her pillow. The weapon firmly in her grip, she rose, heading to the door. A soft rapping sounded an instant before the door opened.

"Jane?" Nicholas entered, but paused at the door, his hand catching the frame as though he needed something solid to support him. His gaze moved from her head to her toes and back again.

Heat flooded her cheeks at his perusal of her in her night rail. Jane lowered her dagger, her fingers suddenly numb at the sight of him. She stepped back toward her bed and reached for her dressing gown, but her fingers would not cooperate in lifting the cloth from the bed. "What do you want?" she asked, folding her hands over her chest, shielding herself from his view.

His face was pale, his eyes as tumultuous and dark as the snow-laden clouds from this afternoon. "What a fool I have been," Nicholas said, his voice raw, harsh. "I never intended to hurt you." He shut the door behind him and moved toward her.

A stark, sudden fear descended. "You went to see Lord Fairfield," she said, her voice barely above a whisper.

Halting before her, he searched her face in a way that no one else did. He saw through her bravado, he saw straight to her soul. "I—I had no idea how deeply I hurt you, until tonight. I never spread those rumors about you, but someone who witnessed our passionate exchanges did. And I did nothing to counter their effects on you."

"I asked you not to go to him." Her mind was reeling, her mouth went dry.

"Which is why I went." His lips curled into a brittle, bitter smile. "Toss me out of the competition if you must, but I had to know why he upset you so."

Tears burned at the back of her throat. "He treats me as so many others do. Whether you spread the rumors or not, the words hurt me in ways you could never imagine."

"Aye," he agreed in a solemn tone. "And I am sorry."

For a second she could not breathe. She had longed to hear those words from him. She looked into the tumult of his gaze—saw his hurt, his remorse.

And all the pain and anxiety she had suppressed rose up and swamped her. Tears built on her lashes and she let them fall as the wall she had built between them disappeared like mist.

He reached out and brushed the tears from her cheeks. "I am so sorry," he repeated. The words fell from him, straight from his heart. "Can you ever forgive me?"

The words tumbled through her brain. She had already forgiven him when he had denied her claim. Now that he accepted what he had done, or what been done to them, she hesitated. "If you want the truth, a scar remains, will always remain. But I do not feel animosity toward you anymore."

"Where do we go from here?" he asked.

"I do not know."

"I do not know all the answers either, Jane. But I do know I want to kiss you." He bent his head, but stopped just before her lips.

"It is a beginning," she said on a whisper. He waited a heartbeat as if to allow her time to sense his hunger, then closed the gap between them. His kiss was soft, tender, coaxing, and one she might have resisted if she had put her mind to it, but she did not.

Jane found herself pulled deeper into his arms and into his kiss. He kissed her until all rational thought vanished, until she was breathless, and achy in strange places, and thinking of things she had no intention of thinking about—sins she had had no intention of committing. And yet she could not pull away.

He lifted his head and looked into her eyes, his heavy-lidded with passion and desire. The fire that had apparently never stopped burning between them leapt once more to life, fully, greedily, eager for more.

But acting upon those feelings would only complicate matters. She ran through all the reasons she should push him away in her mind. She had to finish the competition. She owed the others a chance, if she was to be fair. She did not want to do anything that might impede Jules's progress toward achieving a physical recovery. And, if truth be told, she was still uncertain about Nicholas. But that uncertainty did not hold her back at the moment. Instead, she allowed the flames of desire to surge forward. Throwing all her reservations aside, Jane lifted up on her toes and pressed her lips to his. He moaned at the contact and cupped her face in his hands while he returned her kiss.

Jane tasted him, really tasted him, as she had never done before. As they explored each other, she could feel him all the way to her soul. She had missed his warmth, his presence, the way only he could make her feel.

In his arms she was no longer invisible, as the women in her father's castle were supposed to be. With him, she was free to rejoice in the pure sensuality he brought her, without guilt and without reservation. Someone had called her a passionate seductress, but only for him had she ever felt such need, such desire.

Heat poured through her, welled, and spread to every nerve in her body. She could feel the same helpless reaction in him. Need and desire infused them both as his hands left her waist, smoothed over her sides to grip her back and pull her into the hard ridge of his desire.

"Jane," he whispered against her lips. "If we continue in this way, there may be no going back."

"There was no going back from the moment you stepped into this chamber." She pressed against him in flagrant invitation. She reached up and tunneled her fingers through his hair, then ran her fingers over his chest, slowly, provocatively, until he shuddered.

They had been moving toward this moment since he had first arrived at Bellhaven. And in this moment, she knew there was no turning back. With a desperation she had never felt before, she longed to touch his body, to delight in the powerful sinew that outlined his chest, to experience his flesh against her own.

Need and desire infused her. Without taking her lips from his, she pushed the plait of his plaid over his shoulder at the same moment he released his belt. The fabric fell from his body to pool onto the floor.

Her night rail followed along with his linen shirt until they both stood flesh to flesh as his tongue plundered her mouth, taunting, inciting, demanding. He gave her what she longed for as he joined her in their sensual exploration. She was not certain when they moved back toward the bed. But as the back of her knees hit the edge of the bed, she allowed him to lower her down against the cool linen sheet.

Nicholas lay down beside her as all reservation fled and only desire ruled. Scorching heat flowed between them as his hands explored her back, her buttocks, rocking her against his passion.

Jane savored the firm yet silken flesh beneath her hands, branding him as hers. His lips left her mouth to travel over her neck, her shoulder, and finally to her breasts. Rational thought incinerated in a torrent of flames as desire swelled.

A primitive shudder of anticipation ran down her spine as he brushed his fingers over her breasts, the flat of her stomach, and down further still as he claimed every inch of her skin. He moved skillfully and slowly, claiming her, branding her, with each caress. It was as if he were memorizing her body while he laid his heart and soul before her.

The yearning tension on his face propelled her forward. She arched against him. Fire, hunger, and emptiness drove her. *Emptiness.* She had no notion why she felt that way, only that there was something more she yearned for, needed.

He must have sensed that need because he moved over her, parting her thighs with his knee. He moved between her thighs and brushed his hand over the curls surrounding her womanhood. "So soft," he said, bending down to touch her nipple with his tongue.

The muscles of her stomach clenched as a bolt of heat shot through her, igniting every nerve in her body. Again that sensation of emptiness filled her. "Nicholas." His name was a yearning and a prayer.

"Soon, my love. Very soon," he said as though understanding what it was she needed. His hands settled between her thighs, to stroke her, part her folds, and he slid a finger deep into her sheath, filling her as he slid in and out. She moaned when a second finger joined the first, stretching her, reducing her to gasping, trembling need with every slow, possessive thrust.

She gasped when he drew back. Her senses slowed, and she nearly cried out until he leaned in and she felt the blunt head of his erection at her entrance. He reached down with his hands and tilted her hips up just as his lips captured hers in another mind-numbing kiss.

He thrust forward.

She tensed, overtaken by pain, then fullness at their joining. The pain faded as sensation after sensation coiled inside when he slowly began to move. He stretched her, filled her, possessed her.

Completed her.

She closed her eyes and let the feeling swamp her senses with both pleasure and need, until she arched against him, wanting even more. The sensations were all-consuming, intense beyond measure, surging deep inside in a fiery shower that had her gasping and struggling to breathe. Her climax came hard and fast, rolling over her, claiming her. In that instant she surrendered to the glorious bliss that disconnected her from the earthly world and sent her to hover among the stars.

Nicholas shuddered as a wave of delight more intense than he had ever experienced rocked every nerve in his body. His breathing ragged, he collapsed beside Jane, still entwined with her as intimately as before. What had come over him? He had not come here with the intent of seduction. He had wanted to apologize to her, to beg her forgiveness, nothing more. When his strength returned, he disengaged and lifted off her to settle against her side.

They lay there entwined forever. Then with a trembling laugh, Jane tried to draw away. "We should right ourselves before—"

"Morning?" he suggested. He reached down and drew the edge of the coverlet over the top of them. "Let me remain a few moments more."

She smiled.

He lifted a hand to her face, touched her cheek, traced the outline of her upper lip. He wondered suddenly how a man could survive longing for a woman so much. Battle, he was used to. Abuse, he had endured. But if Jane wanted to reach inside him right now and grab his soul, then crush it in her palm, he would let her. He would do anything for her. He would marry her this instant if she chose him. He would even walk away from the competition if that was what she needed him to do.

For a second his heart contracted. Could he walk away after what they had just shared? He had been the first. But now that he truly had initiated her, would she fall into the arms of any of her other suitors?

He bit his lip, afraid suddenly to ask that question or to say any words that, once spoken, would end this moment between them and return her to the others. His heart raced as he turned to look into her face. He saw peace and satisfaction there, and that lessened his anxiety somewhat.

"That was not supposed to happen." She drew a long, shuddering breath. "We never were able to control our passion for each other."

"That is not a bad thing in a couple." He let the words slip past his caution. He studied her, gauging her response.

"I imagine it could prove inconvenient at times," she said as she nestled against his shoulder.

"Passion is never inconvenient. It is a gift. You will see that in time." A long, tender moment ticked by. His heartbeat gradually slowed, his breathing eased.

She looked up at him. "I should throw you out of the competition for ignoring my wishes."

At the words, his whole world tilted. He had to speak the words she did not. He had to know. "Must the competition continue? After tonight—"

"Tonight changes nothing," she said softly, stroking his chest with her fingers. He could see the storm that had gathered in her eyes. She was as confused about what they were to each other as he was. "I made a vow when the competition started to see it through to the end. I will follow through on that commitment."

He understood, or at least he told himself he did. "If you must see this through, then at least allow me to stay in the competition. For how will I win if I am not involved?"

Her fingers stilled and a teasing smile came to her lips. "Then by all means, you must compete."

201

He stroked a hand lovingly down her back, her waist, her thigh. "I might have to remind you again what you would be giving up. . . ."

In response to his touch, she arched against him, then caught herself and pulled back. "You do not fight fair." Her voice lowered, her tone provocative.

"With you at stake, never." Tonight, together, they had taken a step back through time, as though the past two years had not mattered. Every kiss, every touch, every moment had been the fulfillment of what they had started so long ago.

He cast a sidelong glance at Jane, breathed in the scent of roses that clung to her skin. While he could not claim her as his tonight, he was not about to hand her over to his competition, either.

In fact, now that he had had a deeper taste of the raw passion and unquenchable need that flared between them, he would not give it up without a fight.

20

❄

The following morning, Nicholas and the other four remaining suitors gathered in the kitchen. Bryce sat in a chair near the table at the center of the room. He had recovered from his trauma of last night. He appeared as eager as the rest of them to get this morning's competition over with so they could continue to search for clues to Jane's attacker. This time, Bryce's intentions seemed honest. Last night's danger had changed him, seemingly for the better.

Bringing his attention back to the moment, Nicholas looked about the small chamber. Marthe stood in the corner near the hearth, surveying her domain. Nicholas knew she did not like having to share her space with others, but today's cooking competition demanded it. The cook smiled at Jules, then frowned at Nicholas, her eyes narrowing.

At least now he truly understood why.

Nicholas returned a bright smile, one designed to weaken the knees of women in even the foulest of moods.

Marthe's cheeks turned pink a heartbeat before she turned away.

Nicholas's confidence grew. Before the day was through, he would once again be in Marthe's good graces, and receive the one gift he considered most sacred—time alone with Jane.

"Good morrow, gentlemen," Jane said as she entered the kitchen, followed by Lord Galloway and her aunt.

"What a fine day it is for our second to last competition." Lady Margaret appeared to be in the best of health this morning. In fact, in Lord Galloway's presence, the woman's appearance had altered. Her cheeks had taken on a rosy tint and her gray eyes sparkled. She appeared far more vibrant than she had three days prior.

Margaret stopped beside Marthe and whispered something to the cook, to which she bobbed her head, then left. On her way out the door, she gave Jules a conspiring wink.

Jules preened, and Nicholas knew a moment's fear at the realization that Marthe had helped Jules come up with something to cook that might just win him the prize.

Nicholas caught Jules's gaze and curled his lips into a bitter smile. Nicholas was prepared to battle it out on the field of honor or over a hot flame. He cared not which. Jane would be his tonight, and all nights thereafter.

"Just as with the sewing competition, you will each have access to the supplies available on this table and in this room. Nothing more. You will be given two hours to cook something with a holiday theme for Lady Jane. Use your imagination and do your best."

"We can truly cook anything we choose?" Colin asked. He sat opposite Bryce at the big table in the center of the kitchen. "I could make blood pudding in the shape of a wreath, if I choose?"

Margaret's smile slipped. "I repeat, you have two hours and you can make whatever you like. Jane will be the judge, so I would keep that in mind as you prepare your entry." She looked pointedly at Colin. "I might suggest playing to the judge if you want to win."

Colin's expression turned serious as he stared at the items on the table. "Eggs, butter, flour, oats. What if we do not know how to bake?"

"You have to cook something," Lady Margaret said, edging for the door.

"Just try your best," Jane reassured Colin with a smile, then glanced about the chamber. "I am eager to see what you all come up with."

Margaret allowed Jane to precede her out of the chamber, then turned back to the room, gazing at each man. "No cheating this time." On those words she closed the door behind her.

Colin groaned the moment the women were gone. "I am doomed to failure."

"Cheer up," Bryce said with a half-hearted smile. "None of the rest of us know how to cook or bake either."

"Speak for yourself," Jules replied, scooping up a portion of the butter from the crock on the table and heading toward a wooden bowl on another, smaller table near the open window.

David added his own groan to the bunch. "Great, a true baker to show us all up the way Lord Galloway did with the sewing."

Nicholas moved to the table and inspected the items left there for their use. "Do not write off this competition yet. We each have the same chance to win if we actually prepare something. The only way to assuredly lose is to not even try."

"Well said," Bryce commented, reaching for the oats at the same moment David did.

David snatched them away.

Bryce stood, then paled and sat back down.

"I need oats, too," Colin growled, moving toward David with his hand on his sword.

"Use them when I am done," David moved to a small table near the hearth with such deliberate slowness that Nicholas knew it was his way of letting Colin know just how small of a threat he thought the warrior was.

Colin growled, drew his sword, and lunged for David.

Nicholas grabbed an iron pan from the wall and stepped between them. A loud clang resounded as the sword hit the pan. "Enough. You are squabbling like little girls."

205

Colin's lips thinned. "The only other thing I know how to make is with oats," he groused.

When the fight died in Colin's eyes, Nicholas stepped away, moving toward the shelf and grasping another bowl. Without argument, he took the bowl of oats from David and poured half into the new bowl, then set them on the table between Colin and Bryce. "I trust you two can share?"

"I never said I would not share," David grumbled and turned his back on the room.

"We had best stop fighting and get to work. We only have two hours to come up with something acceptable." Nicholas turned back to the table, inspecting the ingredients once more.

"Something palatable," Jules offered as he stirred what looked like sugar into the butter he had claimed earlier. Satisfaction warmed his features as he surveyed the others. "Lady Jane will decide which offering tastes the best. If they all taste like oats, it will be the unique taste that wins this challenge."

Colin's face darkened again. His fist curled. "God's blood."

Nicholas locked gazes with Colin. "Cooking, not fighting, will win you this event."

Colin released a pent-up breath. "I hate cooking."

"So do the rest of us," Bryce added with a half smile. "Ignore Jules, Colin. Cook whatever you can. Who knows, maybe it will be Lady Jane's favorite."

Colin fell silent as he took another bowl from the shelf and poured some of the oats into it, then set to work.

For the next hour, the men chopped, mixed, and molded. Colin, still angry with David, picked up a handful of flour and tossed it in his direction, coating his dark-hair in a film of tannish-white.

"Very nice," David said, blowing flour off his face. In retaliation, he picked up a scoop of flour and dusted the blond warrior from head to toe, as well as all the surfaces around him.

"Do not insult a man's cooking before you have tasted it," Colin quipped.

Over the next hour, David and Colin continued their battle back and forth, sometimes catching Bryce or Jules or Nicholas in the process.

David focused his attention on creating a Scotch Pie with what appeared to be a thin, flaky crust filled with kidneys and potatoes. As for the oats he had fought to control, he merely ground up a small portion with a pestle and tossed them into the gravy as a thickener. The puffs of flour that headed his direction with regularity did not seem to harm his recipe in the least.

Colin spent the first hour trying to mix pork blood and oatmeal together to make blood pudding, but when he realized he had nothing to stuff the concoction into, he abandoned the mixture and simply mixed butter, oats, flour and salt together to make oak cakes that he cooked in a pan over the fire.

Bryce remained seated at the table for the first hour, concocting a mass of dough with flour, breadcrumbs, currants, suet, honey, spices and milk to bind it together.

"What are you making," Nicholas finally asked when Bryce dumped the mass of dough in a square of linen, then set it in a pot that fit inside the huge cauldron over the open flames.

After setting his dumpling to cook, he returned to his seat at the table. "My mother used to call it a Clootie Dumpling." He preened a moment before a swath of flour hit him square in the face.

He frowned. "Your flour cannot harm my dumpling," he shot back at David.

"Perhaps not, but I can make you look like a fool with flour all over you," David said with a chuckle.

Bryce's frown deepened. He batted at his hair.

Nicholas ignored their continued discussion as he turned his attention to Jules. Jules had had his back turned to them for most of the time that they had been cooking. When he turned around, it was to reveal a pan of thin almond cookies in the shape of holly leaves.

At the sight, Nicholas's frown deepened. Marthe had helped Jules come up with one of Jane's favorites.

Jules smiled with satisfaction as he crossed the room, heading for the bread oven. He carefully set the delicate pastries on the heated surface to cook.

207

A moment of self-doubt hit Nicholas square in the gut as he looked over his competition. Would his simple dessert be good enough to go head-to-head with David's pie, or Jules's cookies? He drew a deep breath and let the anxiety slip away. He was doing the right thing. The recipe he had found would be the perfect creation for Jane, for the competition.

Jules had been right about one thing, if everything tasted like oats, what did not would certainly stand out. Nicholas looked about the kitchen for the proper tool. The butter churn sat in the corner near the door. He picked it up and chuckled to himself. His creation would be safe from flour or anything else that might attempt to sabotage him. On that happy thought, Nicholas set to work.

Time passed rapidly. When the chapel bell tolled the second hour, Jane and Lady Margaret, escorted by Lord Galloway, stepped inside the chamber.

Jane appeared serene as she walked through the door, but Nicholas knew she was anything but. He caught the telltale hitch of her breath, the shadow of nervousness in her violet eyes, and the slight defiant lift of her chin. "Your time is up, gentlemen," she said, then stopped, mid-step, as her gaze moved about the chamber.

"Good heavens," Lady Margaret cried as she entered the kitchen. "What has happened here?"

Flour was everywhere. On the floor, the table, the ceiling, and on each of the men. Nicholas dusted the flour from the front of his plaid, then scrubbed sugar from his fingertips.

Marthe slipped in behind Jane and came to a halt at the door. "Merciful heavens. You have ruined my lovely kitchen." Her wild gaze traveled about the chamber and came to rest on Nicholas. "Which of you rapscallions did this?"

David's expression clouded and Colin's lips thinned.

"We are all responsible and we will all clean up the mess when Lady Jane is through with her judging," Nicholas replied.

The cook muttered under her breath and crossed her arms over her ample chest, watching all of them from the doorway. "No one leaves until *I* say 'tis clean."

"Anyone want to go first?" Jane asked, no doubt eager to turn the conversation away from the horrible mess they had created.

"Will it make you look more kindly on our cooking?" Bryce asked. "If so, then I volunteer."

With a smile Jane stepped toward Bryce. "I am certain all of your creations are wonderful." Her smiled faded a moment later as she looked upon Bryce's offering. The overly large brown blob of dough with currants poking out at odd angles was wet and shiny, and left a film of brown liquid on the platter beneath.

Jane worked her lower lip with her teeth. "What is it?" she asked hesitantly.

"You do not have to eat any since it is not quite ready yet," Bryce explained, with a sheepish look. "The Clootie needs to sit by the fire to dry for a while, but I ran out of time."

Jane nodded as a look of relief washed over her face. "Then let me judge your creation by smell." She bent down and inhaled deeply, then smiled. "It smells good." Her voice held a note of surprise. "Why would you consider this a Christmastide dish?"

"My mother used to make a Clootie Dumpling every year for Christmas Eve." Sorrow lingered in his tone. "Cooking this treat today made me realize how much I miss her." He stared down at his dish with a frown. "It might be the memory that is more delicious than the actual dumpling," he admitted.

Jane nodded. "Sometimes that is the case, but I am certain we will all enjoy your treat when it is finished."

Jane moved to David next. Her gaze skated over his pie with intrigue. "Very impressive, David. Why did you make a pie?"

"It is the only dish I know how to make. I did add a small flourish of holly cut from dough." He pointed to the center of the pie with his knife. He cut her a thin slice with a portion of the holly leaf, then offered it to her.

Jane took a bite of the savory pie and chewed, and chewed, and chewed.

"What is wrong?" David asked.

Jane brought her hand up to her mouth. "It is a little tough."

David cut a small bite and popped it into his mouth. His expression darkened. "The crust is like leather." He glared at Colin. "Too much flour."

Colin picked up one of his oatcakes and tasted it. "God's teeth," he growled and tossed the uneaten portion back into the pan. "They taste like wood. Nay," he clarified, "they taste worse than wood." The depths of his disappointment shone in his eyes.

"At least you both *can* cook when, perhaps, less flour is involved," she offered with a note of cheer as she moved on to Jules.

Jules's earlier confidence was no longer present as he held out a plate of brown and black cookies toward Jane. "Your favorite?"

"Almond cookies." Her gaze moved to the cook hovering near the door. "I see Marthe has a clear favorite." Jane accepted one of the less burned offerings and took a small bite. She chewed carefully, then flicked the remnants of charred almonds from her lips. "They are delicious, Jules. A little burned, but delicious nonetheless."

"Ye burned the cookies?" Marthe shook her head. "How could ye burn the cookies? I gave you precise directions of what to do." She frowned at Jules.

Jules bristled. "The oven was hotter than expected. They might look a bit burned, but they taste all right. Jane said so herself." He popped one of the thin cookies into his mouth, then frowned. "No they do not." His gaze caught and held Jane's. "They taste terrible." He snatched the cookie from her hand and returned it to the plate. "So much for my cooking skills. Only one more contestant to go."

All eyes turned to Nicholas.

Nicholas's heart sped up as he reached behind him for a shallow pan with a thin piece of linen over the top.

"What is it?" Jane stepped closer, peering at the dish with raised brows.

Nicholas pulled the linen back to reveal his snowy white creation. Not a hint of flour dusted the surface, only a thin layer of glistening sugar. "I call it snow."

"Snow?" Jane, Lady Margaret, and Marthe all repeated at the same time.

Marthe hurried across the room to peek at his entry. She frowned. "It doesn't appear to be cooked at all. 'Tis just cream."

"There you are wrong." He handed Jane a spoon. "I frothed cream, rose-water, and sugar together, then dusted it with more sugar. If you look closely, the sugar on top has been crystalized with heat."

"It looks like snow." Jane exclaimed as she punctured the delicate surface with her spoon. On her spoon, his creation sparkled like diamonds in the candlelight. She brought it to her lips and tasted it.

Nicholas watched Jane work her tongue against the fluffy cream, and heat stirred in his veins. He had to win this competition. If only to keep the others away from her. "What do you think?"

She closed her eyes and drew a slow, even breath. "It tastes like heaven," she moaned. "Sweet, light, and unique. It looks like a snowy Christmas morning. Definitely a winner."

The words he had longed to hear.

Groans of disappointment filled the room. Those groans turned to appreciative responses as Jane passed the "snow" about the room for the others to try.

The last to judge his creation was Marthe. She scooped up a big spoonful and tasted. A heartbeat later her eyes widened and she smiled. "Wherever did you get this recipe?"

"From you." He moved to the back wall and reached on the top shelf of the cupboard for her one and only cookbook. *Excellent and Approved Recipes and Experiments in Cooking.* "Without your help, I never would have won this competition. Thank you." He leaned close and pressed a kiss to the cook's cheek.

"You devil you." Marthe turned red from her neck to her forehead. "You have won yourself time alone with Lady Jane, after you men clean up my kitchen." She looked pointedly at each of them.

"Not to worry, Marthe," Jules said, picking up a broom from the corner. "We can clean better than we cook."

"What are your plans for Lady Jane?" Bryce asked with suspicion. "I hope you will do something to keep her safe."

"That was my intention," Nicholas replied, catching Jane's gaze. "For our time alone, I give you the gift of time alone."

At Jane's quizzical expression he explained, "I want you to enjoy a bath in your chamber while the rest of us spend the evening tearing this castle apart. It is time for us to gain the upper hand before the villain strikes again."

"That is quite a sacrifice." Lord Galloway took Lady Margaret's hands and drew her to him, holding her close. "You would give up time alone with Lady Jane in order to protect her?"

"I will do anything and everything to see Lady Jane safe."

"A true hero." Lady Margaret nestled into Lord Galloway's arms.

Not a hero, Nicholas corrected. Simply a man desperate to win Jane's love for a lifetime.

Nicholas gathered with the men in the great hall after supper that evening. "We will work in teams of two. I want every room in this castle thoroughly inspected. Look at every wall, every surface. Use the candelabras to determine if there is airflow in a room where there should be none."

"The villain is getting around the castle without being seen. There must be an explanation for this," David added.

"Another explanation besides the supernatural." Jules arched his brows in amused challenge.

"Besides a ghost," Lord Galloway echoed. "What need have they for secret passageways?"

"I still cannot believe you gave up time alone with Lady Jane for this." Bryce shook his head.

"Perhaps that was my plan all along." Nicholas smiled. "What better way to earn Lady Jane's good graces than to sacrifice our time alone for her welfare?"

David raised his brows. "Excellent foresight."

Jules frowned. "Let us stop wasting time. I want to find whoever is after the Lennoxes and their heirs. So tell me, Nicholas, what exactly are we looking for?"

"You gave me the idea after you said you retrieved Jane's doll, Meriwether. We now know there is at least one priest's hole left over from the persecution. The Lennoxes would have been sympathetic to the plight of the Catholics. They could have built one or more secret passageways or hiding places."

"Are we to tear down the paneling and pull up floorboards?" Colin asked.

"Nay," Nicholas replied. "Priest holes were usually situated in places where there might have been empty space—as an offshoot of a chimney, in an attic, beneath a staircase."

"We should be able to hear the hollowness of the walls by tapping on them," David offered. "I know at Hathaway Hall we have a priest hole that connects with the garderobe. My ancestor's theory was that no one would ever want to look there, therefore those hiding in the empty space off the exit hole would be fairly safe."

"Brilliant," Jules agreed.

"Often the hiding places were subterranean in nature, with the passages evolving into a thousand windings to discourage the priest hunters," Nicholas explained. "Do not discount the floorboards."

"Where do we start?" Lord Galloway asked, coming to his feet.

"You and Bryce take the great hall, the buttery, and the servants' hall," Nicholas said, motioning toward the doorway. "David and Colin, you take the south and east wing and towers. Jules and I will explore the north and west wing and towers. Whoever finishes their exploration first, move down to the storage rooms."

The men departed to their assigned spaces, leaving Jules and Nicholas alone. "Where do you want to start?" he asked his friend.

"I want to go back to the north tower. All the sightings of Lady Lennox's ghost there have to mean something." Jules straightened and a look of determination shone in his eyes.

"Sounds as good a place as any other," Nicholas agreed.

They left the chamber and proceeded up the stairs to the hallway where he and Jane had previously explored. For the next hour, they tapped on every inch of the walls and floor, finding nothing.

"If we continue at this pace, it will take us well past Christmas to complete our search." Disappointment laced Jules's voice. "I say we split up and cover twice the territory."

Nicholas frowned. "You may be right; however, what if you come into contact with—"

"Do not be my nursemaid, Nicholas." Jules's hand went to the sword at his left hip. "I am stronger than I look."

Nicholas knew better than to argue with him. He simply nodded and asked, "Where do you want to look next?"

"I will take the west tower. What about you?"

Nicholas returned his gaze to the long hallway before him. "I will keep searching the bedchambers."

On a nod, Jules left him for the tower.

Nicholas drew a fortifying breath and moved to the bedchamber on his left. This chamber had been assigned to Lord Galloway. Nicholas entered. He inspected each wall, each nook, each divot in the floorboards, to no avail. He had similar results in Colin and David's chambers. Bryce's chamber had a layout similar to the others he had just inspected. However, when he studied the chamber, he could not help but think something in this room was different.

The room faced northwest, receiving the light from the morning sun through the chamber's only window. Nicholas frowned. That was odd. The other rooms he had searched had sported two windows that had once been shuttered and were now fixed with glass panes.

Nicholas closed his eyes and tried to imagine what this wall of the castle looked like from outside. This aspect of the castle faced the open field where they had sparred. He put himself back there and turned toward the castle, counting the windows. They were situated in pairs of two. Ten windows he recalled.

He opened his eyes and went back out into the hallway, counting the bedchambers. There were five rooms along the outside wall of the castle. Five rooms with two windows apiece.

Except for Bryce's chamber.

Nicholas's heart jumped, pounding at the discovery. He returned to Bryce's chamber and bent close to the wall where the other window should have been. He felt along the cool stone, searching for any anomaly. The wall was clean of cuts or levers. Disappointment welled as he moved to the hearth. The small bedroom fireplace abutted the adjoining wall. Nicholas tapped and tapped the stone, expecting nothing, when all the sudden he heard a soft echo beneath his hand. He rapped again, not believing his ears. The sound came again. The fireplace. There had to be an opening near the fireplace.

Nicholas dropped to his knees, inspecting the floor. He ran his fingers over the wooden floorboards. Rough texture brushed his fingertips, then suddenly something smooth. He grabbed the candle and inspected it more closely. Fine lines were etched into the floor. He followed the lines to an almost imperceptible crack in the wall. Slowly creeping his fingers up the wall, he came to a small pebble that stood out from the surface.

He pressed.

A door swung open easily, and noiselessly, on well-oiled hinges.

Nicholas stood in the opening to reveal a black space that ran alongside the stone of the hearth.

A secret passageway. Grasping the candle, he stepped inside.

Jane eased herself into the steaming water of her bath and forced a stab of disappointment away. She was grateful to Nicholas for this time alone. She had had so little time to herself since her suitors had arrived at Bellhaven. Even so, the thought did not quell the sensation of loneliness that enveloped her.

With a sigh, Jane settled back against the copper tub, hoping the scented steam would work its magic. Before her suitors had arrived at the castle, she had had no idea how alone she had been, or how isolated she had forced herself to become.

She closed her eyes. In two days' time, she would no longer be alone. She would be married.

And despite his winning only one challenge so far, she knew which of her suitors her bridegroom would be.

Her heart had decided long ago.

A creak sounded, a whoosh of cool air shimmered across her skin, and she sensed a presence.

Jane startled and reached for the linen sheet draped at the edge of the copper tub. "Who is there?" Where had she set her dagger?

She pressed the sheet to her breasts, shielding herself, then twisted to look behind her.

Nicholas. Her pulse danced and skittered at the sight of him.

He stood by the hearth, frowning. Behind him was a gaping hole in the wall. "Good heavens." Her eyes widened. "A secret chamber?"

"Aye. It leads from Bryce's chamber to yours." His gaze warmed at the sight of her.

"Turn around," she commanded.

He turned.

She stood and wrapped the bath sheet around herself.

"Who assigned the bedchambers to your guests?" he asked, his tone harsh.

"I did, and believe me, when I did, I had no idea there was a direct route from Bryce to me." She shivered at the thought of who might have entered her chamber unbeknownst to her. She shivered again as she stared at the lean backside of the man who had entered her chamber now.

"Keep your back turned," she insisted as she dropped the bath sheet, replacing it with a dressing gown. She picked up the towel and rubbed it against the ends of her hair that had dipped into the tub. She had just finished toweling her hair dry when he turned around, his eyes searching hers.

He came forward and took the linen from her hand and tossed it aside. He lifted his hand and ran his finger along her jawline. His calloused finger was rough against her flesh, sending chills through her. She knew he wanted to kiss her, and she was amazed by how much she wanted to kiss him.

But he did not kiss her. He simply waited, staring at her with those dark, hungry eyes.

Then he ran the pad of his thumb over her lips and she barely bit back a moan at how good it felt, at how good he smelled, at the tension that rippled between them. The force of it took her breath away.

Just when she thought he would kiss her, he pulled away and shut the false wall. "I need to block this opening so that it can never be opened again from the inside."

Her heart pounding, she nodded. "Let me help you."

Together, they found a thin piece of wood in the holder near the hearth. Reaching for her dagger that she had left on the floor near the pile of her clothes, he whittled the wood down. Before he slipped the wood under the door, he took her hand and guided it toward a lever alongside the fireplace. "In case you ever need this tunnel," he explained, "push the small mechanism and the door should spring free."

She nodded as he slipped the wedge of wood under the edge of the door, effectively blocking it from opening.

"There," he said, standing back to admire his work. "That should keep whoever is using the tunnel out."

"You are certain someone is using the tunnel?"

He nodded. "There were no cobwebs over the pathway and footsteps showed in the dust on the floor. Though the chamber most likely originated during the last century, it has been used much more recently."

Calmly she met Nicholas's gaze. "I am glad it was you who came through the passageway and not someone else."

He gave her a smile, but it slipped away. "I have a feeling there are more tunnels like this one throughout the castle."

She frowned. "Then we will find them and block each of them as we do." She hesitated a moment, thinking of the implication of the secret tunnels. "If there are a series of them, then that certainly explains how someone can appear then disappear all of a sudden."

"But that person would need to have a history of this place to accomplish that task." Nicholas's brows knit together. "If you did not know about the tunnels, then who else did? Your father, your brother, Bryce?" He shook his head at that. "Bryce seemed genuinely baffled by the idea of secret tunnels earlier."

Jane pressed her lips tight. She refused to accept that any of them would use the tunnels to cause harm. "I believe in Bryce's innocence. I think he is just as in the dark about the true nature of this castle as I am."

A scowl darkened Nicholas's features. "I do not understand the man. I have no idea if he is good or bad."

Jane shrugged. "I imagine it is somewhere in between, as we all are. I do not think life has been entirely kind to him. That fact has made him cynical and angry."

Nicholas ran a hand through his hair. "The anger I can understand." He paused, then after a long moment continued, "I do not know whether to trust him or not."

"I do," Jane said quietly.

"He will have to prove it to me."

"He will, in time."

With a weary sigh, Nicholas moved to tend the fire that had died down during her bath. "You always did have a soft heart, especially for the downtrodden."

Her thoughts shifted from Bryce to the Nicholas of her past. He had been handsome and charming and breathtaking upon his arrival. Yet in the days that had followed, she had also seen another side of him; one that was much more fragile than he would ever admit. She could sense deep suffering in him.

She flinched. Was that the reason he had taken her brother's dismissal from Bellhaven so hard? Did his pain go so deep that he could not tolerate even one more rejection?

Jane stepped closer to the flames, closer to Nicholas, and ran her fingers through her wet hair, watching him stoke the fire. She became acutely conscious of the strength of his hands as he spread the coals, then added more wood. Flames leapt and writhed on the long-dry wood. But it was not the flames that drew her attention.

She watched the muscles of his thighs peek out from beneath his plaid, the bunching of his shoulders beneath his soft linen shirt as he settled the screen back into place. Suddenly, she wanted to reach out and touch him, freely, as she had in the past when it was just the two of them. As she had just last night.

"Nicholas," she asked, stepping closer to him. "Will you answer a question for me?"

He stood and turned toward her. "What kind of question?"

"About your past. Your darkness." Their gazes met, locked. She could not breathe. She could not look away.

"What about it?" His voice was low, filled with sudden tension.

She reached up and cupped his stubbled chin with her palm. His eyes held a thousand emotions, making her ache all the way to her toes.

"Why did you come to Bellhaven in the first place?"

"Because I had to get away."

"Away from what?"

"It matters not." He pressed his hand to her cheek, then let it travel down her neck, to her collarbone, her shoulder, her arm. His lips followed the same path. "This is all that matters," he whispered against her neck.

A soft burr sounded in his voice as it did when he was aroused; she had learned that last night. A primal shudder ran through her at the thought. Her nipples hardened, pushing against the soft linen of her dressing gown.

He pulled back and looked in her eyes. He was waiting, watching her, allowing her to make the decision if they moved forward or back. His eyes said it all; desire dwelled there, with no barriers, no walls, simply stark and hopeful.

He reached for her hand but did not draw her to him. Again he waited for her to respond. His eyes locked on hers as he brought her fingertips to his mouth and kissed each one. He let his lips linger just long enough for her to feel their heat.

Jane closed her eyes, enjoying the sensation. Without her vision, her senses sharpened. The scent of cinnamon, bay leaves, and maleness wrapped around her. The sound of the fire crackling and popping in the hearth came to her ears. Warmth from the flames bathed her flesh.

Jane knew she should not fall into his arms again tonight. It was getting harder and harder to pull herself away and act like she did not care. She tried to focus on anything other than the sensation of his lips as they moved from the back of her hand to her wrist. Her pulse leapt wildly at his soft caress. His lips moved over her skin, not with expectancy, but with a gentle promise of more to come.

He drew her closer still, not seducing, but luring her closer to what her head might protest, but her body desired above anything else. When she made no attempt to step away, his lips came down.

Soft kisses rained upon her forehead, her cheeks, her nose, her chin, before he captured her lips. Heat flashed through her, a welcome heat, a heat that had become a part of her existence.

"Tonight, let us throw logic to the wind and let our passion be enough."

She opened her eyes and studied him. "Will that be enough?"

He kissed her again, a light, sweet, tantalizing touch that made her senses soar.

He did not answer her.

She let the question go unanswered as she slipped her hand inside his shirt and splayed her fingers across his chest, each finger as hot as a brand on his chest.

She deepened the kiss and let the passion she always tried to rein in when he held her spill unbidden into her every response. Lovingly, he pulled her against him, deepening their kiss degree by degree, until a tide of longing swept them both away, swept away all restraint, all thought, until there was only sensation to cling to.

He was hers for tonight, for forever, if she only said the words. No matter how much she tried, she could not hold herself apart from him. She wanted to bury herself deep inside him, so deep that she could not tell where he began and she ended.

Slowly he lowered himself to his knees on the rug near the fire, and she followed him, her fingers still exploring the hard surfaces of his chest, his shoulders, his back that lay hidden from her beneath his soft linen shirt. Then, suddenly, she grew restless as the fabric became a barrier to her desire. She unpinned the brooch that held his plaid on his shoulder. Released from the binding fabric, she easily worked his shirt up over his head.

He found her lips and kissed her again, slowly, hungrily as he lowered his hands to her dressing gown and released the tie. He slid the garment over her shoulders, down her arms, down her body until it slithered over her hips and down her legs to pool at her knees, leaving her naked.

His kisses grew hungrier, more demanding, as he held her close enough for the peaks of her breasts to brush against the soft hair of his chest. She shivered at the sensation and tried to pull herself against him, but he held her back, staring down at her as he never had before.

"You are so beautiful," he said, his voice a throaty whisper. In the glimmer of firelight, he bent down and kissed the soft swell of one breast, then the other.

She shivered and released a tiny moan, then arched slightly toward him. He took a nipple in his mouth and rolled the sensitive bud with his tongue. He claimed first one, then the other, until her senses reeled on the outer edges of a vortex of pleasure where only he could take her.

He lowered her from her knees to recline on the rug, then stretched out beside her. His lips returned to her lips, her neck, ignited a trail of sensation from her chin, across her neck, and over her shoulders. His hands slowly traced her waist, her hips. He claimed every inch of her skin, slowly, sculpting her with languid thoroughness, as though he were taking his time to learn every nuance of her body, every intimate detail. His fingers traced the outline of her buttocks and her back.

Her hands were on his shoulders as he stoked the heat rising within her to a fevered pitch until sensation after sensation rocked her.

She gazed into his eyes, watched their color grow darker, stormier as he shifted above her. Jane moaned at the feel of his hard, lean body on top of hers. Heat from the fire encircled them, warming them as she wrapped her legs around his hips.

He was all sinewy power, and it rippled from his body into hers. She ached to feel him inside of her, ached to claim him as her champion. She could do no such thing just yet. If she showed her heart, revealed her intentions, Nicholas would be at risk. And she could bear almost anything except losing him again. Perhaps this time to death.

Slowly, carefully, he worked his way down her body again as he held her gaze, looking at her with a raw possessiveness that stole her breath. His hands burned her as he ran them beneath her buttocks. He slid his tongue down her hipbone to her thigh. He spread her legs wider and slowly kissed his way up her inner thigh. She held her breath, writhing in anticipation of his touch as his hands slid beneath her, gripped her bottom, shifted her up and he set his mouth to her most secret core.

On a half gasp, half moan, she let her head loll back. He tasted her there, everywhere. Jane cried out as a wave of heat rose, then broke over her, and ecstasy rolled through her. She lay there consumed by the heat of passion. When she could take no more without giving in return, she reached for him. He rose upward, his hungry gaze feasting on hers. "Look at me, Jane. I need to see you when I take you as mine."

Consumed by passion, she could only nod.

He moved his swollen shaft toward her opening, pressing into her body inch by inch until they were one. Slowly, with his eyes on hers, he moved back and forth. The gentleness of his thrusts was agonizing, exciting, intense. She arched up into him, wanting more, but he continued his slow, methodical pace, exploring every nuance of her body as they came together and parted.

The intensity built, sensation rippled across every nerve as he filled her, igniting her senses with an all-consuming fire. Passion surged from deep within and finally wrenched all control from him.

He thrust harder and faster and longer and stronger, stroking her body until the flames wrenched out of control, broke over them, dragging them down into a vortex of pleasure that was hot and white and pure. It broke over them in glory and thrust them into a void where only fulfillment existed.

As they drifted back to reality, they lay together, their bodies entwined, a seamless whole wrapped in the golden warmth of the firelight.

Jane sighed her contentment. Her hands roamed freely over his back, then paused. She moved them slowly over the rough surface. He laid completely still as she trailed one finger up, then down the ridge of a scar, then another, then another. "Nicholas," she whispered, realizing what the puckering skin meant. "Who did this to you?" She sat up, staring into his face.

His lips thinned. "It was a long time ago."

"Your father?" she asked, incredulous.

He nodded. "He thought it would cleanse me, or him. I was never certain which."

She touched one scar that crept across his left shoulder. Her eyes swam with tears. "He filled you with pain. Merciful heavens, no wonder . . ." She let her words trail off.

No wonder he took Jacob sending him away so hard. It was but another rejection from people he had allowed himself to care about. He had carried his scars throughout his life, always hurting, always wanting, always alone.

"So much pain," she whispered.

"Nay, Jane," he said. "I let go of that pain the day I met you. The day I knew love, I knew no one could ever send me into that darkness again."

She leaned down and captured his lips with her own. He cupped her face in his hands while he returned the kiss. And Jane could feel him all the way to her soul, with every fiber of her being.

She brought her lips to his left shoulder and kissed the remnant of his scar. No man should be hurt the way he had been hurt. No man should have to suffer what he had been forced to endure at the hands of a parent; someone who should protect you from harm, not cast you into it.

She drew breath, preparing to put into words what she felt in her heart when a rap sounded on the door.

They both turned toward the sound.

The rapping came again, stronger this time. "Lady Jane, I must speak with ye." Angus's voice sounded from the other side of the door.

"One moment, please, Angus."

Nicholas gained his feet. He pressed her dressing gown into her hands a moment before he hastily donned his plaid and boots. "This can be nothing good."

Jane nodded as she heard the tension in Angus's voice. A shiver walked down her spine.

Jane drew a fortifying breath and opened the door.

Angus stood, looming in the doorway, his features pale and pinched. "Milady," he said in an odd, thick voice. "The castle is under attack."

❄

Jane's heartbeat slowed. Time seemed to stand still as the news pierced her brain. Her worst nightmare was upon her.

A wholly unexpected loneliness washed up from the depths of her soul, painfully intense. In that moment she mourned the loss of her father and her brother all over again. This was their fight. Their castle. And yet now that duty fell to her.

Except, this time, she was not alone. She had Nicholas and five others to help her fight this battle. Despite the danger, Jane drew a slow, deep breath and her heartbeat quickened. Time returned to its proper place. "Who attacks?"

A momentary surprise flared in her servant's face before worry once again creased Angus's brow. "The MacGuires. I recognized Seamus MacGuire leadin' his clan from the tower lookout."

Nicholas drew his sword. "How many men?"

"Nearly a hundred, I'd venture to guess."

"A hundred to our sixty," Nicholas said. "My men and I have fought worse odds."

Angus's expression grew stark. "That's not the worst of it."

"Tell us," Jane demanded, her panic rising as she met Angus's anguished gaze.

"They've two siege weapons, and they've already breached the outer wall."

Jane clenched her fists at her sides. "Secure the inner bailey." She turned to Nicholas. "Prepare the men while I dress. I will meet you in the courtyard shortly."

Outside, beneath the dying of the sun, her five suitors and Lord Galloway, their men, and her remaining few servants gathered. The men were wrapped in their plaids, weighed down with weaponry that made them fearsome foes.

In the distance the rumble of the siege weapons hitting the inner wall mixed with the roar of the attackers and the skirling, soaring melody of the bagpipes. The music of war.

The weight of what she must do settled upon Jane like a yoke. These men before her were her army. They might be a misfit bunch brought together to help her cause, but they were more than she ever dreamed she would have.

Gratitude filled her voice as she said, "This conflict is far more than any of you bargained for. I would understand if you were to turn away from the battle ahead."

The six men exchanged glances with one another, then Nicholas stepped forward. "Each of us came here for you—to fight for you to the best of our ability, and in any way possible. We are prepared to see this through. To death if necessary."

"To the death," they all echoed, lifting their swords toward the sunset with a shout for victory.

Nicholas's warm eyes searched hers with an aching need that nearly brought her to her knees.

Then he was gone, leading the men to battle.

Jane swallowed the lump in her throat as she turned back toward the keep. The men would defend the castle, but it was her responsibility to see to the safety of the few women and even fewer children that still remained in her care. She would see them ensconced in the great hall where they would wait out the battle. And, if necessary, Jane would hide them in the newly discovered tunnel above stairs. If the men failed—Jane reached down and patted the dagger on her calf—then she was prepared to defend those in her care until the bitter end.

Inside the castle, Lady Margaret aided Jane in gathering the women and children. "I believe that is everyone," Margaret said with a tired smile as she settled near the hearth to wait. She picked up Angel, who was scampering nervously at her feet, and set the puppy in her lap, stroking her gently.

The animal did not close her eyes as she might have had the danger not been so prevalent. Instead, Angel sat there, eyes open, ready to protect her mistress.

With a soft smile at the dog's heroics, Jane searched the small group that filled the chamber for a familiar blond head. Her smile slipped a moment later when she did not see who she searched for. "Where is Clara?"

Lady Margaret frowned. "Curious, she was right behind me when I brought the other maids down here from above."

Jane reached for her dagger and handed it to her aunt. "Take this, just in case. I will go find Clara."

Margaret accepted the weapon with a frown. "Do you truly think I will need this?"

"I pray not." Jane hurried across the hall and up the stairs. She headed for the north hallway. "Clara?" she called. "Clara, where are you?" She hastened down the hall. All the doors were closed except the one to Jane's room.

Frowning, Jane walked inside. "Clara?"

The door swung shut behind her. Jane gasped in alarm. She reached for the latch. To her horror, it refused to move up or down.

Her heart hammered in her chest as she searched the room for alternative ways out. *The door Nicholas had found.* Jane hastened to it and, following Nicholas's instructions, she soon found the hidden mechanism that opened the passageway. The door swung open. She would head to Bryce's room. There she would be able to open the door. She stepped into the cool, dark space.

She took two steps when suddenly that door snapped closed behind her, leaving her in pitch darkness. Jane's heart pounded in terror. She took the few steps back to the false wall and searched for a similar latch on the inside of the wall. There had to be some way to spring herself free. Finding nothing, she pressed against the stone, trying to force the panel open.

No response. She groaned in frustration and turned back toward the tunnel. As her eyes adjusted to the darkness, the inky blackness turned a shade of darker gray. Refusing to give in to the panic knotting her stomach, Jane drew a deep breath of the musty air and pushed herself forward, feeling her way along the wall. Up ahead a glimmer of light appeared. Had she reached Bryce's chamber already?

Silence surrounded her, pushed in upon her. Only the sound of her breathing came to her ears as she followed that sliver of light. Four steps more and the tunnel opened up off to the right as well as continuing straight ahead.

Judging by Nicholas's description, Bryce's room would be straight ahead. So what was off to the right? Her curiosity got the better of her as she shifted toward the right. She could still feel the cool stone of the castle wall beneath her fingertips, felt the floorboard beneath her feet as she counted her steps—five, six, seven, eight.

With each step the light grew brighter. Then she saw it—an open doorway. Her heart hammering, she entered the open space and stepped into a secret room.

The space mirrored her own bedchamber, from the tapestries covering the walls, the knotted carpet on the floor, the bed frame and linens, to the wooden chair in the corner near the window. At the sight of the chair, Jane's breath stilled. Folded across the back was her father's standard, and leaning against the wall was his missing sword.

Jane's gaze shifted to the bed, to the exact needlepoint bed curtains, coverlet, and bedside table with a brace of candles that sent a warm glow across the room. The only difference in the chamber, other than the stolen items returned to Jane by the MacGuire clan, was a small pewter frame near the bedside that held a miniature painting of her own father with a woman and child Jane did not recognize.

Her heart lurched at the sight. A million questions crowded her mind as she drew her finger across the image of her father's face.

Gooseflesh stippled her arms as she realized she was no longer alone. Jane twisted around and froze.

The flaxen-haired woman from the hunt. The one who had approached Nicholas and her in the cottage. "We meet again, Lady Jane Lennox."

"Your name is not Clara, is it?"

"Nay. I lied."

This time, beneath the light of the candles, Jane studied the woman before her. She was tall and thin, with a frightening hardness in her light gray eyes—eyes so very much like Jane's own father's. "Then who are you?" Jane asked, although she already suspected the answer.

"Amelia MacGuire. Your half sister," she said in a low, ominous tone.

Her sister. Swallowing, Jane stared at the girl. "What is this place? Why did my father never tell me about you?"

Amelia's gaze narrowed. "My mother and I were kept hidden so that you and Jacob could prosper and thrive."

"How long have you—"

"Lived in here?" Amelia said with a forced laugh. "Eighteen years. I was born here at Bellhaven and have been nothing more than a prisoner for eighteen years."

Amelia had been born after Jane, while her own mother was still alive. And on the heels of those revelations came another question, "Where is your mother?" Jane asked.

"She died two years ago." Ice laced Amelia's voice.

Two years ago. Was that timing a coincidence? That was when her father had taken Jacob back under his wing and demanded he start taking an interest in warring and the estate, and when Nicholas had been forced to leave her behind.

Jane shook her head as she tried to come to terms with the fact she had a half sister, and with what Amelia was saying. "Why would my—our—father do this? He might have been cruel at times, but to lock you away for eighteen years?"

"He built tunnels around the castle like the one you found tonight so that we could move in the shadows, but never truly face the light of day."

"Until Father died." Her chest tight, Jane tried to imagine what life would have been like for anyone so separated from the world. It must have been every bit as horrific as what Jules had suffered in gaol. Hard on the heels of that thought was another. "How do you receive basic supplies? Food?"

"Lately, Clara. Before that, another MacGuire servant who was brought into your house to look after my mother and me."

Jane frowned. "Why the MacGuires?"

"They are my clan, my mother's clan." Amelia shrugged, but her gaze darkened.

"I do not understand," Jane said, confusion lacing her words. "Why did you not go back to your clan? My father appears not to have locked you in if you were able to get out of the castle as you did during the hunt."

"It was easier to stay. Besides, that's what my mother wanted. She wanted it all, everything that was due to her—your father and this castle."

"And the MacGuires helped?"

Amelia nodded, her features hard. "They are ready to take what should be mine."

"They attack the castle now," Jane informed her.

"Yes," Amelia replied. "They have come to accomplish what I could not. They are here to kill you, Bryce, and Lady Margaret, then take Bellhaven and her people for me."

Jane stiffened her spine. "I am very sorry for what you have suffered. No one should be locked up and hidden away like you have for so many years, but you have no legal right to this castle."

"With you dead, unmarried, and childless, I do."

"Give this insanity up, Amelia, before it is too late," Jane said. "I have an army now. Your people will be harmed if they try to take Bellhaven. Is that what you want? More blood on your hands?"

Amelia opened her hands and turned to look at her palms. "I will do whatever I have to do to take my revenge against you." A strange light entered her eyes as she moved closer to Jane. "You lived the life I wanted. The life I deserved, since Lord Lennox was also my father."

Jane held her ground. "I do not know why my father did what he did, but his actions do not give you a right to strike out at those people around you who knew nothing about you, who would have helped you had they known. Your clan does not need to fight its way in, when I will let you walk out."

"Would you?" Amelia asked, her tone harsh. "You would let me walk away when I am to blame for your own suffering?"

Jane frowned at that. "The attacks?"

"That and so much more." Amelia offered her a tight-lipped smile. "You truly have no idea?"

She laughed again, the sound harsh and unfeeling. "Explain yourself."

Amelia came closer, moved in front of Jane. "Since you will not be leaving this room, what does it matter if I tell you?" She smiled as she came forward, backing Jane against the wall like a lion cornering its prey.

Jane reached for her calf, for her dagger, then froze when she remembered she had left it with Margaret.

The air in the hidden chamber sizzled with tension. Amelia's smile dipped, her gaze hardened. "You want the truth?"

Jane kept her back straight, refusing to be intimidated. "Yes. All of it."

"Your mother?" Amelia asked. "She died in childbirth?"

"Yes," Jane said as a chill worked down her spine.

Amelia shook her head. "My mother poisoned her just as I tried to poison you a few nights past."

Jane's mouth went dry. "Poison? Why?"

Amelia smirked. "Because my mother wanted her to die so she could have Father all to herself. She had hoped the poison would have worked sooner so that your brother would never have been born, but alas, your mother was stronger than she anticipated, her love for your brother too strong to give up before he was safely into the world."

Pain and anger and sorrow coiled inside Jane at the confession. "Did Father know?"

Amelia nodded, her own amusement growing at the sight of Jane's pain. "Not at first, but eventually he saw what my mother would do to keep him for herself. He was furious with my mother for months."

Jane swallowed back her anger, forcing herself to think. She had to stay in control of her emotions and find a way out. She drew a sharp breath as the details of her life started to fall into place. "It was after my mother's death that Father changed. He pulled away from Jacob and me. He sent for Lady Margaret to care for us then."

"My mother begged him to allow her to care for the child, but he refused." Amelia's face hardened. "He threatened to send us back to the clan. But my mother threatened to poison his precious children if he did."

Why did her father not raise an army against them? Why not turn his own men on these two women? Why would he allow such extortion to occur? Was he that ashamed of what he had done? Jane leaned into the wall at her back, needing the support for her suddenly unstable legs.

Instead of fighting back, her father had distanced himself from Jane and Jacob, not because of anything they had done. It was because of Amelia's mother, and perhaps his own secrets that he hoped they would never discover. He had allowed himself to become a victim to a madwoman's scheme.

"There's more." Amelia's evil smile returned.

Jane's body shook, despite her attempt to control her response. "What more could you do to us than steal our mother and our father?"

"Two years ago, I watched the way you and Nicholas Kincaid looked at each other. I knew it would not be long before you were happy once again, and I could not allow that."

"You made Father send him away?" Jane asked in disbelief.

Amelia gave her a penetrating stare. "With my mother gone, I had to pick up where she left off, controlling your family, torturing you for what we had suffered."

"You are mad," Jane said with a catch in her voice.

"Probably." Amelia shrugged. "The whole of my life has been spent watching you. Hating you." Her eyes hardened. She grabbed Jane's throat, pressed her head against the wall, ringing her flesh.

Rage suffused Amelia's face.

Jane let her pent-up anger flow freely. She slammed her foot down on Amelia's foot.

Her sister's hands slackened.

Jane darted for her father's sword. Extending the blade, she held Amelia at arm's length.

"You are the cause of all that is bad in my life." A throbbing vein stood out against Amelia's temple.

Jane gripped the hilt tightly. "I am not responsible for your pain, Amelia. You are."

"No, it is your fault I was locked in here," Amelia screamed in fury.

"I am sorry for you," Jane said quietly.

"Sorry for me?" Amelia screamed in outrage. Her gray eyes darkened dangerously. She swept the candlestick from the bedside table and held it against the bed curtains. "I will take everything away from you, everything that you love. I will strike your most beloved castle from the inside and out. I will hurt you and hurt you until you beg me for death."

Jane's hand shook on the sword as flame leapt from the wick to the bed linens as easily as water rolling down a hill. Fire wicked onto the threads, came to life, and continued to grow and spread across the dry surface.

Amelia threw the candlestick aside, let it roll across the floor until it came to rest at the bottom of the tapestry. Again the flame from the wick leapt to the dry cloth, slithering like a snake up and across the threads. "If you are going to kill me, then do it. I want you to have the stain of my murder on your soul. If you do not kill me, then I will kill you. Only one of us can survive," Amelia cursed as she charged forward.

Jane hitched a breath, turned the sword sideways, hitting Amelia on the side of the face with the hilt. The blow sent her backwards. "We need to put out the flames."

Amelia clutched her face and cried out. "You will pay for that."

The flames on the bed jumped from one corner of the bed curtains to the other. Jane leapt toward the chair and scooped up her father's standard. She lowered her sword and batted at the fabric, desperately trying to stop the spread of the flames.

"Smother the flames," Jane shouted to Amelia, but Amelia lunged forward and picked up the chair. She hurled it at Jane.

Jane leapt sideways, missing the blow. "If we do not put out the flames, neither of us will have a castle left to inherit."

Amelia shook her head. "I would rather die than help you."

Jane clutched the sword in her hand, and despite her anger, a murderous response would not come.

"We both will die if we stay here." Smoke filled the chamber, burned Jane's throat, stung her eyes, and made it hard to breathe. She moved back toward the entrance to the chamber. "Come with me. We can figure all this out when we are safe."

Amelia's gaze turned stony. "This is a trick. You want me to go with you so you can seek retribution."

"In that you are wrong. I am not like you." Jane lowered the sword. "You are free to leave. No one is keeping you in."

"Leave?" she cried.

"Yes, leave. You are free to leave Bellhaven, go back to your people. No one is left to hold you back. I will help you, Amelia, if you will only let me."

"I cannot leave. This place is all I know." Her face crumpled. "I did not think about anything beyond killing you."

"Amelia," Jane cried as the flames intensified. "We have to leave now!"

She shook her head. "I have nothing."

"Yes, you do. You have your clan. You have me. We are half sisters. That has to mean something to you."

"You mean nothing to me," she said, her voice no longer hard. Only fear echoed in her words.

"I know you must be scared, but I will help you." Jane backed into the tunnel as the heat became oppressive. Bryce's room was their only escape. She took another step back as the heat of the flames grew hotter. "Amelia." Jane tried again. "You have to leave."

"No. You hate me."

"No, Amelia. Despite everything that you have done, I do not hate you. I can forgive you, for all you have suffered. I will be true to my word." Jane reached out her left hand again, urging her half sister forward.

Amelia hesitated, then reached for her hand. But instead of coming with Jane, she jerked her back into the chamber, into the heat and flames. The sword fell from Jane's fingers as the two of them tumbled to the floor.

Amelia clawed at Jane's face, catching her on the cheek. Jane fought back; she landed a blow in the center of Amelia's chest. It was enough to break the girl's grasp and Jane scrambled away and onto her feet just as the glass of the window shattered, sending shards in all directions.

Jane coughed and doubled over as the thick smoke filled her lungs. Her vision blurred. She staggered toward the secret door. "I am leaving, Amelia. Are you coming with me?" Time stood still as Jane met Amelia's gaze. Her sister's face went through an entire cycle of emotions—fear, anger, and finally resignation. "Nay."

Behind Amelia, the flickering yellow light of the fire glowed. Fed by the air in the chamber, licking tongues of flame curled outward, jumped, and spread to anything in its path.

With one last look at the half sister she would never know, Jane ran into the tunnel. Flames followed on her heels as she beat a path to Bryce's chamber, praying the door would be unlocked. Heat from the flames burned her back. She came to the end of the tunnel. Felt for the lever that would release her. One click, the door opened. Jane jumped inside the bedchamber just as flames licked at the floorboards where she had stood moments before. She left the door open, even though it left an easy path for the smoke and flames, which filled the chamber quickly. She would leave the way open for Amelia should she change her mind.

In an effort to preserve herself, Jane leapt toward the outer door, depressed the latch, and moaned when the door refused to budge. She pounded on the thick oak. "Help! Is anyone there?"

No response.

"Clara, if you can hear me, please set me free."

Nothing.

Jane looked around the chamber for another means of escape and found nothing.

Smoke curled through the air, clogging the room. Her eyes burning, Jane felt her way to the unlit brace of candles, grasped it, and returned to the door. She brought the hard metal down against the lock, determined to free herself from the building inferno.

She struck the latch again and again, until she felt her vision blurring. Her throat burned. A cry of despair escaped her lips as she felt the life drain out of her.

Through the haze that had settled in her brain, Jane thought she heard footsteps over the increasing roar of the flames. She looked behind her in the bedchamber, expecting Amelia, when the sound came from the outside of the door.

"Lady Jane!" Angus's voice called out.

The door pushed in. Angus spilled through the opening. "Praise heaven I found ye."

He reached for her hand. Jane took it, grateful for his assistance as her lungs burned and she doubled over, coughing. Angus lifted her into his arms. "I need to get you out of here."

"Amelia," Jane said, her throat raw. It hurt to speak.

"Who?"

"A secret room. My sister." A fit of coughing robbed her of further words. She pointed toward the open tunnel. Angus understood. He set her in the hallway and raced through the tunnel. Jane's heartbeat pounded in her ears as she stared back through the room and down the hallway. Fire was everywhere.

Angus joined her a moment later. Through a veil of tears she saw him shake his head as he gathered her in his arms and, with long strides, hauled her to safety.

In the great hall, the women and children headed out the doors. Jane turned to Angus. "Is there nothing we can do to stop the flames?" she asked, gasping air into her aching lungs.

"The fire spread quickly. Too quickly." He reached inside his tunic and pulled forth an oiled cloth. "I found these outside in the hallway. Someone set this fire intentionally."

A flash of fire streaked across the great hall, igniting the long wooden tables, benches and tapestries.

"Come, let's join the others. The flames are too intense, their stranglehold on the castle too strong." Angus guided her out of the keep and into the night air.

Outside, her people gathered. Margaret organized them into groupings where the more able-bodied could help either the young or the old as they made their way across the courtyard and to the inner bailey. Margaret clutched the puppy, Angel, in her arms. At the sight, Jane drew a breath of fresh clean air and felt her muddled senses clear. "What about the battle?" she asked Angus. "Will we be safe if we leave the inner bailey?"

"The MacGuires are still a threat, but the fire is certain to kill us if we stay."

Jane turned back toward the keep. A reddish aura rose from the growing core of heat and flames that spread into the night sky, while a heavy choking mass of gray smoke billowed around them.

Jane shivered as the cool night air touched her heated skin. Tiny flecks of white fell from the sky, and for a moment Jane thought it was ash. But as she held her hand up, tiny flakes fell upon her flesh, hovering for a moment before melting. *Snow.*

Jane tipped her head back. The moon peeked out from behind dark clouds, bright and full, mixing its light with that of the fire to cast a look that was nearer to daylight than evening across the land.

Bellhaven Castle was burning. There was nothing she could do but let it burn.

The MacGuires brought down the wall of the inner bailey with a final strike of their catapult. Stone exploded, landing against the ground with a mighty thump. A roar went up as the MacGuires charged. Nicholas and the others were prepared. They held their swords and bows at the ready, waiting to strike. The clan climbed up over the rubble and prepared to engage when they stopped cold, staring gazes and slackened jaws, at something behind Nicholas and the other men.

Nicholas turned and looked in stunned disbelief at the roaring inferno that was Bellhaven Castle. He heard David's harsh imprecation, but could not tear his gaze away from the macabre sight before him.

The roofs of Bellhaven were being devoured by flames.

"Lady Jane," Jules cried.

The shocked murmurs of the men sounded behind him.

"We have to get Lady Jane and Lady Margaret out of there." Lord Galloway's sword found its sheath as he bolted forward, only to stop a heartbeat later as dark figures appeared through the haze of smoke.

Nicholas saw Jane, illuminated by the flames, as she came rushing through the gate to the outer bailey with Lady Margaret, Angus, and many of the servants in tow.

Nicholas ran to her and grabbed her into his arms. He did not care that the others looked on. "Praise the saints you are unharmed."

Lord Galloway swept Lady Margaret into his arms. "My love, my heart. You are safe."

The MacGuires, released from their momentary shock, climbed over the rubble and entered the inner courtyard with lowered swords. Lord Galloway and Nicholas both swept the women behind them.

"The castle . . . is burning." Seamus MacGuire came forward, clothed in the green and blue of his clan's colors. "Our cannon fire was not responsible, was it?"

"No," Jane said, stepping from behind Nicholas. "Amelia and Clara were."

"Amelia?" Seamus's eyes widened.

A million questions crowded Nicholas's thoughts, but he forced them aside. There would be time for questions later.

"You know the truth?" the aging laird asked.

"She told me."

Seamus's gaze searched the crowd of people gathered around them. "Where is she? Where is Amelia?"

Sorrow reflected in Jane's gaze. "Amelia refused to leave the castle. Her anger forced her to seek revenge, but it was her fear that ultimately took her life," Jane said softly. Nicholas could hear the regret and sorrow in her voice.

Seamus's face turned red. "No!" he cried as he swung his sword at Jane. Nicholas blocked the strike, knocking the weapon from Seamus's hands. David caught his arms and pinned them behind him.

The MacGuire men surged forward. Colin, Jules, and Bryce stepped between Seamus and his men, prepared to take on the clan with their swords at the ready.

"Stop," Jane commanded. "There will be no more destruction this day." Her angry gaze skewered each of the MacGuire men. "Has there not been enough loss already? Your kinswoman is dead. Bellhaven is in ruin. Tomorrow is Christmas Eve. Please, I beg you, withdraw before any more blood is shed."

Seamus's cheeks reddened as he no doubt fought to keep his anger in check. "Amelia is gone?"

Angus nodded. "I went into the flames tae rescue her, but 'twas too late for the poor lass."

Seamus's shoulders slumped. "I dinna want things to end like this."

"Are they at an end, MacGuire?" Angus asked, surveying Seamus's clansmen.

The angry murmurs of Seamus's men sounded over the pop and hiss of the flames. Then, at a nod from their leader, they sheathed their weapons. Their voices died down.

David released the clan chief. Seamus stepped away and reached down, picking up his sword.

Jane's men raised their weapons once more, but halted a moment later when the old laird slid his weapon back into its sheath. "As much as I want revenge for Amelia's death, I fear we are more to blame for that outcome than you are. We must now be satisfied with the fact we have taken Bellhaven from you. Not in the way we had anticipated, but the castle is gone nonetheless. Because of this, the MacGuires consent to retreat. When the flames die down, we will return to claim Amelia's body."

Jane nodded, then lifted her chin. "Had I known about Amelia, I never would have kept her from you."

Seamus's face reddened once more.

Nicholas tightened his grip on his sword, prepared to step between them if the old laird moved a handbreadth.

A moment later Seamus's shoulders slumped. "She was my granddaughter. I failed her. We all failed her." On a sigh, the clan leader signaled his men back over the rubble. He caught sight of Clara and waved her to his side. "You had best come with us. I doubt you will be welcome here after what we tried to do."

The girl followed behind Seamus, leaving the defenders of Bellhaven to stand alone amongst the ruin.

"Colin and I will see them off the Lennox land," David said.

"Were any of our men hurt in the battle?" Jane asked as David and Colin disappeared over the rubble.

"A few are wounded, but those wounds will heal with time."

Jane released a sigh. "I am grateful for that small miracle."

"Come," Nicholas said. He offered Jane a hand. "We should retreat to the outer bailey while the fire blazes. Distance will guarantee our safety." Jane and Nicholas hung back to assist the others over the loose rock and gravel, until finally they made their way into the outer bailey.

"The outer buildings have yet to catch fire." Nicholas felt a small catch of relief. All was not lost. He organized the female servants to pull water from the well, in preparation for the flames to come. In the meanwhile, he and the men dug a trench just outside the garden wall in an attempt to keep the flames from spreading.

When their work was done, Jane found her way back to Nicholas. He set his shovel aside and turned to watch as the tops of the trees in the garden caught fire, forming an arch of flames that hopped from one skeletal frame to another.

"Fear not," he said in a calming tone. "The fire lines will hold. We will cling to what remains of Bellhaven for your sake."

"Thank you." Jane's voice was raw from emotion as she stared at what had been the north side of the castle. All that remained was an empty shell that was being devoured by obscene tongues of red and orange and blue.

Burning branches from the trees fell to the ground and ash floated down around them, mixing with the ankle-deep snow on the ground. Silence settled. Nicholas pulled Jane closer against him when an explosion rocked the earth. Another explosion sounded, then another. As heat from the fire mixed with the cool stone, the stone expanded, sending stone and wood and debris to rain down upon them.

Tears rolled down Jane's cheeks, leaving rivulets in the soot and ash that clung to her skin. "This castle has seen many wars over the course of its seven hundred years and now it is a ruin."

Nicholas covered Jane's hand. "But Bellhaven is not gone. The lands yet exist. And with care, you can rebuild and restock."

Her hand turned and held tight to his own.

He gave her hand a squeeze, trying to impart warmth, comfort, anything that might strengthen her as they glanced at the sight of the flames.

"I am sorry, Jane, for all you suffered today."

"Nothing lasts forever," she said softly.

"You are wrong." He tipped her face to his. "My love for you will last a lifetime, whether you choose me as your husband or not."

Jane stiffened beside him. "In all the chaos, I had forgotten by this time tomorrow it will all be over."

Before the sun set on Christmas Eve, Jane would have to choose one of her suitors to spend forever with.

24

❄

The following morning, after bedding down in the stables for the night, Jane and her people stood in a new layer of snow. Despite the damage from the fire, the snow had a cleansing effect on what remained of Bellhaven. The once pink-gray stone that had been charred black last night was covered in a blanket of snow, softening the broken line of the battlements. In the apple grove, the scorched, twisted skeletons of the trees were covered in crystals of white.

Bellhaven no longer looked dead. It looked like it was sleeping, waiting to be reborn. She stood, back straight, absorbing the thought, letting it fuel her determination.

The MacGuires had come peacefully early that morning to find and retrieve Amelia's body. They had taken her charred remains, wrapped in a shroud of white, with them for burial.

Amelia. Her sister. Jane shuddered at the memory of how the young woman had died. Things could have been so different for the two of them if only . . . Jane left the thought at that. There was no going back, no changing what had happened. She'd had a sister for a few moments, but now that sister was gone, along with all the mysterious attacks on her, Margaret, and Bryce.

Margaret and Bryce remained. They were her family now. The three of them could bond together and be all that each other needed. But would that bond include marriage to Bryce? Despite what her heart demanded, should Bryce be the logical choice?

"How do you feel?" Margaret gently touched Jane's arm, interrupting her thoughts. "Is there anything I can do to help?"

"No." Jane turned away from the ruins and shifted her gaze to the familiar faces gathered nearby. David, Jules, Colin, Lord Galloway, Bryce, most of the household staff, Angus, Ollie, Egan, and of course Nicholas.

Jane offered them the beginnings of a smile. Christmastide was one of her favorite times of the year. Despite the secrets that had been revealed last night, and the fire, she still felt a glimmer of the usual happiness that this time of year brought. If she forced the disaster from her mind, and truly looked at what was in front of her, she still had one of the greatest gifts of all—love. She had the love of her people, her family, and her suitors.

Her suitors.

"Today is the final day of the challenge. I know we had planned a melee for today, but given the circumstances I thought we would change things up a bit."

"Cousin Jane." Bryce stepped forward. "None of us expects you to continue with the challenges. We know the depth of your loss. Make your decision now. Any one of us who remains in the competition would accept you willingly. And the others will bow out graciously once you choose."

"Thank you. That means a lot to me," Jane said as she turned to address the others. She drew herself up as a sudden lightness came over her. Christmastide was upon them. It was the season of peace, of giving, and of joy. Despite the ruin that surrounded them, those gifts of the spirit could remain.

Jane smiled, a true smile—one that she felt from the bottom of her soul. "Your final challenge is to find whatever you can among the ruins of

Bellhaven. Things we can use to make ourselves more comfortable. Find as many items as you can, but choose one to offer to me as a gift this Christmas Eve."

David frowned. "We should stay with the others and help prepare the outer buildings before the pending storm lets loose."

"Angus and Ollie are quite capable of organizing the other men to see to that task. Please, David, do this one last thing for me."

"As you wish," he said with a bow. "I could never deny you your heart's desire."

"You have two hours," Jane said, before dismissing them to head off toward the ruins.

"I will help Ollie and Angus." Lord Galloway pressed a kiss to Margaret's lips, then he was gone, leaving the two women alone.

"Are you certain it was wise to send them off on a scavenger hunt when we could really use their help to rebuild a warm, safe haven?"

Jane remained silent while she waited for the men to be out of earshot. Finally she said, "We need the useful items they will find every bit as much as we need shelter. I also sent them away because I need time to prepare. Margaret, I need your help. I must find four gifts of my own to give to the men who I will not take as my husband. Please help me send them away with something with which to pursue their own dreams."

Margaret's eyes widened. "You know which of the five you will choose?"

"I do," she said, then smiled at the words that slipped so easily off her tongue. "I will say those words again before the sun sets this day."

"You shall reveal him to me this moment," Margaret demanded in an excited tone.

Jane simply smiled. "You will have to wait and see like everyone else."

Margaret growled. "I have my suspicions. But I will wait to be surprised with the rest of your people." She took Jane's hand in hers. "Come, let us find those gifts so that we can make certain this marriage happens as it should."

Jane stilled as a thought suddenly occurred to her. "What about the minister? The wedding needs to be official."

Her aunt smiled mischievously. "I sent for the man two days ago. He should arrive before noon."

Jane laughed as joy bubbled up from her toes to greet the crisp morning air. "My heavens, a fortnight ago you would have had to drag me to the altar. Now I can hardly wait to get there."

Margaret returned her smile. "It is odd how life reveals itself to us sometimes, is it not?"

Odd was not the word Jane had in mind. Miraculous seemed more suited to this event.

Miracles and Christmas Eve. Did it get any better than that?

Over the next two hours the sun had worked its way through the clouds to cast a bright white glow over the land. The sunshine helped fuel Jane's renewed sense of purpose. Her suitors had returned from their hunt. They gathered in the outer bailey outside the stables and the kitchen. Lord Galloway, Angus, and Ollie had led the others in creating a new, temporary home with several of the useful items found during the competitors' hunt—scraps of uncharred wood that could be used to build, furnishings that had somehow survived, several mugs, plates, an iron cauldron, along with various weapons and shields.

One by one the voices in the bailey fell silent. The earnest faces of her suitors and servants turned toward Jane.

She drew a steadying breath. "This is our final competition, which means it is time for me to say farewell to four of you. Choosing a winner was difficult for so many reasons. And I want you to know that those of you who I will not select as my husband will forever hold a fondness in my heart." Despite her best efforts, her voice cracked with emotion.

Jane turned not toward her suitors, but to Lord Galloway with a smile. "I am so grateful that you came to this competition, and even more grateful that you found your own prize."

Lord Galloway slipped his arm around the woman beside him, pulling her close. "Lady Margaret," he said. His smile widened. "Soon to be Lady Galloway, is a treasure, indeed."

247

Margaret blushed. "Oh, Hollister, you are embarrassing me."

Jane knew a moment's contentment that her aunt had finally found someone worthy of her love. Beginning her own life with one of her five other suitors would be much easier knowing her aunt was happy and making a life of her own.

Forcing her gaze away from the happy couple, Jane turned back to the other men. The time had come to say farewell. She reached behind her for the largest of the gifts she had gathered, then took her first steps toward David.

"I am the first to go." He laughed, but it was a hollow sound.

She looked up at him, knowing her eyes were full of the emotion she was afraid to release. "Thank you for your strength, your skill, and your willingness to compete with the others for my hand. Having you here meant the world to me."

David bowed and held out his gift to her. It was wrapped in a piece of linen that was gray with ash. "Open it," he said, a half smile on his lips. "It will make me happy to know you have this with you when I am gone."

Jane set David's oddly-shaped gift on the snow-covered ground. She accepted his gift, unwrapped the cloth then smiled at the contents. *Her dagger.* "I cannot believe you found this in the ruin." Filled with joy, she rose on her toes and pressed her lips to his. "Thank you, David." Jane picked up David's gift by the sides and stretched her arms out to him. "My gift to you."

A high-careening squawk came from beneath the cloth-covered gift. David's brows drew together as he pulled back the cloth to reveal a cage containing a sleek gray falcon.

"You are giving me Falco?" he asked, his voice filled with wonder.

Jane nodded. "Our finest hunter. I want you to have him because I know you will care for him and use him well."

He flashed a grin filled with happiness. "I will."

Jane went back to select another gift and moved to stand before Jules.

He groaned. "And I am to be the second to leave you behind."

Jane saw the uncertainty in his blue eyes, the need, and it touched her deeply. She reached for his hand. "You are my friend now and forever. And I honestly believe there is someone out there for you who will love you as you deserve to be loved."

"I have a gift for you this Christmas Eve," Jules said.

He reached inside his sporran and withdrew a long metal chain, and suddenly Jane realized what it was he held. *Her mother's girdle.* The rubies sparkled in the light of the sun. Tears filled her eyes when she looked up at him.

"Thank you." The words were raw and the only ones she could force past the emotion clogging her throat. When she had sent them on their hunt, she had had no notion of what they would find. That they had found two of the things most precious to her was more than she had dared hope for.

She batted at the tears spilling on to her cheeks, then lifted her closed hand out to Jules. She drew a breath and forced her voice into steadiness. "I had a very difficult time trying to find the perfect gift for you, Jules. What I ended up with is more symbolic than helpful, but I hope you will keep it with you to help you remember what it is you have gained."

She opened her palm to reveal a small skeleton key. "This is the key to your new life. The past is gone. The future is what you make of it." She stared down at the key, unable to look him in the eyes.

He touched her chin, tilted her face, and brought her gaze to his. "My dear friend, thank you for your role in helping me start anew. You were part of whatever forces transpired to set me free. That is your gift to me, the ultimate gift—freedom."

Jane gave him a heartfelt smile. "Sometimes the world has to turn us upside down to show us what we need. What is truly important to us."

Jules laughed. "I would like to try being right side up for a while."

Jane thrilled to see the shadows vanish from his eyes. "You will find your way, Jules. I have no doubt."

Jane felt a shiver of peace move through her as she returned to the gifts she had gathered and selected her next offering. She made her way toward Colin.

Regret shadowed his face for a heartbeat before his expression cleared. He straightened and offered her a nod. "I am honored to have been included among your suitors. I am only sorry I did not have more to offer you."

"Do not think for a moment that your lack of a past has affected my decision at all." Jane reached for his hand with one of her own, disturbed that he thought that was why she had failed to choose him as her mate. She stared up into his face, deep into his silver-gray eyes. "None of that matters to anyone but you, Colin. You are independent, resourceful, courageous, and one of the most beautiful men I have ever met." At the admission, she felt heat rise in her cheeks.

Colin's mouth turned up into a grin. "Admirable traits—and still they were not enough."

She stared at him long and hard, then quietly said, "Your past, or lack thereof, makes you who you are. I would not change a thing about you. But that is me. You need to find peace with yourself. And this might help you." She extended the folded sheet of paper in her hands.

His brows drew together as he extended his hands to her, offering her his gift. "Let us exchange our gifts, then."

Jane nodded and accepted a small wooden box stuffed with straw.

At her quizzical look, Colin said, "What you seek is hidden in the straw."

Jane plunged her hand into the soot-tinged contents until she felt something hard and cold. She drew it out to reveal a forged piece of metal no bigger than her hand, bearing the Lennox crest of two broadswords in saltire behind an imperial crown. "Where did you find this?" Her father had had the miniature crest created many years ago and had mounted it at the top of her mother's headstone in the church graveyard. It had gone missing, and now she understood why. Amelia had no doubt taken the memento from the family she would never have. A pang of regret moved through Jane at the thought of her half sister's death.

Jane stood there a moment, simply breathing in and out until she found her equilibrium again. Had she not been lecturing Colin about letting go of things beyond their control?

"Thank you, Colin. This means so much to me. It is a link to my family that I will treasure." She motioned to her gift, feeling a sudden connection to this man. She realized how bruised and vulnerable he was; how those tiny chinks in his armor affected him. "I want you to find a link to your family, if possible."

He stared down at the paper in his hands. "The papers the informant delivered to Bryce?"

Jane nodded. "I am so grateful I stored this information in the stables and that they survived the fire."

Frowning, Colin carefully unfolded the document. "I asked the informant about them. He did not know what had happened to them after he gave them to Bryce, and he could only recall some of the contents. I have it all now." He looked to Jane. "How did you come to have these?"

Jane turned toward her cousin. "Bryce willingly turned them over to me."

"I would like to say I had gathered the information for your benefit, but that would be a lie," Bryce said in a strained voice. "I only hope you can use the leads my informant found and discover the answers you seek."

"Thank you," Colin replied with a hopeful smile. "For the first time in my life, I have a beginning to that journey."

Leaving Colin to study the papers, Jane gathered her last gift, then moved to stand between Bryce and Nicholas. She passed her gaze over both. "One of you will win my hand. One of you will win something else that I hope will become a new start for you."

A hushed silence fell over the crowd. A mixture of regret and excitement coiled in Jane's chest. Her heart fluttered and she stepped toward Bryce.

He remained silent.

She stood there, staring at him, waiting.

"I want to hate you for this, but I do not," he finally said. "This was a hard decision for you, divided between family and love. Love won out, as it should." She could hear the rawness in his voice, his need to understand.

"You are a good person, Bryce. You will find someone of your own," she whispered. Jane wanted to turn toward Nicholas, to fall into his gaze. Instead, she kept her focus on Bryce. He deserved that much from her.

He shook his head, his face pale. "I have nothing without you or Bellhaven."

The pain in his voice was like a knife. She reached out to him, touching his chest, feeling his strong heartbeat beneath her fingers. "Oh, Bryce, you have everything you ever needed right here. When you finally let go of your anger, you showed us all what a kind and gentle heart you have."

She withdrew her hand from his chest to gather his fingers in hers. She pressed her gift into his palm. A piece of stone.

He stared at it. "What is this? It looks like one of the stones from the walls of Bellhaven Castle."

"It is. I am giving you one-third of the estate."

His pupils flared. "Why?"

"Because this is your home, too," Jane said simply. "I am dividing the estate between you and me and saving a portion for my brother, as a token in the hopes that he still lives."

Tears shimmered in Bryce's eyes as he looked at her. "I was so horrible to you. . . ."

Jane shook her head. "You were angry because you thought the world had cheated you. I forgive you for your behavior. Please know that I understand."

He stiffened, and she could tell he was grasping for self-control. "I do not deserve this gift. . . ."

"Yes, you do. You deserve a home of your own and a family to share it with."

He swallowed roughly. "Where do I start?"

"With that one small stone."

He nodded, straightened, then reached behind him for a long, wrapped object. "I found this for you," he said offering her his gift.

She pulled the linen cloth from the long object to reveal her father's sword. Jane smiled. Only a few days past, this memento from her father had meant everything to her. But she realized now that she needed nothing but her memories to keep him close. "I thank you for this, Bryce. It is all I have left of my father." She held the weapon back toward her cousin. "But I want you to have it. As the next male in line for the estate, you should carry this sword."

He accepted the weapon from her. "I will use it to protect our family."

"I like the sound of that."

Finally, she turned her gaze to Nicholas and her heart soared.

"Jane." He said her name, the sound as smooth as honey. He gazed at her with an intensity that made it hard to breathe. Warmth spread through her as a happiness she had never experienced before settled in her heart.

"You chose me."

She nodded, unable to keep a smile from her lips.

"'Tis everything I ever hoped for." The weak winter sunshine bathed his face in a radiant glow that matched his smile. Reaching out, he pulled her close. She stared into his eyes. In that moment, the last vestiges of old hurt and bitterness, fear and loneliness, vanished. She and Nicholas were united by joy, bound together by love.

"Nicholas?"

"Aye." The word was a raw whisper.

"I love you." It was so easy to admit what she had fought for so long, to speak the words she had longed to speak to him since the last time they had parted.

"For always and forever, I love you," he said thickly.

With him she would finally have the life she had always dreamed of. "There is only one last thing that we must do."

He pulled her close and pressed a long, passionate kiss to her lips. "Is this anything close to what you had in mind?"

She pulled back to smile at him. "After the wedding."

"Which reminds me. . . ." He studied her eyes intently, then leaned close again, gently cupping her face with one hand. He brushed her lips with his. "Would you like your gift?"

Happiness swelled in her chest, filled her heart to overflowing. She raised her hand to place it over his, feeling his gentle strength, his love. "Nothing would make me happier."

He smiled at her as he captured her hand in his. "If you want your surprise, you will have to come with me." He drew her toward the inner bailey before he stopped and turned back to the crowd. "Perhaps you should all come with us."

"What are you up to?" Jane asked.

His lips twitched. "All will be revealed."

25

❄

To Jane's surprise, Nicholas led her to what remained of the chapel. The east wall lay in a crumpled heap, but the other three walls remained standing. He did not lead her to the door of the chapel, instead he took her to the open side, down a path that had been cleared of rubble and lined with sprigs of green holly with red berries.

Nicholas stopped the procession at the entrance he had created and turned to face her. "This is the first part of your gift," he said, pointing to a row of large stones laid in a line atop a blanket of snow.

"What is it?" she asked, puzzled.

"The beginning of our new home. Bellhaven Manor." His expression turned serious. He dropped to his knee in the snow. The green and black and red of his kilt mixed with the nearby holly to create a splash of color in a sea of endless white.

He took one hand in hers, pressed a kiss to the back of her fingers before raising his gaze to her face. "We have missed so much during the last two years. I do not want to miss a moment more. I want you in my life forever. I

GERRI RUSSELL

want to go to bed with you every night and wake up next to you each morning. I want to raise our sons and daughters in a house filled with love. I never want them to suffer or know a day of loneliness in their lives."

A smile broke across his face. "I love you, Lady Jane Josephina Catherine Lennox. Will you marry me?"

His words sank deep inside her, twining around her heart. It was all there in his words, everything she had ever wanted—commitment, family, and most of all love. "Yes, Nicholas, I will marry you."

The words barely left her throat before he was up beside her, holding her, kissing her so passionately her world began to spin.

The crowd around them cheered.

Despite their audience, Jane clung to Nicholas, loving him so much that her emotion spilled over, brought tears of joy to her eyes. At the sight of her tears, he only kissed her more. He kissed her until they were both breathless and wanting before he pulled back.

"Now that you have said yes," he said with a soft burr in his voice. "I will show you your next surprise." He took her hands. "Close your eyes."

"Nicholas," she protested.

"Please?" he asked with a heart-melting grin.

On a soft sigh, she complied.

Silence surrounded them as he tucked her hand into the crook of his arm and led her forward until they came to a stop once more. "All right. Open your eyes."

She looked from Nicholas to the ethereal fairyland he had created. Her breath caught in her throat.

Inside the three-walled building, he had laid fresh evergreens, holly, and mistletoe around the entire circumference. The altar was covered in greens as well, with candles interspersed among the boughs. The flames from the candles were soft and gentle, nothing like the inferno from the night before. In contrast, the yellow-gold flames threw sparkling beads of light across the entire chamber. The scent of pine mixed with the crisp freshness of the snow, cleansing away the horrors. The snow, the greens, the candles—he had created an enchanted playland.

"It is beautiful," she admitted in awe.

Her gaze left the whole to focus on one item in particular. A tapestry frame stood off to her right that he must have found amongst the ruins. It was not the frame that drew her attention, but the light green brocade gown that was displayed across it.

"Your wedding gown," Nicholas said softly.

"But everything burned in the fire," Jane whispered as tears anew came to her eyes.

Nicholas's expression grew serious. "Not the chapel or the labyrinth beneath. It is as if something was protecting them. There is no soot below, and not even the scent of smoke. That is where I found this dress."

Jane looked at him, stunned, as she fingered the sleeve. "This was my mother's gown. The one she wore when she married my father." She blinked back tears. "How is that possible?"

"'Tis your mother's doing," Lady Margaret said, coming to stand beside Jane.

"My mother is gone," Jane said. Amelia had admitted to her own mother poisoning mama.

"Why do you say that?" Margaret touched Jane's cheek in a motherly fashion. "Many of the castle's residents have reported seeing Lady Lennox over the years. Perhaps, just perhaps, some part of her remained here, with you, until she could see you happy and safe."

Jane gathered the dress in her arms. "I would like to believe that."

Margaret's expression became tender. "I remember my sister-in-law as a tenderhearted person who loved her daughter more than life itself."

"Do you truly think some aspect of her is here with me?"

Margaret nodded. "She loved you so much. I would even go so far as to say that your mother is why Amelia was never able to harm you, no matter what she tried. Your mother knew, and she made sure you were one step behind a falling object or a thrown dagger. It was her love that kept you safe."

Jane could only nod as emotion thickened her throat. She desperately wanted to believe that her mother was the reason she had not fallen victim to Amelia's attempts to harm her and Margaret and Bryce.

"The minister has arrived. Would you like me to help you with your dress?" Lady Margaret asked with a soft smile.

Jane nodded. The two of them moved down the stairway off to the right to go below into the labyrinth. Once there, Jane slipped off her soot-stained gown. She used a ewer of water to wash the grime from her body before stepping into her mother's wedding gown. Once the gown was buttoned, she fastened her mother's gold-and-ruby girdle at her waist. A bittersweet memory of her mother tightened Jane's chest as she smoothed the fabric of the gown into place. "Will I do?" Jane asked Margaret, returning her thoughts to the here and now.

Her aunt tilted her head, studying Jane carefully. "You look lovelier than I have ever seen you. I am so proud of you for seeing this competition through, Jane. I know your father and brother would be, too, if they were here."

Jane sobered. "I miss them."

"Yes, I imagine you do. They are here with you in spirit, and what you do now will protect their memories and guarantee your future. Marry to keep what is yours, but also marry for the love I know you have always had for Nicholas." Margaret's no-nonsense approach steadied her.

"You are pleased with my choice?" Jane could not help but smile at the thought of her betrothed.

"You and Nicholas were meant to be together. I am only sorry it did not happen before this, and that you had to undergo such doubts of your love during the last two years."

"We needed to go through that, I fear, to appreciate what we have now." At the thought Jane laughed, the sound filling the chamber. "We have nothing at all except each other."

"You have everything," Margaret corrected. "A fresh start and enough love to last you a lifetime."

Jane took her aunt's hands in her own. "And Lord Galloway? Are you happy, truly happy, with him?"

A blush crept up Margaret's throat. "I never imagined a future with another husband, and yet that is what I received from this mad scheme to find you a husband."

"Marry Lord Galloway tonight, alongside Nicholas and me," Jane insisted. Seeing her aunt settled on the same day she would start her own new life would make everything complete.

Margaret shook her head. "This is your moment, dearest."

"No," Jane said. "This is when both you and I get to embrace our new future with the men we love."

Margaret hesitated, then finally released a sigh and nodded. "Let there be laughter and passion and lots of growing old together in the days ahead."

"And miracles," Jane added. It was a miracle this moment was upon them after all they had been through. She prayed their lives would be filled with many more. Jane took Margaret's hand and they ascended into the chapel. As they approached, every head turned to stare. Nicholas waited at the back of the chapel, cleaned up and dressed in his plaid, looking even more handsome than he had a short time ago.

"You are breathtaking," Nicholas greeted her, and gathered her to him. "Are you ready?"

"In a moment." She turned toward her aunt.

Margaret moved to Lord Galloway's side. "Are you ready to marry me tonight?" she asked. "The minister is here, the chapel is decorated. It would be a shame to wait."

"Dear woman, I would have married you three days ago if we'd had the chance." Lord Galloway took Margaret's hand and the four of them proceeded up the altar to kneel before the minister where they would repeat the vows that would bind them together for an eternity.

Jane knelt beside Nicholas, her heart so achingly full. They had won this new life together. They had made it through to their togetherness, despite all those who had stood in their way. And tonight, before the stroke of midnight on Christmas Eve, she would be a married woman.

At the thought, Jane smiled. Suddenly, a laird for Christmas did not seem like such a terrible thing at all.

Epilogue

Standing atop the newly renovated north tower of Bellhaven Manor, Jane looked out across the view she had missed so desperately. A soft summer breeze ruffled the ends of her hair. A deep sense of contentment moved through her.

"Welcome home, my lady," Nicholas said, coming up behind her and slipping his arms about her waist.

Jane leaned back into his embrace. "I cannot believe you did all this in such a short time." He had managed to complete the main wing of their new modern manor house along with two of the four planned towers in the past six months.

"You are pleased?" he asked.

"Yes." Jane twisted around. "You are smiling like a man who is quite content with himself."

"I am smiling like a man who is in love with his wife." He kissed her gently.

The taste of him, the scent of him, and the feel of him, combined to send her senses reeling. "Do you think Margaret and Hollister are as happy as we are?"

Nicholas tucked his chin against the top of her head. "I have never seen a couple so happy."

"Truly," Jane agreed. "Once Hollister made it through their wedding night, Margaret finally allowed herself to have the dreams she had kept hidden in the depths of her heart for so long."

"You mean the baby?" he asked, pulling Jane closer.

"Yes. Hollister is convinced it is a son," she laughed.

"A son would be nice," he said somewhat wistfully.

She could feel the beat of his heart against her chest—so steady and strong. Attributes he would need in the near future. "Did you plan for a nursery in the manor?"

He stepped back then turned her to face him, his expression puzzled. "You know I did. It is located next to our chamber."

"Can you have it finished in the next six months?"

"Of course."

"Good," she whispered, rising up on her toes to kiss his lips. "Because Margaret and Hollister are not the only ones expecting a child. We are pregnant, my lord, about three months along."

Nicholas gave her a smoldering smile. He brought his hands to cover her abdomen. "Ah, Jane, you have made me the happiest man alive."

Jane wrapped his love around her, embraced it. She looked up at Nicholas, felt the new life flutter inside her, and knew her heart's desire was not a place, but a feeling. With her heart full to overflowing, she knew that love had won in the end.

THE END

Acknowledgments

As always, thank you to my wonderful friends, critique partners, and plotting pals: Pamela Bradburn, Teresa DesJardien, and Karen Harbaugh. Your advice, patience and support mean the world to me.

About the Author

After a long career in journalism, Gerri Russell left to pursue her passion for historical romance. Since 2006, she has published 7 titles, winning two Romance Writers of America Golden Heart Awards and an RT Book Reviews American Title II Award. An expert and enthusiast of Medieval and Renaissance history, when she's not reading and writing she's a living history reenactor with the Shrewsbury Renaissance Faire. She lives with her husband and children in Bellevue, Washington.

THIS LAIRD *of* MINE

Argyll, Scotland

Jules MacIntyre, through no fault of his own and much to his dismay, was now the fourth Earl of Kildare. The father he never knew had a heart had died when it stopped one week ago, and his brother had drowned himself in whiskey two days later. They both lay dead in the family crypt, alongside the woman who had sent him to gaol for sixteen months and twenty-seven days.

He had been blamed for her death. A death Jules had always suspected was self-inflicted in order to make him suffer. But at the moment he did not care about his stepmother's machinations. He was free, and he had more pressing issues to contend with today.

Jules leaned back in his late father's wooden desk chair and contemplated the fanned display of swords that took up the far wall of the study. If a sword was the answer to his problem, he had many to choose from.

Jules frowned at the multitude of unpolished steel. A sword was what had started all his problems. It would never be the solution. He was not as weak as his brother, or quite as desperate. Yet.

With a flick of attention toward three stacks of letters on the corner of the desk, Jules stood and paced the room. The larger stack contained duns from creditors. His father and brother had lived extravagantly for the past several years, well beyond their means. And now the estate was in ruin and the creditors had already threatened him with debtor's prison. For a second, the memory of his dark, dank cell came flooding back. He could feel the heavy manacles at his wrists and ankles. He shuddered, forcing the memory away. Never would he go back to gaol. He would rather impale himself on one of those swords than allow himself to be cast back into that hell again.

With a sharp breath of the musty air that enveloped Kildare Manor, Jules turned to gaze at the second stack of letters on the desk. They were from Jane and Nicholas, checking on his welfare, begging him to find a wife, annoying him with their constant prattle about how happy they were and only wanting the same for him.

The problem was that he still had feelings for Jane. He loved her, despite the fact she had married another man. Jules had tried to put her out of his mind for the last seven months, but to no avail. His thoughts returned to her time and again, even though he knew she was happy, that her new husband, Nicholas Kincaid, was a decent sort of man, and that she had married for love.

With a groan of disgust, Jules paced about the chamber, contemplating the faded walls where paintings once hung. Even if he ignored his own emotions, he still had a problem with Jane and Nicholas's appeal to seek out happiness with a bride.

Did Nicholas and Jane not understand that what they had was special? Most people did not find that kind of love.

Jules continued his pacing and stopped before the massive display of weaponry. He reached up and fingered the dull tip of one of the swords. The metal was cool to his touch, echoing the emptiness of his soul. Happiness was a rare commodity. And wanting something more than what life had offered him so far was only setting him up for more disappointment and pain.

Which was why he had created her.

Jules smiled as his gaze moved to the third letter on the desk. A letter from Claire. His newly *created* wife. She was the perfect woman. She never complained, did not mind his late nights out, or his discrete dalliances. She never spent money. And best of all, she always kept her opinions to herself.

She was the perfect creation.

His Claire was the perfect invention, and his only salvation. She would keep Jane and Nicholas from interfering in his life. She would allow him the time he needed to deal with the mess his father and brother had left behind. If he were lucky, she would also keep the creditors at bay. Who wasn't sympathetic to a newlywed couple in their first weeks of life together?

A sound at the doorway brought Jules's gaze around. His father's servant . . . his servant, John Finnie, stepped into the room carrying a tea tray that Jules had not requested.

"I brought ye somethin' tae ease yer pain." Fin said, setting the tea upon the dusty desk.

It would take something stronger than tea to accomplish that. But Jules was not his father or his brother. Whiskey at ten in the morning was not for this MacIntyre. He would not repeat his brother's foolishness.

"Thank you, Fin," Jules replied, meaning the words. He was grateful for the refreshment and just as pleased not to be utterly alone. Jules studied his companion. The aging retainer was dressed in the same threadbare jacket and breeches he had worn for as long as Jules had been alive.

"Beg pardon, mi-," the old retainer said, coughing before he could finish his words. Fin cleared his throat and tried again. "Beg pardon, milord. A messenger brought these fer ye." He shuffled forward, holding three letters.

Jules frowned at the messages. He recognized the tight and neat hand-writing on the top letter as that of his solicitor. The other two were most likely duns or more pleas from Nicholas and Jane for him to pursue happiness and love. His frown deepened at the lack of a silver salver or even a wooden platter to deliver the messages upon. The silver had long since been sold, along with most of the paintings, furnishings, and anything else that could fetch a price and perhaps keep the creditors at bay for a few days more.

Jules reached for the first letter. As expected, it was from Grayson, but the contents were not what he had expected at all. His fingers tightened on the paper. He could only focus on a sampling of the words. *Your father . . . no money . . . unknown benefactor.* Jules closed his eyes and concentrated on his breathing. Then, very slowly, he opened his eyes and read the letter in its entirety.

It was then that the truth crept over him. His father had had nothing to do with his release. And Grayson had been unable to discover who had secured his freedom.

A chill worked its way across Jules's neck. If not Jane or his father, then who had released him? The knowledge that he was indebted to some unknown benefactor shook him to his core. He would be beholden to no one, whoever that someone might be.

Jules drew another slow, deep breath at the blatant proof that his father had abandoned him. He stared up at the ceiling, feeling empty inside. God, it hurt to know that the man he once loved had never loved him in return.

But with his next heartbeat, he forced that pain and isolation away. He might have been denied a loving and decent family, but something good had come about regardless. Whoever had released him had given him a second chance. His life had come down to this moment, when he was broken and alone. Yet the opportunity to change everything was only a heartbeat away.

This was his moment and his crossroad. He could go down with his family, or fight for the life he wanted, despite it all.

Jules's throat tightened and his palms grew damp.

4

"Milord," Fin said, bringing him back to the present. When he failed to retrieve the other letters, Fin stepped closer, jiggling the folded paper in an attempt to gain his master's attention.

Fin's worn boot caught on the carpet and he pitched forward. The letters fell to the carpet in one direction as Fin fell the other.

Jules caught the old retainer before he went down, then guided him to the chair behind the desk. "Sit here, Fin. Catch your breath."

"But the letters—"

"Are probably more debtor notices," Jules said, flexing his right arm as he stepped back, grateful he had regained his strength over the last seven months. His time in gaol had stripped him of more than his soul.

"Nay," Fin protested. "Lady Jane wrote one, but the other letter is in an unfamiliar hand."

Jules's curiosity won out. He bent to retrieve the letters. He paused for a moment as his fingers brushed the thick, intricately designed floor covering. It seemed odd that when everything else had been sold to pay the estate's debts, the carpets still remained. He frowned and scooped up the letters. As Fin had stated, one letter was in an unfamiliar hand. The other was from Lady Jane Kincaid.

He broke the seal on Jane's letter after tossing the other on the desk.

Dearest Jules,

When I first heard from the lady herself that you had married, I must admit that I was hurt. I had so hoped to be included in your celebration. However, after meeting the glorious creature you now call wife I can understand your haste. She is, in every way, your perfect match. I forgive you and congratulate you on a job well done. I look forward to seeing you in two days when you can introduce all of us to your new bride properly.

Your friend always, Jane

It took the words a few moments to sink in. But when they did he dropped the letter on the desk. Jane had met Claire? How was it possible to meet someone who was merely a figment of his imagination?

"Milord?" Fin's voice broke in.

5

He looked across the desk at his servant, trying to find the words, but all he had was a stark sudden fear. "This cannot be."

"Beg pardon?" Fin's eyes narrowed with concern.

Jules reached for the next letter and broke the seal. A feminine hand stared back at him.

Jules, my love,

I have been to see your friends, Lord and Lady Kincaid, as well as Lord and Lady Galloway, and invited them to visit us at Kildare Manor. Sir David Buchannan has agreed to escort me northward in two days' time. Please have the house readied for our guests. Until then,

Yours truly, Claire

Jules swallowed hard, thinking. What madness was this? This letter was not written in the hand of his solicitor—the person he had hired to falsify his new bride. Claire did not exist. Would never exist.

Yet she was meeting his friends, and coming to him in two days' time.

"Milord, yer scarin' me. Ye got that look yer brother had right before he sliced himself through with a sword." Fin's voice brought Jules's gaze around.

He shook his head in an effort to clear his thoughts. The motion did nothing as questions raced through his mind. For his servant's sake, Jules pasted on a smile. "You need not worry, Fin. I am not so weak a man as that. I have endured much worse than this." At least he hoped he had.

Jules continued. "It looks as though Kildare Manor will have no time for grief. We will be having visitors on Saturday. I will arrange for a few maids to come up from town to help with the preparations."

Fin's brow furrowed. "I mean ye no dishonor, milord, but we've no funds fer food, let alone cleanin' women."

Jules nodded as he dug his booted toe into the thick carpet beneath his soles. "I have a notion of where I can gather a few funds, at least enough to hold off the creditors for a while longer while I figure things out."

Fin stood. "Very well, milord. You'd best enjoy yer tea before it grows cold. That was the last of the tea leaves. If ye need somethin' stronger, there's lots of whiskey still."

Jules nodded as the servant shuffled out of the chamber, leaving him in silence. Whiskey seemed like a better option, Jules thought as he reached for the tea and poured himself a cup. Perhaps, in time, it would be his only option, just as it had been for his brother. But for now, he had work to do and a wife to meet.

In front of his friends, he would have no choice but to accept her, whoever she was. But once they were alone, he would discover what was behind this imposter's game. In the meanwhile, for better or worse, definitely poorer than richer, a living, breathing Claire MacIntyre, Lady Kildare, would soon enter his life.